Far Away
From
Where?

A novel by

Yehiel Grenimann

Mazo Publishers

Far Away From Where?

ISBN: 978-1-936778-89-8

This is a work of fiction. Some of the characters and incidents are based on real people and events, but there is no claim to historical accuracy in the details. The milieu and general historical events are tragically all too real and forever seared in many memories.

Contact the Author:
farawayfromwhere@gmail.com
www.farawayfromwhere.com

Published by:
Mazo Publishers
USA: 1-815-301-3559
Israel: 054-7294-565

Website: www.mazopublishers.com
Email: cm@mazopublishers.com

Cover artwork by:
Nehama Grenimann Bauch
nammyg@gmail.com
www.nehamaketubah.com

Book production by:
Prestige PrePress
prestige.prepress@gmail.com

With love, dedicated to

Boris, my father,
May his memory be blessed.

Chana, my mother,
May she have many more meaningful years.

and my brothers Sam and Jack.

To the thousands of survivors and their children.

To the Jewish community of Melbourne, Australia.

Contents

Acknowledgments

I have many, many people to thank for their part in this creative endeavor and am sure I will inadvertently forget some, so I begin with an apology. Forgive me.

Firstly, I thank G-d for having blessed me with a wonderful and supportive family, and the conditions which made it possible to write.

In particular I would like to thank the following people:

My publisher, Chaim Mazo, and my cousin-in-law John Adler of Pomegranate Books for their invaluable help in editing. John and my beloved wife, Debbie, for their literary insights. Debbie for her sensitivity, and patience in helping me see the writing process as a craft. She sees it through the eyes of an experienced and professional editor. (One of the best in Jerusalem!) My apologies for not taking all of their advice! The faults are mine, the strengths partially theirs.

Diane Greenberg, in whose creative writing class this novel got started, and Margalit Jacob-Frutkof for helping me struggle with my writing blocks, and for their encouragement. Judy Labensohn and Fern Reiss for their helpful comments on the way and the wonderful support they provide in their blogs for writers in Israel.

Nora Gold for her editing tips when publishing the chapter "The Seder" in her "Journal of Jewish Fiction" and her friendship over the years.

My talented daughter, Nehama Grenimann Bauch, for the artistic cover, and the many previous sketches.

My friends: Mark Silver, Jeff Green, Meyer Eidelson, Tom (Irene) Kalinski, Bogna Pawlisz, Mordecai Goldberg, Gershom Gorenberg, David Young, Daniel Avitzur, and many others for their help and encouragement.

David Niven, who taught me many moons ago at Melbourne High School and inspired me with his love of literature. Sidra

Ezrahi and Steve Copeland for their profound teaching of Jewish literature.

Elie Wiesel and Arnold Zable for their inspired writing.

The late Lola and Adam Kalinski for their inspiring example of a loving relationship.

May we all be blessed with joy and gratitude in the ongoing adventure and miracle of life.

Rabbi Yehiel Grenimann of Jerusalem
(formerly John Green of Melbourne, Australia)

July, 2011

To everything there is a season,

And a time to every purpose under the heaven;

A time to be born,

And a time to die;

A time to plant,

And a time to pluck up that which is planted;

A time to kill, and a time to heal...

Ecclesiastes, 3:1-3

1
Yanosh and Eva

The old oak tree in Pilsudski Square, Warsaw, provided them with privacy. It was house-like in its immensity, its thick branches crowned with a canopy of leaves. Agile children would climb up into their safe haven, whispering secrets, telling jokes, teasing those below. Brave boys hung from them shouting, imitating Tarzan. As evening approached, it grew colder and became a quiet spot.

There Yanosh and Eva would meet after school. He was learning in a Polish state high school, she in the Peretz Yiddish school. His parents did not approve of the relationship, neither did hers. They were "too young." She was too politically radical and too "Jewish" for them; he from too assimilated a family, lacking Jewish loyalty, or pride.

He inscribed their initials into the bark, etching in the date in Roman numerals. He translated it for her. June 7, 1933.

She laughed watching him. He worked away at the tough material with his Swiss pocket knife. It glinted in the afternoon sun.

Yanosh loved this handy red knife. Marek had given it to him as a birthday gift when his father last returned from overseas. Marek's father, a diplomat, would enchant the boys with stories of exotic faraway places, like Jamaica or Australia. He brought his son gifts, souvenirs from his travels. Marek already had a pocket knife just like this one.

Yanosh promised Eva that when they were old enough he would marry her and they would travel to one of those distant lands. There no one would stop them from seeing each other, no one would attack or spit at Jews or Communists anymore, like they did in Warsaw.

October 1944, Warsaw

Throughout the long night, the sounds of explosions and shooting outside had terrified them. A strange, eerie silence now reigned.

Eva looked pale. She was curled up in the corner, wrapped in her blanket, staring at nothing.

Yanosh crawled over to the window to peep outside. He lifted the curtain, and glimpsed out. Night was receding before the first rays of the morning sun. Down below he could see silhouettes moving between the still smoldering ruins of once elegant buildings.

The tanks were gone. So were the German soldiers.

Yanosh crawled back and took her cold hand. He rubbed it gently, trying to warm her. She managed a smile, gave him her other hand.

"I think it is over, Eva. Listen..."

"I don't hear anything."

"That's right. They've gone. Warsaw is free, at least until the Soviets arrive. This nightmare is over."

"Yanosh, have they really left? Are you sure?"

"There are no tanks down there. I don't see any soldiers. I think it is now safe to go outside."

Eva was trembling. Was it fear or the cold? He put his arms around her to hug her. She pushed him away. She whimpered. He began to cry too. Was it really over?

The sound of footsteps were heard in the hall. Voices too. Who was out there? Yanosh strained to hear what they were saying. They were speaking Polish, these were familiar voices! Turning to Eva he saw that she too had heard. They helped each other up, in anticipation.

The door flew open. Marek stood before them, a weapon strapped across his back. He was smiling from ear to ear. He looked gaunt and tired, deep dark circles around his eyes gave him a spectral look, but he was back, still alive! The gold cross he wore was visible, resting on his red chest hair, under the rifle strap.

Marek had been bringing them food, water and news from the Polish underground over the past year, but had disappeared during the week of the heaviest fighting, leaving them with no sustenance and no news.

Yanosh thought of the many people he knew; Henryk Wolinski, Julian Grobelny, Ferdynand Arczynski, and Ewa Brzuska "Babcia" came quickly to his mind. They were involved in the Rada Pomocy Zydom, the council to aid Jews, otherwise known as "Zegota." He feared that their Zegota friends were dead.

Some, like Marek were childhood friends. They had clandestinely helped each other and hundreds of others escape the Nazi murder machine, risked their lives and those of their families with Aryan papers, false identities, jobs, money, and contacts. There had been executions, hangings, torture in the Gestapo cellars; many had paid dearly for their participation in this particular resistance against the German occupiers.

Despite the thousands involved in the effort to save Jews from Nazi brutality and the mass murders, few had been saved, fewer still had remained hidden in Warsaw and participated in the revolt. Many had lost their lives because of the ubiquitous *szmalcowniks*, the blackmailers and informers; a cancerous growth in Warsaw society.

"Thank God you are still alive!"
"Thank our luck, not God!"
Marek laughed.
He hugged and kissed each of them, then stepped back to introduce his friend. Yanosh didn't recognize her. Marek presented her as Pawla. Standing beside him gripping a rifle, a cigarette in the corner of her mouth, she was radiant with happiness. Looking at the two of them standing there, Yanosh wondered about their relationship. Were they a couple?
"The Germans are gone! The bastards fled. They ran like

frightened rabbits, leaving their dead and wounded behind like the cowards they are," Pawla said, flicking away cigarette ash in disgust.

Yanosh noticed a thick red scar under her chin. Her long blond hair was tangled and dirty. She was a well-endowed, shapely woman, but he could not keep his eyes off the scar. She noticed that too, but ignored it. A proud woman, he thought, seeing the angry spark in her eyes.

"Yes, they've left. We are free now – for the time being. But the Soviet Army will be here soon. Now you have to take care of yourselves and we have to disappear before the NKVD tracks us down..."

Marek frowned. He was a tall man, towering over his friends. His height and sharply cut red beard gave him a striking appearance. Yanosh imagined a biblical prophet must have looked like this.

"What do you have to say, my friend?" Yanosh asked, looking up at him.

His face had changed from initial radiant joy to a dark shadow of concern. He crossed himself before speaking.

"Pawla is right. There are many dangers ahead. We will move on, leave Warsaw, go into hiding... I advise you two to do the same, as soon as you can. It is a miracle that you are still alive. Many dangers still lurk out there. You must be careful."

He paused, thoughtful for a moment, then added:

"And you must have faith."

Eva and Pawla nodded.

Yanosh did not respond. He lowered his head, struggling to hide his negative feelings at hearing this comment.

Pawla walked over to the window, with a quick movement of her wrist tossed the dead butt out, and turned to face Yanosh and Eva.

"We've brought you something."

She walked back out of the room and bent down to pick up an object in the hall next to the door.

It was a battered old brown suitcase. Yanosh had not noticed it there before.

"It's yours, Yanosh. Don't you recognize it?"

Yanosh shook his head.

"Well it is yours." Marek repeated, smiling.

Yanosh looked at it more carefully. Perhaps it did look familiar. He took the suitcase, shoved aside the things on the table and placed it there, ready to be opened.

Before he could do so Marek offered him his ruddy hand.

"We must go now," he said, shaking hands with Yanosh, who wouldn't let go of him, trying to pull him closer, to hug him.

"Yanosh, I must go. Good luck to you, and God protect you," he added, freeing himself.

"You take care of yourself too, Marek."

Yanosh wanted to thank them for all they had done, but could not find the words. He stood in the doorway awkward and silent. Marek and Pawla turned to leave. Eva said something about meeting them again. Yanosh nodded.

"We will meet again in better times," he managed to say.

"I hope so," Marek answered.

He and Pawla smiled, then left.

He watched sadly as they descended, hearing the wood creaking on the stairs below as they disappeared from view.

He closed the door, turned towards the table and looked at the suitcase. It was dark brown, had a gold-painted handle. Bits of a maroon material still decorated the edges in some places.

It does look familiar, he thought to himself.

He tried to open it, but the rusted lock would not budge.

"Break it, Yanshuk. Use that," she said, pointing to the bronze candlestick standing on the floor beside the table.

He bent down and lifted the candlestick. It felt heavy in his hands.

He wondered whether Sonia had used it in the past to light Sabbath candles. What had become of her? The question had occurred to him before while looking at it. She probably died in Treblinka, like the others, he answered himself.

Yanosh pushed the thought away, focusing on the suitcase, again sensing the solidity of the candlestick. He gripped it, lifted it, and began to hammer the lock with its base. Once. Twice. On the third attempt the lock gave. Putting down the candlestick, he opened the suitcase.

Yanosh looked down at the open suitcase, and then over at Eva. She was staring at him, still shaking and clutching her blanket. He beckoned her to join him. Barely able to walk, she came over and together they looked down into the suitcase. It contained old, used clothing, women's things.

He watched as his wife started sifting through the blouses and skirts, until she found a dress she liked. She held it up to show him. It was green, with white lace at the collar and sleeves.

"Do you like this one, Yanosh?"

"It would look good on you. The color matches your eyes."

"Yes, it does. It is in good condition too. Almost new."

Most of the clothes now lay strewn around her feet. She appeared to be happy with the dress she had picked, but that didn't last long. She soon looked up at him, her eyes revealing her disappointment. She had reached the bottom of the case, had found nothing more useful than clothing.

He had remained silent watching her, struggling with his own emotions, his throat tightening. He looked more carefully at the suitcase. A name had been inscribed on it.

"Kaminski," he read aloud, pointing to the golden inscription.

He hadn't needed to. She had seen it. His mother's clothes.

He remembered her as she had been before the war. Her round, lined face shining with love. She was smiling, dark, kind eyes looking directly at him. She was wearing a red and gold embroidered scarf, the one she wore on holidays. She looked younger, fuller than she had when he had last seen her in the ghetto, not yet shriveled up and grey.

At the memory of the ghetto her face disappeared, leaving cold and emptiness. He wept.

Eva came over to him and put her hand on his shoulder. He appreciated her touch. Over the last week she had given him strength, while they sat there in the dark apartment, clutching for sanity as the battle continued outside, wave after wave of terror washing over them with each explosion of shooting and screams.

A thought crossed his mind. He bent down to look again at the clothing, started to rummage through the pockets as his grandmother had done before Pesach when he was a boy.

"There is something in this pocket," he told Eva, showing her the pocket of a brown coat of silky texture. He remembered first noticing the coat and its bulging pocket when he had opened the suitcase.

His hands slipped in and closed on a small but bulky paper package. Might there be money inside?

He pulled out the object. Eva crouched down beside him to see. Her sudden movement made him jump, bump his elbow on the corner of the table and in his pain drop the package. She picked it up.

"Give it to me!"

She handed it over. He unfolded the wrapping. There was a small photograph, some zloty bills, a few coins and a plain gold ring.

He looked at the photo. It had been taken at their wedding. A group photo of Yanosh's family at the event. Yanosh's parents, his four sisters, two brothers-in-law, their seven children, his nephews and nieces, and he and Eva, newlyweds in the center. It seemed so long since that picture had been taken; felt like looking back at another planet, a world turned to ashes.

They stood there looking at the photo, surrounded by his mother's clothes, crying like two lost children. Yanosh finally stopped it.

"Enough," he said, drying his eyes, "enough of this!"

He angrily shoved the suitcase off the table. It crashed to the floor.

"What are you doing?" she asked.

"We can't wallow in sentimentality," he explained.

"Let's count the money!"

He placed their new treasure on the table and began to count.

"Four hundred and fifty zloty."

He pocketed the money, and looked at the ring carefully.

"I wonder how much it is worth?"

"The ring is gold. It must be worth something," she commented.

"Yes. I think so."

He looked up at Eva, and softened. How hard it had been for her to part with her own wedding ring, when they had needed to exchange it for food! He would never forget that terrible moment.

"Here," he said, "take the ring. You wear it now."

"No, I can't wear your mother's wedding ring. Yanosh, I'm sorry."

She returned it, watching him put it back in his pocket.

"Yanosh, there is writing on the paper!"

She bent down, picked it up and handed it to him. Yanosh, feeling Eva's tension as he read the letter, could hear her heavy breathing. He noticed that his hand was shaking too. He read the letter aloud.

April 15, 1943

My dear children, Yanosh and Eva,

Your father and sisters are dead. Shot in the ghetto street. I will not survive this hell either. That you might get through, this gives me comfort. The contents of this paper will help you, I hope. Say Kaddish for us. I love you.

Your mother,

Shula Kaminski.

Yanosh folded the letter, and put it into his inner coat pocket.

He and Eva stood there stunned for a moment. Then he pointed to the door.

"It is time to go out," he said.

She nodded.

He led the way towards the door, opened it and they went out. Walking down the stairs, he heard the boards creaking beneath them. They descended, holding hands.

The morning sun was warm; its caress met them as they first stepped out into the street. It had risen over what was left of the buildings across the road.

October 15, 1944

Eva and I came out of hiding on the 3rd of October, 1944. It had been eighteen months since we had last walked the streets of Warsaw. We took our first steps outside. The light was absolutely blinding. It took awhile to become accustomed to daylight. I took her arm, lowered my hat over my eyes, and led the way, down the steps of the building. We looked around to see the ruins of Warsaw. The site was devastating. Barely a structure was standing undamaged. Whole blocks were nothing but rubble, with parts of buildings jutting out like macabre blackened ghosts of a former time, a time when Warsaw had been peaceful and prosperous. That seemed long ago, so much had happened since we went into hiding four years ago.

We walked along the street, and across what had been Pilsudski Square. Few trees were left in what was once one of the finest squares in the city. I glanced at Eva. She was silently rubbing tears off her cheeks as we looked around. She was thin. My beautiful Eva, so little was left of her body, yet her eyes still glowed, despite all that we had been through. She was so precious, so beautiful to me. If not for her I would have given in to the angel of death, who lurked behind every corner, constantly stalking us during these terrible years. She had always been optimistic, a source of energy and hope when they were needed, able to joke and smile. During the last difficult weeks she has grown somber and weak. It is my turn to find strength for her. She needs me now, I know.

I remember thinking at the time that what we were doing reminded me of a Jewish custom. I remember that when my grandmother died we sat at home for seven days. That was how we mourned her death. People would come visit, bring food, and share words of comfort with my father and uncles. When the last morning came, the rabbi led the family out into the street and told us to take a few steps, to return to life. I felt as if we were doing the same now, but in reverse. We had left our hiding place, our little haven where, in the midst of all the destruction, we had planned our rebellion, where we had lived desperately each day, fighting for our lives and for our freedom. Now, outside, faced with the dimensions of the destruction we could begin to mourn Warsaw, mourn the world we had known. I understood then that we would have to leave. It was just a matter of time until Eva would agree.

2
First Steps Outside

Yanosh looked at his wife. Walking beside him in what was once a pretty green dress, now draped with a piece of orange curtain, she looked frail and fragile. "We need to find some food and water, we having nothing left."

His parched throat made the sounds. She just nodded.

They made their way through the rubble until they came upon a German barracks. It was deserted, apart from one old man in uniform, asleep by the gate. They crept past him and went in. His snores followed them into the still smoldering building.

"There must be a kitchen here somewhere..."

Through the second hall they could smell something familiar. The faint odor of burnt oil and then a pungent pong of rotting potatoes.

They entered the room. There was no one else there. The scent of food was overpowering. It had been five days since they had eaten anything. They had also run out of water the day before. When Yanosh spied a dripping tap he was overjoyed. He shuffled across the room in what was left of his shoes, almost tripping twice on the way. Behind him Eva slid down along the wall and then just sat there. She had no energy. Yanosh heard her moan behind him but didn't stop. He was so thirsty he could think of nothing but drinking.

On the way to the sink he picked up a bowl he'd found. He placed it under the broken tap. Only drops came out. Behind him he heard Eva's breathing and began to feel guilty that he had left her behind in his rush to drink. He drank what he could out of the dripping tap and carried the bowl, with its refreshing little pool of water, over to her. He put it to her lips and she sucked out what there was. She looked up at him, trying to smile in gratitude. He smiled back, then turned away to look around him again. He soon heard her snoring quietly behind him.

Across the room Yanosh saw a heavy skillet. Did he have the strength to lift it and break the tap with it? He walked across the room, picked it up with both hands, returned to the tap. He smashed the tap. The handle came off, landing on the floor beside him with a crash, then rolling away. He grasped the side of the pan before it fell and continued hitting the tap with as much force as he could manage. The noise woke Eva, who watched him working at it from under her blanket. After a while the tap snapped. Both of them were sprayed by a gushing fountain of water.

Shivering from cold, they drank with the help of the bowl, and their cupped hands. It was good to drink their fill again.

"We must find a container to collect some water for later, to bring back to the apartment," Eva said.

Yanosh agreed. He began looking through the cabinets and inside the boxes strewn around the room, but found nothing.

"Yanosh, look outside. Maybe there is something we can use out there."

Yanosh walked outside into the backyard. It was covered in soot. There was a large a crater right in the middle of the yard, a reminder of the past week's battle. In the far corner he saw a pile of rubble, a wall which had collapsed. He sifted through the rubble, moving broken blocks of cement and timber in his search.

Eva had crawled over to the kitchen door and was watching him. He looked up at her, smiled sadly, and then went back to his digging. He felt like a dog digging for a bone. It was to no avail.

A thought crossed his mind. He got up from his burrowing. After the dust had settled a little, he went over to the crater and peered into it. He spotted an object below and began to slide down the side, into the pit.

"Yanshuk, what are you doing!? Be careful!"

From deep within his voice echoed up: "I've found something we can use!"

"Yes, what is it? Show me."

She watched as first a metallic object, then the hand holding it, an arm, then Yanosh's beaming, triumphant face emerged from below. He put down his prize, dusted himself off, wiped his sooty face and then wiped the object clean. The metal gleamed in the sun.

"Do you see what I've found!"

She looked at it blankly.

"What is it?"

"It's a tank shell. A source of death, but for us it will be a container of life," he said.

Yanosh must have looked strange in his tattered, dirty clothes, sopping wet, running streaks of black soot on his face, holding the tank shell up with both hands to show her. She looked skeptical.

"It doesn't look like a very practical water holder to me."

"You'll see!"

He filled it with water, fastening a small pot over the top, secured with strips of cloth they'd scrounged around the yard. They headed out of the yard, carrying their precious water supply, some good potatoes they'd found and a small jar of oil. They walked over the rubble, out through a hole in the fence and towards Prozna Street.

Yanosh knew Eva wanted to get back to the safety of the apartment as soon as possible.

Looking around he saw that they were not alone in their venture. Others were also digging around in the rubble, carrying their finds back to hiding places. The previously empty road was now peopled with sad little groups and solitary figures. Survivors of the maelstrom, like us.

Men and women, mainly in blackened dirty rags, some missing limbs, were everywhere, trying to take their first steps back into life. They were strangely silent, murmuring amongst themselves, looking furtively around as they carried their prizes back to their human rat-holes. Yanosh noticed as they limped back to their own haven, that there were no children to be seen anywhere. Where are the children? he wondered. Have they all been killed?

They turned the corner of what was left of Marshalkofska Street and soon were approaching the apartment with their treasures. A group of people had congregated on the steps, talking excitedly. As they approached, Eva became nervous.

"Let's wait till they leave, Yanosh," she said.

Yanosh agreed. Eva spotted an impressive oak tree by which they could wait. Its thick trunk was perhaps half a meter wide. Their side of it was decorated with engraved names and symbols. Amongst them, he recognized his own handiwork, an adolescent heart, their initials, Y.K. and E.N., inside it. He looked at Eva meaningfully. She smiled sadly back at him, but remained silent.

The blackened branches spread out broadly above them. There were few leaves, mostly on the lower boughs. That this tree had survived the battles, was still standing, amazed Yanosh. The remaining foliage was still green, but beginning to yellow. Autumn leaves, he thought, the seasons continue as always. They will soon fall, scatter in the wind.

They sat down at its base to wait, watching the little crowd on the steps of the apartment building, hoping to see them disperse. The people stood there talking for some time. Yanosh studied them as they sat there. They didn't seem threatening to him. They were better dressed than the others they had seen in the street on their way back. Had they been collaborators with the Germans? No, they had executed the "quislings" weeks ago! So who were they? Perhaps they were Polish patriots who had dug up old elegant-looking clothes, now that the Germans were gone. He decided there was no apparent danger. After all neither he nor Eva looked Jewish. He managed to calm Eva's fears as well. They rose, helping each other up, and continued towards the apartment.

As they approached the building, the voices grew clearer.

They could hear some of the conversation: "We must organize before the Soviets arrive." The words came from an elderly gentleman, leaning on an elegant walking stick, made of dark, polished wood. The gold buttons on his navy-blue jacket shone in the sun.

A younger man speaking from under thick glasses added: "Yes, we should greet them as liberators, but be wary of them. When the Russians take control of Warsaw they will be reluctant to let go again. We must show them that we can take care of our own needs, now that the Germans are gone."

The others, three middle-aged women and a younger-looking man chorused in agreement. A young girl ran up, yelling: "They're coming! I heard the tanks crossing the Vistula. They've built a bridge over it again."

The people scattered. The three women entered the building; the two younger men hurried down the road towards the river. The older man turned the other way, walked slowly down Marshalkofska, tapping his walking stick as he went in the opposite direction. None had noticed Yanosh and Eva as they approached.

By the time they arrived at the steps of the building the people had gone, leaving behind them a litter of papers and cigarette butts. Yanosh bent down and picked up a leaflet. There was a hammer and sickle in the top right hand corner, a photo of Stalin in the center, and the well-known slogan "Workers of the World Unite!" across the left hand side. The slogan and iconic symbols were printed in red ink; the rest was black on white.

The body of the text, in Polish, announced the arrival of the Red Army who had "come to liberate our Polish brethren from the Fascist murderers." The people were warned to keep away from the army passing through and were promised that a civil government would soon be established in Warsaw, after which order would be restored and the city rebuilt.

Yanosh read the pamphlet to Eva, who responded bitterly.

"Where were they these last three weeks while the S.S.

henchmen and the German Army crushed our resistance uprising here?"

They both knew the answer: the Soviets had waited on the other side of the Vistula, pleased no doubt to see the Germans destroy the Polish nationalist resistance movement, the A.K. and their allies.

He remembered well the Soviet treachery in the past, the Molotov-Ribbentrop non-aggression pact, the massive Soviet supply of raw materials to the Germans, the executions and Siberian exile of so many Polish socialists and communists, who had fled to the "Socialist Motherland" when the Germans invaded, Stalin's bloody purges of his own people. So many had simply disappeared.

After a long silence, he said: "We must move on as quickly as possible, go somewhere where we are not known or recognized as Polish nationalist activists. The Soviets will plant their own people here and the purges will begin soon enough. Let's gather our things and move west to a smaller place, a quiet village where we can gather our strength and get organized again."

"But how will we manage without help, without knowing anyone? Here we know people."

"Don't fool yourself, Eva. Marek and his friends have already fled. Most of the Polish underground are underground," Yanosh said, pointing to the earth below them, "dead, or have moved west to escape the Soviets. We must do the same. What do we have left here? A few rags, an old suitcase, this container of water, a few rotten potatoes? We must go!"

"What about the apartment? What about Sonia's apartment?"

"Sonia's dead. Her family is gone. The apartment, the building, anything still standing will be requisitioned by the Russians. We must move on. We must get out of here fast, while we still can."

"All right, Yanshuk. I'll try. It's hard. I'm weak, but I suppose you are right."

They entered the building and climbed the stairs, heard

voices, the sounds of moving furniture from one of the other apartments. They came to the familiar door on the second floor, unlocked it and went in.

The apartment was in disarray, women's clothing all over the floor, the old suitcase sitting empty and open on the floor beside the table. Yanosh realized that his mother's old suitcase would be useful to them. He remembered the money and the ring. He checked to see if he still had them in his pocket. He did.

Eva began to gather up the clothing. She glared angrily at him for a moment. He responded with a loud sigh, which he saw she did not appreciate. He also started picking up things.

When they had finished, Yanosh remembered the water and food they'd brought in from their excursion. He had placed the shell-container of water on the table, next to the now refilled suitcase. He went over to the kitchen cabinet, took out two glasses and filled them with water. He handed one to Eva who took it gratefully. He put down his glass, lifted the suitcase off the table and put it back on the floor, then sat down to drink too. Eva joined him.

They began to make plans again. They would pack the little they had that was useful for their journey, use the suitcase, strapped to Yanosh's back, to carry the things. Eva would make a bundle of bedclothes, a couple of pillows, some blankets and they would set out as soon as dark fell. They would cook up a meal from the potatoes they had found. That would give them the energy they needed to start their journey.

Eva took the pan, the oil and the potatoes. She cut away the worst parts, which were truly rotten, grated the rest, forming what resulted into potato cakes, and began to fry them. She complained that without flour or eggs they would not hold together very well. Yanosh, who was busy organizing their things for the journey, told her he was sure they would be delicious as always. They discussed what to take and what to leave behind.

The smell of the cooking potatoes soon had them in improved spirits. So much so that Eva began to hum a tune to herself.

Yanosh listened. He recognized the melody, a Bundist song. He began to hum too.

He hadn't heard Eva sing anything in so long. Before the war she was always humming or singing to herself. Perhaps she would find the strength to go on after all. They would be able to build a new life for themselves despite all they had been through. A new life somewhere else. He decided to keep these thoughts to himself for the time being. He didn't want to overwhelm Eva, who was only beginning to look a little more lively. He would wait for the right time to have that conversation.

Eva announced cheerfully that the food was ready, brought the pan of potato cakes to the table, indicating to Yanosh that he should move the suitcase out of the way. He moved it, and set the table.

They sat down to their "feast." They ate quickly, washing the food down with greedy gulps of water. Yanosh complemented Eva on her cooking. He refilled their two glasses of water saying, "Let's imagine this is wine!" She responded with a happy smile.

"It's not easy to leave this apartment. It has been our haven over the past year and a half. I am going to miss this place. The meetings of the underground here. They gave us hope, kept us going."

"This was our last supper here," she said.

"The last supper! That's a good one, Eva."

Yanosh laughed. Eva frowned.

"So many of our friends are gone, our families. There are so many ghosts here in this apartment, in this city. I am happy to leave, to put it all behind me."

They heard a rumbling sound outside.

"We have to go!" he declared, "those must be the approaching Russian tanks."

Eva got up to clear the table. Yanosh shook his head.

"No, no," he said, himself rising. "We must go now. Right away!"

He handed over the bundle of bedclothes he had prepared, picked up the suitcase, placing a hand through each of the two ropes he had attached, adjusting them so it sat comfortably on his back. He grabbed the largest kitchen knife, which he shoved into his belt, just above his precious diary, which he had stuffed into his pants earlier, wrapped in its protective piece of old newspaper.

He beckoned to her to come quickly.

They went out the door. Yanosh looked back up the stairs at the familiar wooden door. So did Eva. Our world has narrowed, he thought. Through that peephole they had seen their friends come and leave, watched fearfully to see who was approaching on the stairs. It had been their only direct contact with the world outside. The flat had been their home, their life, and now they were leaving it behind.

He turned to look at Eva, wondering what she must be feeling. She looked frightened. The sight of the knife jutting out of the side of his coat might be disturbing her he thought, but how could she not understand why he had taken it.

Who knows what dangers await us? he thought, as they descended the last steps and went out into the cold Warsaw air again.

As soon as they went out they heard the roll of the tanks. They weren't the only ones who had decided to move on. People carrying bundles and bags were walking in the same direction, away from the oncoming sound. Others were just gathering along the edge of the road, waiting for the Red Army to arrive. There were newly-hung flags flapping in the wind here and there. Some people were happy that the Soviets were coming, but most of the growing crowd looked somber. Again Yanosh noticed the absence of children. Where were the children?

The noise of motors grew louder. They increased their walking speed. Soon they had no choice but to move over. The roar was now coming from a cloud of dust fast approaching them. People were waving flags. Others were taking cover to escape the noise and dust.

Eva took hold of Yanosh's arm, pulling him closer to her. He could hear how heavily she was breathing.

"I must rest now," she told him, "I can't go on."

Yanosh pushed through the crowd, with Eva following. He found a tree where they could sit to rest briefly. He hadn't noticed, but Eva had.

"It's the same tree. It's where we rested a few hours ago."

"Yes, it is," he agreed.

"Yanshuk, do you remember how we would meet at this tree. How we first kissed here?"

"Of course, I do. I will never forget."

They were interrupted by a sudden burst of gunfire.

It was not the Russians who came. The Germans had returned! They watched, horrified, as the crowds fled in terror from machine gun fire coming from the Nazi half trucks and jeeps, sweeping past them in the Pilsudski Square, pursuing the fleeing survivors. These poor people had hoped to meet their liberators at last. Now the streets were soaked in their blood. Death was their liberator. Bodies were piling up along the road. Some arms and legs were still twitching. The screaming was unbearable.

Yanosh and Eva lay hidden among the dead. There were others still moving, still alive. The Germans had gone, at least for now. Yanosh opened the container, poured some water out into his hands and washed the blood off Eva's face, then washed his own.

"We have to get away before they get here. Come on Eva get up. Get up!"

"I can't, Yanosh. I can't hide anymore."

He slapped her.

She got up, stunned. He began to walk. She followed after him.

They heard explosions behind them, at the far end of the road. Two lines of soldiers were slowly advancing, some carrying blow-torches. Others, striped-pajama clad prisoners, accompanied by whip-carrying guards, and dogs, began to collect bodies. They dumped them into open carts pulled by horses in the center of the road.

January 18, 1945

I do not know how I found the strength to think quickly, to keep us moving, to get away from them, but I did.

It was weeks until I felt clean again, weeks before the sense of contamination by all that human blood faded. And, even now, I can still hear the voices of the dying, the screams, especially whenever I am lying quietly hoping to revive my soul with sleep.

I thought I had lost her. The dead and dying around us, the pull to just give up, to join them, so powerful. It would have been so easy to just lie down, to collapse, to give up!

I could sense her slipping away from me.

So I slapped her. I had never done that before nor could I do it again. I will never forget the look she gave me. Was it shock, horror? And the terrible resignation with which she got up and followed me.

She had let go of her own will to live but I would not let her die! Without Eva I would not be able to go on. Not even one step.

We will live! We will live in freedom again.

Will we build our home again – here in this country, in a free Poland? – a Poland without foreign occupiers and murderers like Hitler or Stalin.

But our Poland has become the graveyard of Europe. Can we live where so many Jews have been murdered? Where their ashes are mixed into the soil and their screams hang in the air above us all the time?

I don't know.

3

Goodbye Warsaw

They marched on away from the city in the dust billowing up from behind the wagons, cars, motorbikes and horses, as well as the multitude of human feet. All were seeking refuge from the Germans.

Yanosh turned to look back at his beloved Warsaw, before it would disappear from view around the next bend. He pulled at Eva's arm until she turned around to look as well.

The sun glowed from between two cloud formations over the city. The city glowed too. It was burning. Yanosh realized that what he had thought were natural clouds were clouds of smoke.

"The bastards are destroying Warsaw. They are punishing us for the uprising."

"What about all the people still there, Yanosh? What will happen to them?"

"The smart ones, like Marek and his girlfriend, already got out, most of the rest of our friends are already dead, killed in the uprising, or already murdered by the Nazis before it, like all the Jews."

"Yanosh, don't be so cold-blooded. There must be more than a million people there in Warsaw. What will become of them?"

"I don't know, Eva. The Nazis are capable of anything, you know that. I can't cry anymore, I can't mourn anymore. Let's get moving again, find somewhere to stay where no one will be looking for us anymore, neither Nazis nor Communists."

"You are right, Yanshuk. We have to move away from the city, but to where? Where will we go now?"

"I have an old school friend in Trebisk, which is a couple of kilometers west of here. If he is still alive, I'm sure Peter would help. He was the headmaster of the local school there and has helped the underground over the years. We'll head for there."

"But Warsaw," Eva mourned, "they are destroying Warsaw!"

Eva cried as she walked and thought of the city burning, hearing the distant explosions. Yanosh waited, drank some water, gave some to Eva, and pointed down the road again, away from Warsaw: "Let's go. We won't be safe here on this road for too long."

January 25, 1945

Warsaw, which is no more:
Warsaw gone. There is nothing left to liberate!
Thoughts? What thinking is possible, what can one think or say?
After all the German atrocities this was the ultimate, the worst of all! They have totally wiped Warsaw off the map. There is no such city anymore. It is like what we were taught as kids in school about the destruction of ancient Jerusalem by the Romans.
Nothing left. Nothing but the smoldering ruins, and some Nazi guards.

Warszawa Warszawa of the Vistula!
You were a shining beauty by the river,

A city of culture, music, poetry and love.
You, now a graveyard, torn and bloodied,

Will you rise again, and fly free like the dove?
Or are you fated to die forever?

Three months later, after Waffen S.S. squads had destroyed Warsaw, blowing up building after building until almost nothing was left standing, after they had rounded up the remaining thousands and incarcerated them in a huge concentration camp and then transferred them inland, the Russians finally crossed the Vistula.

The Red Army arrived in Trebisk soon after they entered Warsaw, on January 17th.

Eva and Yanosh had found Yanosh's friend, Peter, there. He had let them stay in his school building, along with a number of other refugees from Warsaw, had supplied them with water, food, arranged heating and blankets. They were grateful to him but were never able to repay his kindness.

Peter disappeared on the day the Russians came. No one knew what had become of him. Yanosh never heard from him again.

The roar of the tanks brought everyone running into the main road of the town that day. They saw the first tank turn into Pilsudski Avenue. It was a greyish-green color.

A smiling, dirty, helmeted soldier was sitting on the turret, holding a red Russian flag and waving at the Polish crowd. A little boy, perhaps seven or eight, was sitting up there beside him, also smiling. His blue cap didn't hide the happy eyes. He was obviously thrilled at his tank ride. The soldier didn't look that much older than the boy.

After this first tank, another rolled past, a soldier peering over the edge of the turret. A third, and then a fourth tank rolled past them, all of them ripping up the roadway with their massive metal wheels and chains, leaving a trail of slush behind them in the snow.

Yanosh saw the Soviet stars painted on them. His heart sank. Would their momentary elation at their newly-found freedom end so soon? It was Eva who gave them some hope this time. She realized that they were only passing through, pursuing the retreating German Army, that it would take time for a Soviet government to be established.

Yanosh could hardly hear her words in the terrible din, but he could see her eyes. He saw the renewed spark in them, understood that his wife was ready to fight for life again. She was now thinking of the future, not only mourning the past. The snow will melt, he thought, and we will move west in the spring.

The Russian tanks indeed passed through. The silence returned. The snow settled. A new snowfall blanketed the mud and slush. The Polish survivors went back to getting organized. The trickle of refugees out of Warsaw into the countryside continued. New, needy people came from the east, just as Eva and Yanosh had done weeks before when they arrived in this little town, carrying their suitcase and bundle of bedclothes. The main enemy now was not the Russians, but the cold.

There was no coal. Mining had ground to a halt because of the heavy fighting and the resultant disorder behind the front. People burned whatever came to hand, destroying furniture, ripping planks of wood off abandoned buildings, using almost anything for fuel in order to produce a little warmth, to keep their cold extremities from freezing, and to heat food.

They huddled around fires and radios that winter and listened to the news. And the news warmed them; the Germans were retreating westwards out of Poland. They were being pushed back by the Allies in the west as well. It was only a matter of time until their "thousand-year Reich" would fall. The rumors about Hitler became stranger and stranger as the German empire crumbled. Some said he was dead, had committed suicide, others that he had fled into the countryside, dressed as an old peasant woman. The allied bombings of the cities of Germany intensified.

Eva would never forget May 8, 1945, the last day of the war in Europe. She had been working as a ticket collector at the town's only cinema theatre, which had been reconstituted after the worst of winter was over. They showed Russian movies, newsreels of the war effort, followed by tragedies or romances, and, rarely, comedies. The film would sometimes tear and would have to be spliced and reeled again as everyone waited impatiently, gossiping or silent.

That day they were being treated to a showing of an American cartoon featuring a mouse whose squeaky voice could be heard over the slow, dubbed Polish translation. Most of the audience didn't laugh at the jokes, some had fallen asleep, others were necking in the dark.

Suddenly the movie stopped. The lights were turned on. People began to talk and complain until a little bald man got up on stage, demanding quiet. The lights flickered on and off, some in the audience joined the call for quiet, increasing the noise level still further.

"Let's hear what he has to say!" the man next to Eva yelled.

Someone produced a hammer and handed it up to the now frustrated man. He banged it loudly on the floor until there was relative quiet.

"Listen to me!" he called out. "I have important news to share. The Germans have surrendered. Hitler is dead."

The hall fell silent and he repeated his message.

"The war is over," he said.

"He said the war is over!"

It caused pandemonium. People were hugging, kissing, weeping. It was hard to believe.

Eva sat down on the top of the stairs leading up to the projector room watching them, stunned, until a hand waving across her line of vision, caught her attention. She looked up into Yanosh's smiling face, and was soon standing wrapped in his strong embrace. They joined the crowd singing the Polish national anthem, *Mazurek Dąbrowskiego*, then left the hall to dance home together in the rain.

May 9, 1945

The war has ended, but not the suffering of our country. The Germans are gone, but Poland still bleeds.

And the Jews are gone, extinguished as a race here. Does that mean anything? Does it matter to anyone? We are the last Polish Jews. Everyone is happy but we Jews. The Jews have lost so much:

faith, hope, family, homes, ideals. We are a shattered, disillusioned remnant. For us, the struggle only begins. What do we have left now? Where shall we go to rebuild our lives, how shall we become human again, rejoin the world of the mundane everyday after what we have been through?

"Yanosh what are you doing?"
"Can't you see. I am writing. I need quiet now. I will finish soon, don't worry."

"But, Yanosh, I am worried. We are running out of money!"

"Eva, you worry too much. Let me finish this paragraph, then we will discuss matters. We will find a solution, I am sure."

August 3, 1945

Life here in Trebisk has been hard. I haven't found work. We survive on the few zloty Eva gets for her work at the cinema and some sewing she does, a one-time payment I received for an article I wrote which appeared in Henryk's journal, and food from the soup kitchen here. Its potatoes and more potatoes, weak but sweet tea, and occasional bottles of vodka to wash away bitterness and frustration. And now it's hot, too.

I have no creative juices anymore, either. Everything I write is flat, lifeless. I start and stop. Over and over again. Is the muse dead after all that has happened here in Poland?

We have lost contact with our old friends. I don't know where Marek and Pawla are now. Henryk said he had received a letter, but with no address and no specific information as to where they were, other than somewhere in Silesia. I have heard that they are still active in the anti-communist underground, but nothing else.

And I? I just sit here isolated in this hole, fretting, worried about the future of our country, but doing nothing substantial to help!

I want to move on from here, to get involved again, to do something.

4
A New Life – Silesia

We are now in the village of Svetyana, Upper Silesia. It's a pretty little place which has somehow remained untouched by the war. I found a nice house here. Left behind by the Germans, the Volksdeutsch, who used to live here. It's a small wooden cottage, windows painted green. A red, tiled roof. A fireplace with a stack of wood, ready for use in the winter. The chimney's not blocked this time. It's wonderful to see Eva smile so much. She has been flowering ever since we arrived here. It was a good decision. Things will be better here than they were in Trebisk.

But money … money is going to be a problem. I've got to find work. At least Eva already has a job in the local factory, but it's not enough. And Henryk still hasn't paid me for my second article. I must send him another reminder.

There are a lot of refugees here, many of them Jews. They have been steadily crossing the border from the Soviet Union. Some are fleeing the Communists, hoping to cross the border from here. The Jews are frightened by the renewed anti-Semitism in the East. Many are crossing the country to settle here in Silesia where there is housing and work.

They look awful. Thin, in rags, dirty and with haunting, haunted eyes. Most of them come carrying small bags of belongings, but some arrive with nothing. Nothing at all. Not even adequate clothing. Some are invalids, missing limbs.

It is good to see children again. To hear some of them singing with their families after work in the evenings. One young man, they call him Yankele, has a small accordion and a group of young people gather around him in a shed nearby sometimes. They use it as a clubhouse. It's a Zionist thing I think. But their "happy" songs

in Hebrew and Yiddish sound mournful and sad to me. Eva tells me
the words are of hope, of building Palestine, the Land of Israel, but I
am not convinced. They are deluding themselves with a false dream,
an impossible utopia.

January 8, 1946

Eva looked out the window hoping to see her returning husband. He had been gone ten days. She was worried. She had received a postcard from Berlin, knew he had arrived safely, but hadn't heard from him since.

Moniek and Jadzja, their new ex-Warsaw friends, had come by to visit her the week before last. Moniek had just returned from Germany. He told many stories about his visit there: his successful business deals, the humiliation of the previously proud Germans under foreign occupation, the influx of refugees from all over Eastern Europe. He had seen Yanosh. They had had a drink together in a Berlin bar. Yanosh had sent her the card with him and had asked him to look in on her, to make sure she was all right, to tell her he would be home soon.

That was two weeks ago. She had heard nothing since and couldn't help herself – she worried. They had not been separated since 1943. She had become ill with worry because of his Polish underground activity. Then it was the S.S. which terrified her. Now she was frightened of the Russians, the French, and the British. She wondered whether she should have agreed to this trip. He had seemed so sure of himself. He had promised that on his return they would have the money they needed, that he would not be caught. He'd known, he said, how to deceive the Nazis during the war, the occupying allies would be much easier to deal with. Her intuition told her that there would be trouble, that he would be caught smuggling, but she had ignored it, had not opposed the trip. They did need the money; perhaps she was just being hysterical, overprotective. And now? Was he now sitting in jail somewhere unable to contact her? Why didn't he come home?

They had been in Svetyana five months. Had moved there from the town of Trebisk, near Warsaw where they had first found refuge, after fleeing Warsaw. When the Jews had begun returning from the camps, the forests and later from the Soviet hinterland, things had taken a turn for the worse in Trebisk. Their former neighbors were unhappy about their return. They feared for their newly-gained possessions, that the Jews would start making demands of them, want their properties back. They were incited by anti-Semitic nationalists who associated the Jews with the newly established, and much hated, Communist regime. There had been violence. Some Jews had been killed. They had been murdered by hooligans. Eva remembered how Yanosh had pulled out his knife when they felt threatened, how he had slept with it under his pillow, always ready for use. She remembered the constant fear.

Their underground connections had been useful, had helped them find work: she as a seamstress in a newly-established, dress-repair shop, he for the local newspaper. But they lived in fear of the growing anti-Semitism. No one knew they were Jewish. They both spoke excellent, cultured Polish. They didn't have that sad, tortured Jewish look, but the fear of being found out was always there, gnawing at them.

The Polish government announced a program of resettlement in Upper Silesia. When the surviving Jews began to move there, they went too. It had been hard to move yet again. The anti-Semitism followed the Jews wherever they went. There were incidents in Silesia as well. As the Zionist groups became more active, the Hassidic groups reemerged, synagogues and Jewish schools were established, and so did the attacks on the Jews increase. The government attempts to curtail such attacks were meagre and unconvincing.

Eva wondered whether the communist leadership, which was clearly unhappy about this new assertion of Jewish nationalism and religion had not acquiesced in the anti-Semitic outbursts. Perhaps they did not regret the new phenomenon of Jewish exodus from Poland, which the Zionists called "*Bricha.*"

Yanosh had been happy here in Silesia for a while, Eva thought, but now he was growing restless. He had begun to speak about leaving Poland too. This made her nervous. She had wanted to stay put, had been happy here in Silesia.

When Yanosh heard how others had made money smuggling goods between Poland and Germany, had made contacts, which enabled them to bring family and friends across the border and on into the free zone, he decided to try his hand at it too. Eva remembered the conversations they had had about it, the way his eyes had lit up with excitement, the fears it had aroused in her. She had agreed ... agreed to his journey, agreed that they would leave Poland at some future time, despite her ambivalence. So he went. And Eva waited.

Two more days passed without a word from him, without a sign of life. And then on Tuesday evening she heard a knock on the door. It was early evening. She was already in bed, but not yet asleep. She had not been sleeping well, was all nerves. The knocking was incessant but faint. She grabbed her dressing gown, wrapped it around her shoulders and went running down the stairs. The tapping had stopped. She hastened to open the door, fumbling at the door handle for a moment. It swung open. There stood Marek and Pawla!

Pawla looked different. She had filled out, but the scar on her neck was unmistakable. Marek was a little balder. He wore the same red beard, now trimmed at the sides, bushy at the chin. She reached up to hug Marek, then hugged Pawla. Despite being a little startled at their unexpected visit, she was glad to see them.

"We knocked lightly. Didn't want to disturb you." Marek said, looking awkward.

"Marek said you were always an early riser, sometimes go to bed early," Pawla added.

"I am so delighted to see you," came the response. " Come in. Come in!"

"Thank you. We will."

"Eva, you don't look well. Have you been sleeping enough? I think you have put on weight."

Pawla poked Marek, who fell silent.

"You're expecting!" exclaimed Pawla in delight.

"Yes, I am."

She managed a smile, touching her belly with her right hand. As she spoke she caressed it.

"I'm due in August. I am so excited about it. Yanosh probably will want a boy. I just want a healthy baby, whatever gender."

"Where is Yanosh?" asked Marek. "Is he upstairs?"

Eva frowned, sat down and beckoned them to do so too. They sat down on the other two chairs in the fairly bare room.

"No, he is not here. He has been away almost three weeks now. On business. I'll tell you all about it, but first I want to get dressed and make us some coffee. I have the real thing. I won't be long."

Pawla lit herself a cigarette. She offered Eva and Marek too, but they both refused.

Eva got up again, headed for the kitchen to put on the kettle. On entering she thought she heard the kitchen window rattle. She looked outside but saw nothing. Thinking it must just be the wind, she turned back to the stove, picked up the kettle, filled it and returned it. She added another coal to the fire and stoked it. Behind her she heard the window rattle again. She turned to peep out but there was nothing there. She could hear Marek and Pawla talking in the living room, nothing else.

She came out to the living room, smiled at her friends who smiled back.

"Did you hear anything?" she asked them.

"No, just the wind blowing outside," Pawla answered, from behind her cloud of cigarette smoke.

"Were you expecting someone?" Marek asked.

"No, just thought I heard something outside. I'm just going up to get dressed," she said, climbing the wooden stairs as she spoke.

"The kettle is on. Make yourselves at home. I will be right down."

Eva opened her wardrobe in her room, rummaged through her few things until she found her favorite dress, the blue one Pawla had given her when last they saw each other. She picked out a matching shawl. She quickly slipped these things on, stockings and shoes, glanced in the mirror to check whether she looked presentable. The dress was a bit tight. Must let it out a little, she thought. The tired look of her face, the new wrinkles in her brow, the baggy eyes, all these bothered her, but this new evidence of her pregnant state was pleasing.

As she headed downstairs she heard the door, and then voices. Marek and Pawla were talking to someone, a man.

She strained to hear. It was Yanosh's voice!

She flew down the stairs straight into his strong arms. It felt good to be there again. They kissed and parted to look at each other, Eva trying hard to hold back her tears.

Yanosh handed her a handkerchief, the one she had given him, inscribed with his initials. She wiped the tears off her cheeks, and dried her eyes. She looked up at him. He looked thinner, but clearly happy to be home. He was smiling broadly, eyes shining. But he turned serious.

"You have been worrying about me, Eva," he commented. "You haven't been sleeping."

"Yes, I have... No. I haven't... You were gone longer than you said. I've heard so many stories about people caught on the border. Did everything go as planned? Are we now rich?"

Yanosh laughed.

Marek and Pawla both sat there poised, each with a cup of coffee in hand. They had helped themselves. They were listening with interest to Yanosh's answer. They, too, were considering a similar project.

"Well," he started, "I was lucky..."

"What do you mean?" Eva jumped in, suspicious and concerned.

"I was almost caught and a guy I was with was caught.

I stayed a little while at the border to help him out. As you know the importing of leather is very lucrative now. Leather is cheap in Germany and in great demand here. The watches I was smuggling were on me, hanging on a chain around my neck, under my shirt. He had a couple of bags of leather hides. I suppose I didn't look suspicious to them. They didn't search me, just walked right past me. But they focused on the man I was with. He was a short, stocky fellow whom I had befriended earlier in Berlin. He had been a Soviet partisan during the war in Byelorussia, had good contacts everywhere and had turned to smuggling. He was experienced already, almost professional. He helped me out a lot when I first arrived in Berlin. He told me incredible stories about his partisan days. He, too, likes to write. He shared some poems he had written. "Bora" he called himself, short for Borowski. After awhile, I learned that his first name is Yosef in Hebrew, and Joseph in English."

Yanosh stopped to sip some coffee, saw he had everyone's attention and continued:

"Anyway, the French gendarmes got on the train near the border and started searching and questioning people. They didn't bother me but they soon found Bora's bundles of leather. They were just hauling them away when Bora spoke up. He told them that the leather was his, that he was legitimately importing it to Poland, showed them papers. They seemed convinced, returned the parcels and were about to go when a young blonde woman came up to the officer and whispered something to him. Bora looked shocked, but remained silent. The officer gave an order in French. They grabbed the leather again and Bora as well, began to drag him off with them. He resisted them."

"So what happened to them?" asked Marek, taking a cigarette from his wife and lighting it.

"They took him outside. There was some yelling. I heard them calling him a dirty Jew (Juif, Juif! They screamed at him). They started beating him. He was all bloodied. He lost some teeth in the fight, but he seemed to keep his cool. He gave as good as he got. Two of them, but he stood his ground. I was looking out the window, wondering whether I should go out to give him some help. He saw me and yelled to me between blows, 'You stay out of this! Just wait for me!' Then he yelled something in Russian before he was finally knocked down. It sounded like 'under the seat!' They dragged him along the station platform, threw some water on him, forced him to get up, and went out through the gate with him."

"And then?"

By this time the windows were crowded with people watching the show. No one interfered or said anything. While they were dragging Bora away I slipped back into the cubicle and looked under the seat where he had been sitting. I found a black cloth bag tied to the back leg underneath. I stuffed it into my coat pocket, and headed for the nearest toilet. There I undid the string which held it closed. There were papers inside, and money. A lot of paper notes. Just as the train began to move again I jumped off onto the platform, determined to help Bora. There was no way I could contact you, Eva. Later I tried, but with no success. I managed to get Bora released, using his money to bribe his guard the next morning. We crossed the border together that night without being caught."

Yanosh suddenly sat down.

"I am tired," he said, "I need to wash and rest, but first, Eva, tell me about you. Is everything all right? You look very tired yourself. And you have gained weight... Have you been eating too much strudel?!"

Eva looked at him incredulous. She wondered how he could ask such a question, but didn't say anything.

"Go wash up. Lie down in the bed for a while. We'll talk later," she said.

Marek and Pawla rose to go. They told their hosts they were staying nearby with other friends, that they would come back later. After hugs, kisses, a few more parting words they left. Eva appreciated their sensitivity.

Yanosh had soon washed and was in the bed. She joined him

there. He was not quite asleep yet. She began to caress him. He was soon aroused. They made love passionately. Yanosh slept. Eva got up, got dressed again, and went out to work.

All day at work she thought about Yanosh's last comment. Could he have forgotten that she was pregnant? She had told him, hadn't she? Now she was not sure whether she had told him yet. Perhaps that's why he'd mentioned that she had put on weight. But then when they had made love he must have noticed the change in her breasts, her slightly protruding stomach. He hadn't said anything, but then he was so tired. Was it possible that he didn't know?

She barely thought of anything else. So much so that she cut herself on the sewing machine. She ate her lunch with her workmates as usual, and was excited and happy to share the news of Yanosh's return with them. They all knew she was expecting. How could it be that Yanosh didn't?

She returned home along her usual, tree-lined route, barely noticing the pretty houses with their little German gardens on the way. It was cold and drizzling. Her scarf was wet. She thought of what they might have for supper that night. Perhaps cabbage soup and potatoes? She thought about how she would bring up the matter of her pregnancy.

As she approached the building, spotting the now-familiar red-tiled roof with its smoking brick chimney, she came up with a plan for the evening. She wrapped her jacket around her shoulders more tightly, closing a couple of buttons before the cold evening wind, and continued walking towards her Silesian home. She thought of its previous occupants, wondering what their fate might have been. She knew they were Germans who had been expelled from this area in the post-war settlement. She imagined them as homeless refugees in Germany. She knew what that meant and, even though they were Germans, felt sorry for them.

Yanosh had woken and was reorienting himself after his three weeks away in Germany. He wandered around the house, checking to see that everything was in place. Eva's paintings and drawings hung along the far bedroom wall. He liked her sketch of the oak tree they had sheltered under in Pilsudski Square when they had first come out of hiding. She had captured well the lonely, defiant stance of that tree in the ruins of Warsaw. Their initials were there, along with the initials of many others. So many others, who had not survived the war.

He wandered into the kitchen, put the kettle on, added a coal to the stove fire, and checked the cupboards for something to nibble. He found some biscuits – maybe Eva had made them. They certainly tasted like Eva's baking. A little stale, but still tasty. They were heart-shaped and dusted with cinnamon and sugar. The kettle whistled. He lifted it off the stove, pouring himself a cup of tea. He took out his diary and pen to write until Eva's return.

He thought about the strange new friend he had made while in Berlin, Yosef Borowski. He was enchanted by his quiet self-confidence and cunning. He had dealt with a terrible situation and jumped back out of it, on his feet again like a cat. Bora had a charming side to him, but he could see that he was tough and ruthless. He had challenged him to join him in settling accounts with the S.S., left him contact details and invited him to call after he got back to Silesia. Should he do so?

Perhaps he would write a character sketch of the man? No. He didn't know him well enough for that.

So what would he write about now? His thoughts on his visit to Berlin? The rage he felt at the Germans he met there, their denial of the atrocities of the recent past, the war years?

He looked at his watch. It was already four thirty in the afternoon. Eva would be home at around five thirty, he thought, which gave him an hour to write. The first page of the diary was marked August 3, 1943. He started to read what he had written. It was written while they were still in hiding, at the time of the final destruction of the ghetto. His strong, clear handwriting surprised him, considering when the entries were written and what they described. He had been trying to put all that behind him: the anguish, the sense of impotence against the Nazis as they murdered his people. It all came flooding back now. He closed the diary again. He couldn't write. He put his diary away.

He saw his mother's face at their last meeting. She was saying something, but he couldn't hear her. The words she mouthed were soundless. She looked old, thin and grey. What was she saying? Help us! Save us! Tserrateven! Tserattaven!

He remembered he had brought them food, had succeeded in getting into the ghetto disguised as a German soldier. He had proudly shown them his pistol. He hadn't understood why they weren't impressed. The stench in the ghetto was overwhelming; there was no escaping it. He remembered how happy he had been to leave, to leave his own family behind in that filth! His mother asked him not to leave them, but he did. He had to go... Eva was waiting... He'd be back, he promised. She clutched his jacket. He released her frail hand and left.

He got up, wandered around the house again, looked out the window. It was raining; the trees and buildings were glistening, reflecting the lights of the windows along the road. Everything seemed so peaceful out there, but inside his mind was churning, burning. Guilt. He felt guilty remorse. Could he have saved her?

It was painful, but he could not escape the flood of thoughts and memories.

He went back to the stove and added a coal. He picked up the worn brown leather-bound book and his pen. He sat again to write, but found it impossible to do so. He put the pen down again, closed the diary.

The door opened behind him. He turned to see Eva standing there. She was dripping. She held a basket, a loaf of bread peeping over the edge of it... He saw a greasy package that looked like it might be butter, and some cheese. He got up, got her a towel, and wrapped it around her. He kissed her.

"Yanosh, wait! Wait! Not now! Let me put these things down," she said, smiling. "Look, I brought us food."

She put the basket down on their little table, and began to take things out. The red towel draped over her hair and shoulders made her look like a good fairy, a Little Red Riding Hood, perhaps.

"Look, Yanoshke, fresh bread. Smell it!?"

He nodded, smiling as she lifted the bread out towards him.

"Butter, cheese, and best of all, a bottle of vodka ... in honor of your safe return," she said.

Yanosh's smile broadened as he watched her place a small green bottle on the table beside the bread.

"Go bring some glasses, a knife and a couple of plates, my love," she said.

"Of course," he responded, walking towards her, arms outstretched, "but first a kiss."

He brought the things and they sat down to their meal together. Outside the rain grew stronger, beating heavily on the roof. The leak in the ceiling began to drip more frequently into the metal basin placed below it. An annoying metallic clink.

The lights flickered on and off a few times, and then finally went out. They saw a flash of lighting outside the living room window, followed a few moments later by the crash of thunder.

Yanosh commented that the storm had probably caused the problem with the electricity, that they had some candles which would help light their meal, that it would be more romantic by candle light anyway, that he knew where they were and would bring them to the table.

Eva sat watching as Yanosh got up to get candles to place on the table. Through the stove window she could see the glow from the embers of the burning coals inside. It gave her some dim light by which to watch Yanosh's movements, as she dried her hair. His silhouette moved around the kitchen area as he searched for the candles. She hummed to herself as she watched him, wondering how she would bring up the subject of her pregnancy.

He turned back towards her carrying two candles and some matches, which he set up in the center of the table and lit. She poured two glasses of vodka and suggested a toast.

"To us!" she said.

"Yes, to the three of us!" he responded, smiling in the impish way he did sometimes.

"So you know that I am pregnant!"

"Yes, of course, what did you think? How could I not notice? I brought you a small gift in honor of the occasion."

"You got me something?"

"Yes, I did."

"Oh, it's so beautiful!"

"I thought you'd like it, Eva ... Someone is at the door. Why don't you put it away for now, and I'll see who it is."

Eva slipped the gift into her apron pocket and got up to join her husband at the door. She was curious to see who would be visiting them in such a storm.

He opened the door and in stepped a dripping Pawla, followed by a very wet Marek. They were both shivering.

"Oh, you are both so wet! Come in, come in. I'll get some towels and find you something to change into."

"Yes, that is a good idea. Then you can join us for a little vodka. We have something to celebrate," added Yanosh.

"But why did you come in such a storm? You could have waited; we would have understood why you didn't come."

"It wwwasn'tt a sstorm when wwwe set outtt, just light drizzzzle," said Pawla, between shivers.

"Here take these towels. Dry yourselves. I'll be back with some clothes soon."

Pawla wrapped herself in the towel she had been given, still shivering. Marek dried his curly hair with his towel. Another round of thunder and lightning, a window flew open allowing cold wind and rain into the room, until Yanosh managed to shut it. The candles had blown out. Eva rekindled them.

"We came because we have to talk to you," said Marek, "we must talk about something important before it is too late. It is urgent."

Pawla nodded in agreement, the red scar on her neck alternately visible in the candlelight and the light of the stove embers, as her head moved up and down.

"That sounds serious, but not yet. First you must get into some dry clothes, and have a drink to warm your insides as well," Yanosh said, half-laughing at his poor friends.

As if on cue, Eva then returned with some clothes. Each willingly took a bundle and headed for the bedroom to change.

They heard giggling from behind the door. Yanosh winked to his wife. She blushed. Another clap of thunder. The laughter stopped.

The rain kept pounding on the roof, the wind whistled, and they waited.

Their friends reemerged after a few minutes looking like a pair of clowns. Marek was a bigger man than Yanosh. The clothes were tight on him, the pants legs and sleeves too short. His nose was painted red. Pawla stood there wrapped in a blanket, lipstick smeared across her mouth and cheeks, complaining that Eva's clothes were baggy on her. Eva and Yanosh laughed at the absurd.

"What have you been doing with my lipstick?"

"Well... We looked like clowns with these clothes, so why not?" he retorted, laughing too.

"I am sorry I don't have anything else for you to wear, Pawla, but I'll put your things on the stove so they'll dry a little."

"She could wear my dressing-gown, Eva. It would be more comfortable than that blanket."

Yanosh went into the bedroom, soon returning with a big blue dressing-gown, which he handed to Pawla.

"Let's have those drinks you promised, Yanosh!"

Yanosh poured two glasses of vodka. Pawla returned from

the bedroom, wearing the blue dressing-gown. They all sat down around the little table.

"To the baby!"

"To the baby!"

The vodka was soon gone, as were the bread and cheese. Eva refused a second drink.

Yanosh got up and lit a cigarette at the stove, and lit another for Pawla. He ignored Eva's disapproving look. The two smokers puffed their cigarettes contentedly, and relaxed.

"Pity we have no more vodka," Marek commented.

"Yes, a pity," Yanosh agreed.

"We will have some tea and talk more seriously now," Pawla announced, flicking cigarette ash into her plate.

Eva grimaced.

"Yes, I am curious to know what brought you here tonight," Yanosh said.

Marek made an effort to look serious, wiped his nose clean of the lipstick, sat up straight in his chair, and then leaned forward in a wobbling movement towards Yanosh and Eva. He had to steady himself, almost falling off the edge of the chair. Pawla laughed at him.

"I think it might have stopped raining," commented Yanosh.

"Certainly the thunder and lightning have stopped."

"It's still raining out there, but the storm has let up a little. What was it you wanted to talk about?" asked Eva, turning towards Marek.

"Well you know that the present Polish government is preparing for elections in the near future, that Stanislaw Mikolajiczyk's Country Party is very popular and that the communists might not be in the next government, if Mikolajiczyk wins enough votes."

"Yes, I am excited about the possibility of getting rid of the communists. So many Poles dream of regaining their freedom after being occupied by the Nazi murderers and now by the Russians. As long as the communists are in government, the Soviet tanks and soldiers won't be leaving our Polish countryside. We all hope to get our country back from them, don't we?"

"Yes, we do Yanosh, but don't fool yourself. It is not going to happen. There will be no elections, the Soviets will not leave. Stalin, I am afraid, is here to stay."

"Why do you say that with such certainty, Pawla?"

"Ask Marek. Ask him. He knows something important."

"So Marek, what's the story? What do you know?"

"I spoke to an old friend who is a member of the party, a high official in the foreign ministry. I can't tell you his name, promised him that I wouldn't. They are planning to announce a state of emergency, people will be arrested, the elections will be postponed. They're looking for former activists of the Armia Krakowa, the wartime Polish resistance. We are on the list. Your friend Borowski is listed too."

Eva's face paled. She and Yanosh were listening to Marek as if they had not been drinking and laughing, been jolly just a moment before. Yanosh put out what was left of his cigarette, lit another, offered one to Pawla, who lit hers from his.

The sound of the steady rain hitting the roof was amplified by the silence in the room. Eva heard the clip-clop rattle of a horse and wagon going past.

Marek turned to Yanosh: "You are on the top of the list. You must leave Poland as soon as possible. Tonight. There is no time. You cannot wait any longer. Your life is in danger. Eva is expecting."

Yanosh puffed on his cigarette before responding. "Tonight! No, we can't ... not tonight. I'm not ready yet to leave."

"Yanshuk, if what Marek says is even half true, we must flee immediately, even though we had other plans."

"But this is too rushed, too soon." He blew a thin column of smoke, which rose towards the ceiling.

"Yanosh, listen to your wife. If she, in her present condition, is willing to go, then you must. Marek is worried about you. We wouldn't have come in such weather if it was not urgent."

Pawla's cigarette quivered between her fingers as she spoke. She was not one who said much, but when she did...

Eva saw that her face was focused on Yanosh, waiting for him to understand. She put her hand on his shoulder, a gentle touch, understanding how intimidating Pawla's stare could be. The room was becoming stifling.

"But how? How are we going to go anywhere now? In this rain, in the night?"

"Yes, we know, we know. But you must pack some things quickly and come right away. A friend will be here soon with a car to take you to a safe place. We have booked tickets for you to Berlin. The train leaves tomorrow morning. Here. Take them. When we get to Berlin we will be met by friends. Antek and Moniek will be waiting there for us."

"What! You've got tickets? A car? Now? Right away?"

"Yes, Yanosh... Now... You must go... Now. We don't want you endangered here tonight. They might be on their way to get you right now. So be quick. Get your things. Eva, come... Let's get ready as soon as possible. Borowski is on his way."

Eva heard the sound of an approaching car coming along the road. The lights moved into sight through the window. They then shone directly into the room, like the threatening searchlights outside the barbed wire fence of a ghetto or camp searching for escapees.

They heard voices outside, speaking Russian. The car engine continued purring for a while, but was soon turned off, as were the lights. Footsteps approached, and then there was a loud knock on the door. Marek had pulled out his pistol. Pawla did so too. They moved towards the door, signaling to their two friends to crouch down.

Another knock, louder than the first. And a third. The two pistols were aimed at the door, Marek and Pawla waiting crouched on either side. Yanosh grabbed Eva's arm and pulled her down low, just under the table. They waited. Eva almost laughed at the sight of her pistol-carrying friends at the door.

They looked comical, the way they were dressed. But this was deadly serious. She stifled her laughter.

Voices. Russian again. More steps. Then everything exploded. The door came crashing down. Automatic gunfire rang out. Two men fell into the room on top of the blackened door, bleeding profusely, each dropping a weapon. They convulsed for a few moments, then "relaxed." They were both dead. They lay there in a pool of blood. The blood spread along the edge of the door, framed it in red.

Behind them stood a short, stocky man holding a Sten submachine gun. His dark eyes shone, a close-lipped grin spread across his face as he stepped into the room to check his prey.

He kicked over each of the two dead men in turn, picked up the two handguns, which he stuffed into the ample pockets of a brown coat, and strode into the center of the room.

"Is everyone all right in here?" he asked looking around the room.

Sweating profusely, the stocky man reached into his pocket, pulled out a cloth and wiped his brow. With his other hand he released the machine gun. It dropped to his chest with a thud, and then continued swinging, pendulum-like, from a leather strap. His thin smile broadened a little.

"Why are you all so serious now? They are only a couple of NKVD goons sent by Stalin to knock off 'enemies of the state'. It was them or us! We must get out of here fast. There will be more where they came from."

Pawla and Marek had slid down beside the door. They sat there staring up at Bora, and at the two dead men. Yanosh let go of Eva and straightened up. He walked towards the man to greet him. Eva sat there hugging herself and shaking.

The two shook hands there beside the red-framed door, ignoring the two bodies still bleeding on top of it, as the others rose to join them.

"It's good to see you again, Bora."

Yanosh turned back towards his wife and introduced him:

"Eva, this is the man I told you about, my friend Yosef Borowski."

"Your wife?"

"Yes."

The man bowed towards her formally, then took her hand and kissed it. She was taken aback considering the bizarre scene.

"I would have preferred better circumstances for such a meeting. We have some things to discuss I think."

"Listen, Yanosh, we don't have time to talk now. We must move quickly. My car is waiting downstairs. All of you ... grab whatever you need to take with you. We have to get out of here fast! I will be waiting for you downstairs in the car. I'll keep an eye on the road while you pack. If you hear the engine turned on, just disappear fast. Marek, Pawla ... Come join me. You can keep watch at the entrance."

The three of them left immediately, leaving Eva and Yanosh standing there. Eva wondered what to do with the two dead Russians. We Jews have seen too much death, too many corpses in the streets of Warsaw, she thought. And yet something about these two bodies disturbed her terribly.

The war was over now, so why was there yet no end to the bloodshed? It seemed indecent to just leave them lying there behind them as they fled. She had to do something. She grabbed a couple of blankets from the bedroom to throw over them. Their glassed-over eyes seemed to stare at her until she draped the blankets over the faces.

Having covered them, Eva breathed more easily.

Yanosh began to collect some things and packed them into his brown suitcase. He beckoned Eva to do the same, pointing at her bag insistently.

"You must pack now," he said. "Leave them alone. We don't have time to do anything for them. No time for that now. Who knows how many unburied, unattended dead these two have left behind them? Leave them."

Clank. Something, maybe a stone, hit the window shutter.

"Hurry!" Marek's voice called up at them.

Eva began to pack. A couple of dresses, the green one and the black, stockings, a sweater, some blouses, underwear, toiletries, a pair of black shoes, a towel, her sketch-book, some pencils, her gloves and a red scarf. She was experienced at packing but had never packed as fast as this.

Yanosh was waiting impatiently, having already packed. He had his jacket on, as well as his grey cap.

"I'm almost ready. Just need to check that I have everything that I need."

"What are you going to sleep in, Eva?"

"Ah, yes ... a nightie! Okay. That's it. I'm now ready to go," she said, as she put a nightie in, got into her coat and closed her bag.

"Did you pack your diary, Yanosh?"

"Of course!" he replied. "Let's go!"

They headed down the stairs, just as they heard the clink of another stone hitting the shutter outside.

The car was an old Volkswagen, a black round presence in the dark. They heard the engine but barely saw the vehicle until they got close to it. The car door swung open. Bora beckoned them to get in. He jumped out and loaded their two bags in the back. Marek and Pawla were already sitting there inside. It was crowded but they all managed to squeeze in. The back door slammed shut. Then Bora got in again, turned the lights on and the road appeared before them in the flickering beams. They began to roll forward, gathering speed, Bora put the car into gear and they started moving as the engine purred more loudly. Behind them they saw the approaching lights of another car.

Bora accelerated and turned a corner. They swung across the car from one side to the other as they went around. The car skidded and screeched. The road was still wet.

"Careful, Bora. Careful ... You could cause an accident this way!"

"It's a wet road. The car's barely stable. Slow down!"

"All right, all right... We're just going around one more corner and then we are out of the city center, then I'll slow down. *Farshtaistzich?*"

He flew around yet another corner. The car almost went into a spin, snipping a lamp post with its tail end as they skidded past. They were now on a wide boulevard, trees lined either side, some car lights were moving along it ahead of them. They overtook a horse and buggy trotting along steadily at a clip-clop. The driver waved.

"*Na Zdrova!*" they heard him say as they drove past. Eva looked back at him in the light of an oncoming vehicle. His wrinkled face showed the mark of years of bonhomie, smile lines etched into the leathery cheeks on either side. Bora, to their relief, had finally slowed down. They began to breath more easily again. Marek stretched his long legs... Pawla sighed.

"Where are we going, Bora?" asked Eva.

"You'll see soon enough!" came the answer.

"Marek tell us. You must know where we are headed," she tried again.

"You'll see," Bora repeated, annoyed, looking into the mirror at Eva and the other passengers, and beyond out the window.

Marek didn't respond.

"Nothing suspicious," Bora said, half to himself, as he drove on. "We're all right."

Yanosh sat beside his wife wrapped in silence.

She looked at him, wondering what was on his mind, but knew better than to ask. She felt his hand resting on her shoulder. It was reassuring to have him there beside her, not far away in Berlin, or running around outside their hiding place as he had done in Warsaw. She reached up to touch his hand. It was warm. He took hers for a moment, warming her, but then withdrew it. He was so faraway, despite his physical closeness. What was he thinking about?

The car slowed down, then came to a stop.

Bora announced to them: "We have reached our destination. Time to disembark!"

Eva looked outside to see the same train station they had arrived at when they first came to Steszin. The tall iron gates were closed, padlocked. A train sat there on the rails, a snake-like creature sleeping, waiting for the warmth of the morning sun in order to come back to life. All was dark. It looked desolate, nothing like the busy, bustling place they had met when they had first arrived months before. Why were they stopping here now in the middle of the night?

Everyone got out of the car, stretched their bodies, appreciative of the fresh, but chilly, night air and that they were no longer squashed into the car. Bora unloaded the bags, handing them out to the two men to carry. Pawla grabbed a bag as well. Bora led them away from the car, having locked it.

"Follow me," he said, smiling to himself mysteriously.

They followed him. He led them around the station entrance, about a hundred meters along a trail by the railway track, and then turned right off the track towards a little wood.

They walked along a thick hedge of bushes for a while until Bora found a break in it through which he led them. On the other side of the hedge they met a row of low tents, the kind used by soldiers in the field. Eva counted four tents.

"Who are these for?" she asked.

Bora laughed, Marek and Pawla joining his laughter. Yanosh gave his wife a little poke, mumbling:

"Don't be silly, darling. This is our hotel for the night."

The four pup tents had been set up in a straight line behind the hedge. The dark olive material which showed in the light of Bora's lantern would be hard to see in the morning Eva thought, the tents sitting along the hedge like that. It would certainly be well camouflaged overnight.

"You will be safe here tonight," Bora told them.

"Come on, Eva; Let's get bedded for the night."

Eva looked at the tent, which Yanosh unflapped, skeptically.

"I put them up for us earlier this evening, before setting out to get those Russian assassins," Bora explained.

"No one is going to find us here. The challenge will be to get on the train tomorrow morning without any problems from those *mamzerim*."

"Why are there four tents?" asked Eva.

"You ask a lot of questions, maidelle!

Eva blushed.

"One for each couple, one for me, and one for our bags," Bora answered her. "We will have to take turns keeping watch through the night. Who will take the first turn?"

"I will," Marek responded.

Oh, no, thought Eva, the middle watch is the worst. Your sleep is broken by the watch. Yanosh is so tired!

Yanosh said nothing.

Bora seemed to read her mind:

"That's all right, Yanosh. I will take the middle watch. I'll wake you for the third."

"That's all!" piped up Pawla, angrily. "I understand that you don't expect Eva to guard since she is expecting, but I'm as good a shot as any man. I will take the third watch. Let Yanosh sleep, he looks so exhausted."

Yanosh smiled weakly in agreement.

"Right, Pawla, you're on then! We are relying on you to wake us before dawn, so we can make that train on time. Good night to everybody."

Next morning, birds were singing above the tents. The rain had started and stopped through the night, beating on the canvas, dripping through in places. Yanosh looked out beyond the flap to see Pawla sitting huddled beside the bushes. She was holding her pistol in one hand, a cup of tea in the other. Yanosh saw the rising steam and wondered how they had boiled water here – it was damp, and a fire would certainly have given them away. How had Bora done it?

Eva lay curled up under her coat and the one blanket

they'd found in the tent when bedding down the night before. Yanosh's bladder and the cold had woken him. Still dark, he wondered what time it was. Had his watch had stopped? It read 2:00 a.m., but the birds told him differently, their chirping a precursor of the coming dawn. Perhaps water had gotten into the mechanism. He awaited the warmth of the morning sun eagerly. Perhaps he could escape the cold which had penetrated his bones by walking around a little, he thought.

He got up out of the tent, found a spot to urinate, watching the steam rise as he did. He then joined Pawla. She was happy to have his company, offered him a steaming cup of tea.

"Thank you. Nothing like a hot drink in this cold. That was very nice of Bora to arrange it."

"There's more. Here, under the hedge ... a flask of tea. I'll pour you some more."

"How did he do it?" he asked her, sipping some tea.

"I don't know, but you know Bora. He always manages to arrange things, to fix things that others can't. He is pretty amazing that way," she commented.

"Yes, he is, but he is not an easy person to deal with."

"He is a strange man ... keeps to himself a lot. I have never seen him spend much time talking to other people. He doesn't seem to have patience for people."

"I spent some time with him, when we were in Berlin together, doing business there. He told me some incredible stories about the years he spent as a partisan fighter in the Byelorussian forests during the war."

"I've heard some of his stories. I know that he gave evidence to a war crimes commission about the German atrocities. You know, Yanosh, as a messenger of the Polish underground I got around a fair bit. I'd heard of his group during the war; Nekomma – Revenge, they called themselves. It was a Jewish group, which the Soviets disbanded. There were some contacts between his group and the A.K."

"You seem to know more about him than I do. I would like to hear more."

"I don't think so. Well, he told me he had been an officer in the Red Army. When the Soviet front collapsed under German attack in June 1941, he managed to escape with some other officers into the Naroch forest. The commander was a Colonel Markov."

"That matches what he told me."

"Did he tell you how they were abandoned by the Russians, set up their own Jewish group?"

"Yes, of course. He is proud of what they did, and bitter about the Soviet behavior."

Yanosh considered whether he should continue talking about this subject any further. Bora might not appreciate him sharing what he had told him.

He saw that he had peaked Pawla's curiosity. She was looking at him expectantly, had put down her cup. She was stroking her scarred neck, as she often did when she listened.

The sky was growing lighter, the birds had stopped chirping.

"Good morning! Is everything all right?" said a familiar, gruff voice.

They turned to see Bora standing there, studying them.

"It is time to get the other two up and get moving," he told them, winking.

They were startled at first, but then got moving. While they'd been sitting talking, the first light of dawn had turned into morning. The shadows were gone, the greens of the foliage around them, the azure and gold of the sky above was being painted again on the canvas of a new day. Yesterday's clouds were gone.

Yanosh went to call Eva, Pawla to awaken Marek, their whispered calls to their loved ones echoing each other between the tents. Bora meanwhile pulled the bags out of the other tent, took down his and the fourth tent, then poured himself a hot drink, stood there waiting, watching as the two couples organized themselves to leave.

They were soon packed. Bora took the tents and stowed them

under the hedge near an old oak. He placed a few rocks in a pile as a marker. Yanosh thought of the stories he had learned as a child as he watched him, something about Jacob, the patriarch, when he fled his brother Esau, or was it the story of Joshua's entry into the land of Canaan? He couldn't quite remember.

They headed out towards the train station, a silent procession of armed refugees carrying bags. Bora led the way, Pawla taking up the rear, her auburn-blond hair flying out behind her in the wind.

They walked back along the railway tracks until they reached the entrance to the station. The car was not where they had left it the night before. Bora stopped where the vehicle had been. The ground was black, as after a fire. He crouched down to look more closely, picked up a handful of dirt and smelled it.

"Gunpowder and petrol," he commented. "There must have been quite a fire here last night. They would have finished us off if they'd found us nearby."

"But we didn't hear anything last night, there was no explosion!"

"You're right, Pawla."

"So what happened to the car?"

"Don't know, but it doesn't matter now. Let's get moving. Right away!"

Bora led them into the station. There was no one there. It was cold, bleak. Everything was wet. It smelled of rotting wood. Some of it was charred. Signs of a fire which had been extinguished?

They sat on the bench under the shelter, waiting. Listening. Yanosh heard sounds of dripping water. Footsteps.

The stationmaster, rubbing his blood-shot eyes beneath silver spectacles, sauntered out onto the platform. He spied the group of waiting travelers and stopped in his tracks. He had seen many bedraggled people carrying bags waiting on the platform early in the morning, some sleeping overnight, but this bunch made an impression on him.

"Lucky these people weren't here last night," he mumbled, "Dealing with a bloody fire here was enough for one night!"

"*Dzien Dobry!* Good morning. You are early," he said to them, breathing out an alcoholic smell as he spoke.

"Did you see the smoke last night? We had a fire here."

"We can see that," said Marek. "What happened?"

"Don't know. I was sleeping, heard an explosion. It took a while to put out the fire. A lot of people were running around here, yelling. Now they are all gone. Left me with the damage to take care of."

"Quite a mess."

"Yep."

"Cold this morning, isn't it?"

"Yep."

"Cold isn't the word. We are freezing," added Eva, shivering demonstratively.

The station master had a round, ruddy face, bushy white eyebrows, needed a shave. He looked at Eva sympathetically.

"You are expecting?"

Eva nodded.

Yanosh wondered how he knew. She wasn't showing yet.

"Hold on a moment, I'll be back."

He walked back down the platform to the little ticket office, pulled out a heavy ring of keys, which jangled and jingled loudly in the early morning quiet. The door creaked open and he disappeared inside for a while. He came back carrying something. It was a small, grey blanket.

"Here, take this," he said, smiling kindly, "but please remember to return it before you board the train."

Eva accepted the blanket. She looked grateful.

"*Dzien Kuje bardzo!* Thank you. That's very kind."

She draped the blanket over her shoulders, and then folded it over her chest.

"When you are ready one of you should come over to buy tickets. Where are you going?" he asked.

"Berlin, sir, by way of Lodz. We already have tickets," said Yanosh, producing them to show him.

"So bring them over to the office ... later on," he responded.

He pulled on a chain hanging from his coat pocket until a pocket watch appeared. It began to swing like a pendulum, until he caught it in mid-arc. He examined the watch, which glinted in the sunlight, commenting:

"It really is early. Only seven ten. The train to Lodz leaves at nine, so there is plenty of time. It won't arrive here until eight forty-five at the earliest."

"We will wait here."

"Suit yourselves. I am making tea. You are welcome to join me for some, if you want. I make it strong and sweet, especially after a wet night, like last night, if you understand what I mean..."

"*Damien Kuje*. You are very kind, sir."

The strong, slightly alcoholic black tea helped warm their fingers and insides. The conversation was bland, no one really wanted to say anything, but all felt the need to be polite. Sometime later they heard the distant sound of the train's horn and then an approaching rumble. Yanosh looked outside to see the column of steam coming closer. He thought of all the trains that had carried so many Jews to their death only a few years before, but banished the thought as soon as it appeared. The train arrived, an old blue-painted steamer with at least ten carriages. He had stopped counting after six.

They boarded at eight forty-eight. The train left at nine, on schedule.

They passed a couple of rivers, crossed over a bridge and under another, saw a small lake and a distant forest, but most of the time the view was monotonous and predictable. It consisted of flat farmlands, with fields full of ripe barley and new wheat crops, sheep and cows at pasture, little towns and villages with thatched roofs and dirt tracks. The churches and occasional aristocratic villas overlooking the bigger towns in this part of the country showed a strong German influence. Many were Gothic in style.

As they approached Lodz, the scenery changed. There were better roads, other rail lines crisscrossed theirs, another train passed them, carrying freight in the opposite direction. There were trucks and cars, instead of the horses and wagons they had been seeing here and there. Then they saw the smoke stacks of Lodz approaching them, bellowing smoke into the afternoon sky.

Yanosh shuddered, "That smoke, those chimneys … they remind me of the stories about the death camps."

"What did you say, Yanosh?"

"Look, you see that smoke rising over there. And there? Behind that old brick building, a great green chimney bellowing smoke up into the sky. Do you see it now? There, near those two blackened trees."

Yanosh pointed out the train window, so that Eva could see what he was talking about.

Her eyes followed the line of his outstretched arm and index finger. He was pointing at the two chimneys and the rising black-grey smoke he had seen.

"Yes, I see what you mean, but they are just factory chimneys, that's all."

"Probably, but the chimneys at Oswiezcim must have looked just like that, pouring out the smoke from the bodies of all those murdered, gassed Jews."

"Yanosh, let's talk about something else. I have heard more than enough about what the Nazis did in that camp. I can't listen to it anymore. Please stop. Please. You seem to talk about nothing else since your return from Germany."

Yanosh didn't answer. He knew she was right. He needed to protect her, but the flood of thought was hard to control. He must keep these things to himself, be more circumspect he thought.

Pawla turned to look as well. Marek was staring out the window already.

"Those are two factory stacks, as Eva says. I know the place... They make rail tracks. It is an iron foundry."

"How do you know so much about it?" Marek asked his wife.

"I visited the place during the war. There was a man there who used to help the 'underground,' the A.K. His name was Karol Shashinski. He would supply us with metal parts for weapons we were making. It's a huge complex. The Germans Aryanized it – it had been Jewish-owned – but they kept the Polish middle management in place. Shashinski was a smart fellow, perhaps too smart. He was in charge of the storerooms, the only one there who knew where everything was. They needed him, couldn't run the plant without him..."

"Shashinski, yes I knew him too. Before the war. I heard he was helping the underground. What became of him?"

"The Gestapo found out about his underground activities – someone in the factory informed them. They arrested him, tortured him. He let them have some names and people were executed. They let him live, sent him back to work again. He was a broken man after that. Someone killed him, I think. The rumor was that one of the families squared their debt with him for speaking with the Nazis, for telling them too much. Dead ... like so many others."

Marek nodded.

"So many others ... Thousands murdered ... Maybe a million dead, or more, by those German butchers."

"Lodz looks so peaceful today."

"Yes, it is amazing to see how well-preserved Lodz is ... compared to the rest of the country, especially Warsaw."

Everyone nodded solemnly in agreement.

The train pulled into Lodz station, with a screeching sound of brakes, the emission of a loud sigh of steam, and a sudden jolt of the carriage. The passengers in the compartment were thrown forward, regained their composure and began to get organized.

A blue-uniformed conductor passed by, announcing their arrival in Lodz, blowing his metal whistle.

"You have thirty minutes until we move again," he told them. "You may leave the train, but please do not leave the station. There are facilities for your convenience right here in the station. When you hear the bell ringing, you must re-board quickly."

Yanosh looked at the man. He looked familiar. He could not remember from where. His face was wrinkled, prune-like. There was a scar across his forehead. The red, scarred tissue was just discernible under the peak of his blue cap. It ran the length of his forehead, reaching just above his right ear.

Nazi whip, he thought. He must have been a slave-labourer during the war.

The man walked on, making his announcement to the passengers in the next carriage. Then Yanosh realized who he was. It was the voice. He still remembered his deep voice. Shashinski! He was still alive. The rumors were untrue. He had somehow survived.

When they left Lodz it was almost night.

Yanosh looked out the window. It was raining. Eva was sleeping. The light was weak, the hour early. He had slept poorly. What future awaits a child here in Europe? he asked himself. It was hard to have hope in war-destroyed Europe. They couldn't live in Poland under the communists. Where would they go? What would they do?

Bora often spoke of building a Jewish homeland, a new life in Palestine, freedom. He always called the homeland *Eretz Yisrael*. Fine words, but there was bitter fighting there. The Arabs didn't want more Jews to come. The British were not about to leave. The rickety old boats carrying Jewish refugees from Europe were being turned back. Some sent to Cyprus, to internment camps. Did they want to bring a child into such an environment?

No. He would not do such a thing. Even if he admired Bora's determination and national pride, understood his passion for national freedom, he would not sacrifice his family on the altar of patriotism or abstract ideals.

No. He wanted a simple life, peace, serenity. Would that be possible in Palestine? No. They would not go there. Despite the speeches, despite the appeals from the Jewish leaders, from the messengers from Palestine, the *shlichim* from the *Yishuv*.

No. No. No. It was life he wanted. Life. Nothing else. Freedom of movement, of thought, of attitude ... without having to answer "the call" anymore. Freedom from slogans. To breathe again. To sing again. Just to be themselves without pretensions, without demands for conformity to rules, orders, commands. The freedom of the sea waves, the stars...

The rattling train was as good as any baby carriage or cradle; it soon had them all asleep.

Yanosh woke with a start, looked around him, rubbing his eyes. Eva was asleep beside him, her head resting on his arm. Marek and Pawla were sleeping on the opposite seat.

He saw Bora's bald pate, framed by the curly brown hair on the sides and back of his head, reflecting the dim light of the passageway as it bobbed up and down with the movement of the rattling train. The man looks so vulnerable now, he thought. Bora opened one eye for a moment, stared at him, then fell asleep again, smiling. Always on the alert for danger, Yanosh thought to himself.

He looked outside but could see nothing much. An occasional distant light shot past now and then, the dark forms of trees and low hills, but mostly it was pitch black. Yanosh sat there dozing occasionally, but not quite able to sleep. He was too tense, felt that they were leaving Poland too abruptly, was nervous about what awaited them in Berlin. He admitted to himself that he knew very little about this man, Bora, who was leading them there.

5
Berlin

Yanosh thought about Berlin as he dozed in the train. It had been the capital of Hitler's Third Reich, a city of culture which had slid into barbarism. A hated place, a place of hate. The capital of the "invincible" German racist empire. What joy they had felt when they had heard of the destructive bombings by the Allies, of the Russian entry and revenge!

He remembered his previous visit to the city, and how he had first met Bora. He had been reluctant to go, but their financial needs had been pressing. Marek had made the first connection with Polish friends already there. He had written that there were many economic opportunities in Berlin, and had sent Yanosh the address of a man he said could be very helpful.

He had found Berlin hard to imagine. After all the destruction the Nazis had caused in Warsaw, he had hoped to find the city flattened, blackened, destroyed. He had wanted to see miserable, suffering Germans, or, even better, dead, rotting bodies in the streets, as he had seen in Warsaw, but had been disappointed.

His mind flashed back to that first visit:

When he got off the train he was disappointed by what he saw. The crowded train station looked in good condition: solid, recently painted, clean, undamaged. There were soldiers there from the four allied occupying armies, wearing uniforms of various shades of brown, green and grey. There were also travellers: poor refugees, dragging baggage, their limited belongings, behind them, business people, well-dressed and carrying small briefcases.

A market place was bubbling with life next to the station. No signs of destruction or suffering there, just foreign occupation. No dead Germans either. The opposite. They looked robust, rosy-cheeked, happy and plump. They were well-dressed, as if there had been no war. How could that be? He saw a young American soldier, looked no more than twenty, flirting with one of the young German women, who smiled coyly in response. He felt revulsion at what he knew was natural human interaction.

So soon? All is forgiven, forgotten so soon? But, then, why not? We are human beings before all else, aren't we, after all?

He left the station, repeating his few German phrases to himself as he went. *"Bitte ... auf wiedersehen ... dankeschon."* How would he manage with so little German? He looked up at the signs on the street corners, dodging a heavy-set, older woman carrying two bags laden with fruit and vegetables. The one on the right read Bracher Strasse, the left was labeled Albert Strasse.

"Albert Strasse! That is the name ... I need to turn left here," he mumbled to himself.

He looked at his noted instructions.

And then turn right into a narrow lane, third door on the right, big brass door handle ... Guntherhaus, it read.

He followed the directions and soon reached a door with the name Guntherhaus etched into it in gold letters. He pulled up the heavy metal clanger and knocked. Once, twice, thrice. Then waited.

He heard footsteps approaching on the other side of the huge wooden door. A heavy thud and then it creaked open. There stood a short, stocky man, perhaps in his mid-thirties. The man was balding, but had thick curly brown hair on the sides, a thin smile on his lips.

"Are you Yosef Borowski?" he asked him, a little hesitant and nervous. The man's deep-set brown eyes were studying him. Yanosh felt naked before their piercing gaze.

"And who are you, sir?" Again the ironic smile.

"Yanosh Kaminski. Just arrived from Poland. I wrote to you a few weeks ago. Marek's friend."

"Ah, yes. Come in. Please come in."

He offered him his hand. A powerful grip, vigorous handshake.

"Call me Bora. Everyone does," he said.

He escorted him into a small courtyard, with a well-kept little garden of shrubs, white and yellow flowers and a potted lemon tree. He had first closed the heavy door and bolted it behind them while Yanosh waited.

The man crossed the cobbled courtyard, Yanosh following him. His strides were short but firm and fast. Although Yanosh was a bigger man, he had trouble keeping up with him. Across the courtyard there were two doors. Borowski reached out and turned the door handle on the right door, which opened into a poorly-lit room. There was a wooden table and a couple of wooden chairs lit by a flickering lantern sitting in the center of the table. A pile of books and an open notebook flanked the lantern.

Bora pulled out a chair for Yanosh.

"Sit, please," he said. "I will return soon."

He attended to the lantern for a moment, turning a valve until the flame inside grew and it glowed more brightly.

"You can look at these books while you wait, he said, shoving the pile across the table."

He left through a door on the far side of the room.

Yanosh looked down at the pile of books. The one on top was black. The title on the first page read *Der Schwartzer Buch – Der Churban* (The Black Book – The Destruction). He started to leaf through the book. It had been published in Moscow, but nevertheless was written in Yiddish. He read passages here and there as best he could. It was soon clear that what he was reading was a description of the destruction of European Jewry by the Nazis. He had heard since the war that what had happened in Warsaw had happened in other places, that there had been other ghettoes, other places of mass murder, like Treblinka, but he had never before seen or read a detailed account of what had happened all over Europe.

As he skimmed through the book, all that he knew and had heard fell into place. What the Nazis had done they had done systematically, according to a plan. They had called it "The Final Solution of the Jewish Question," their euphemism for the total extermination of all the Jews of Europe. Not only Poland. The book's conclusion was that between five and a half and six million Jews had been destroyed – three to four million in six death camps in Poland, one and a half to two million by shooting in the eastern regions of Latvia, Estonia, Lithuania, White Russia and the Ukraine and hundreds of thousands through starvation and torture in the ghettoes, work camps and concentration camps.

"Interesting reading, isn't it, Mr. Kaminski?"

Yanosh looked up, startled. He had not noticed the man's return. He had been so deeply engrossed, so lost in a whirlwind of terrible memories, that he had not noticed him reenter the room.

Borowski, stood there looking at him intensely, studying him again. It was unnerving.

"You might find this photo album interesting. Here, let me show you."

He flicked it open and began turning the pages showing his guest the contents. After a few minutes Yanosh asked him to stop, turned away.

"I have seen enough, Mr. Borowski, I've seen more than enough."

"You have seen nothing. This is just a small sample of what they did. One S.S. man's souvenirs, sent home to his wife from one place," Borowski responded.

"Why are you showing me these things? What are you getting at?"

"Some of us have organized to achieve some important purposes here in Germany, Mr. Kaminski. To do justice ... We know you have been active in underground work in Poland,

and that you do not deny your Jewish origins. We would like your help here in Berlin."

"Yes, go on. I am listening."

Borowski picked up the album again; he flicked through it toward the end and handed it back to Yanosh open, pointing to a photograph.

"More atrocities?"

"No, not this time."

He looked down at the photo. It was of a group of men in uniform. Three of the faces had been marked by a penciled "x." Yanosh looked more carefully at the picture. He saw the dreaded S.S. insignia, the sign of death.

The train began to slow down as it pulled into the Berlin station, the sudden burst of sound from the engine startled Yanosh. He heard the familiar metal ringing, announcing their arrival, warning the waiting crowd to be aware of the approaching locomotive.

Yanosh looked up to see Bora standing above him, "Time to get up," he announced.

"I must have been sleeping."

"You were snoring!"

"I don't believe that. You are just teasing me!"

"Well now is no time to discuss it, we have to get organized. Get up."

Marek began handing down luggage to Bora who parceled it out.

Yanosh got up, stretched his legs and began to help. They followed Bora out onto the platform after the train stopped.

"We will meet at that clock," he said, pointing to a large black timepiece suspended from a metal stand in the center of the platform.

"Wait for me there. I will call a friend to fetch us."

Yanosh walked over to a phone booth, joined the queue. He watched Eva and Pawla disappear into the crowd, talking. Meanwhile, Marek went looking for a toilet.

Yanosh carried their bags over to the station clock. He looked up at the thing. It looked very old. It had fading black Roman numerals, and was cased in copper on which gold-tinted words were inscribed. They too had faded. He wondered what this clock must have been witness to. The station was noisy but he thought he could hear the clock's steady ticking, ticking as it probably had through the war. It must have been keeping time then as now, as the crowds came and went in this station, as they had in so many other stations throughout Europe. Its cogs and wheels were turning as soldiers and their wives, parents and children parted, as refugees passed, some perhaps looking up to tell the time, others, such as this old woman now passing, not noticing it all. It must have been beating out the time as the condemned had arrived, waited and left this station for unknown destinations in the east. Why had it not stopped, why was it still ticking at all? He turned away, blocked out the imaginary sound to listen to and watch the passing crowd.

He saw Pawla coming. She had returned without Eva, and Yanosh began to worry about her. It was only after some anxious confusion in the crowd that he found her again. They kissed and, holding hands in the crush, managed to rejoin an impatient Bora.

"Where were you? You left the bags unattended. Lucky they were still here!"

Yanosh looked down for his battered brown bag, was relieved to see that it was still there. He picked it up and followed as their little group began to walk towards the exit at the end of the platform.

They filed past a uniformed and bespectacled old ticket-collector who examined them suspiciously. Bora handed him their tickets while the man counted them. Eva's hand felt cold and sweaty as they passed him.

"We have arrived in Berlin, at last."

"Yes, and I want us to leave here as soon as we can," Eva whispered to Yanosh. "I am not having our baby here!"

Yanosh nodded. He understood how she felt.

"This is not the place for our child to be born."

He remained silent, but knew she was right.

It was not the place for a new birth, not here in the heart of what had been the kingdom of death, not here in Berlin! But ... but ... it was time. That he knew. The time had come. These past five years had been a time of death and survival, death and revenge. They had discussed and postponed having a child during the war. But the time had come to live, nothing was more appropriate now than to bring a new life into the world. No, he would not join Bora in his passion for revenge. He could not. The time for killing, for vengeance was over. It was now a time to celebrate life, for new hope, not more death, a time for birth, a time to be born.

"Yes," he said, "you are right, Eva. The baby will not be born here!"

Yanosh shuddered. He felt Eva's hand in his again and calmed himself. She must have felt his tension, he thought. He noticed that she too had fallen silent as they followed Bora out through the wrought iron station gate, with its intricate German sign.

Bora led them along a deserted street, past a row of shattered buildings, and then across a busy square. It was being used as a marketplace. As they passed, Yanosh noticed the people in rags, their thin bodies, the facial sores and hollow eyes of hungry people. It was not a new scene, but he hadn't expected to see it here in Berlin.

They reached a lone stone building, two stories high, standing somber guard over what looked like the aftermath of an earthquake. It was surrounded by acres of debris, as far as the eye could see. The streets were barely recognizable as such.

Everything smelled of dust.

"Welcome to my fortress!" Bora exclaimed, smiling as they walked up to the door.

He knocked three times. It was slowly unbolted, then swung open with an angry creak. Two heavyset men holding submachine guns stood there. They nodded at Bora, then stepped aside to let the group pass. Yanosh was surprised to see a mezuzah on his right as they walked through.

As they walked in, Eva took Yanosh's hand: "I don't like this place, Yanosh."

"Don't worry. We will only be here temporarily ... until we find something better," he promised.

She squeezed his hand.

January 12, 1946

We arrived in Berlin today. My second time here. But now I see what I missed the previous time – the extent of the destruction. Perhaps my anger blinded me to it then. Indeed the train station and the streets around it are pretty much untouched, buildings still standing as if there had been no war. But beyond that, a little further on, when I first went out for a stroll after we'd settled into Bora's "fortress," the scene that met my eyes was almost as bad as our Warsaw when we left her.

I saw rubble, heaps of broken stones, buildings torn asunder, missing roofs and walls, roads strewn with debris, potholes everywhere from the American and British bombings, and remnants of Russian tanks.

And the children! There are gangs of children of all ages roaming aimlessly through the dust, many of them barefoot, often in tattered clothes. They look no different than the children we saw in the villages near Warsaw as we went through them. But there are more of them here.

I will not let my pity get the better of me! They brought all this on themselves. They called themselves the master race. Now look at them! Humiliated, defeated. Where is their arrogance now, where is their superiority and pride? There is no reason to feel sorry for them in their miserable state today. They started the war. Remember what they did in Poland these last six years! How could I ever forget or forgive? They deserve their fate. Curse them. Curse them!

January 31, 1946

Bora's "fortress": Everywhere I look here I see armed guards. There must be at least eight guys here with Bora, carrying weapons. They don't smile much, but they have plenty of food, and money too. They come, they go, don't say very much. They bring other exhausted refugees who stay for a while, until they have rested a couple of days. They then move on. Most of them go to a camp called Wittenau in the French sector. Bora finds the others places to live, jobs, papers. Where does he get the energy to do so much? He is always listening, moving, organizing, giving orders. I don't see him sleeping or eating much. Only drinking tea all the time, and sucking sweets. I couldn't live at such a pace.

It is clear that he and Pawla know each other from before, but there is tension there. Pawla has become moody. Sometimes I hear her and Marek arguing in the other room. Marek is impressed with Bora, just as I am, but Pawla avoids contact with him, obviously doesn't like him and is influencing Eva too – against him.

Eva is often nervous lately. She tells me she hasn't eaten as well as this in years. I see that she does have a healthy appetite now. But she stays up late talking or reading, complains that she sleeps poorly here. She doesn't like the look of Bora's "friends," former partisans and smugglers who have been "working" together for a while now here in Berlin.

I understand her doubts about them, but there is something about these men that I do like nevertheless. I'm not sure what it is, but I feel that under their tough exteriors and rough language there is some idealism. It is hidden under cynicism, but they are helping people flee Poland, just as they have helped us. Bora leads them and I think we should appreciate our luck at having been taken under his protective wing.

6

The Festival of Freedom

1946, Waldenburg, Germany
The American Occupied Zone

It had been a cold winter. There had been a shortage of coal, wood and other basic commodities. If not for the American airlift, many would have starved. Yanosh and Eva seemed to be well-supplied with most of their needs, as did all those connected, however indirectly, with Bora and his group.

Eva didn't know why they were so well off when so many others starved and froze, but she suspected that Bora and his "gang" were involved in criminal activities of some kind. She wondered how many had been robbed to supply their needs so well. They were always carrying weapons, swaggering in and out of their "headquarters" as if they owned the world, often arm-in-arm with young German women who offered their services in exchange for thick winter coats, silk stockings, perfume or other luxuries.

Winter passed. The snow began to melt, the constant rain and rivers of mud of that early spring made good boots valuable, and Bora supplied them all with new boots. The grey began to lift, the skies cleared, and there were sunny days again.

Eva's pregnancy continued to develop. After they had been in Berlin only two weeks she had started to show, even when fully dressed. She had to let out her clothes. People were getting up for her in the trolley cars, much to her embarrassment. The special attention Yanosh and his friends gave her, bringing her extra food, particularly dairy products, was wonderful, but it would sometimes get annoying. She did not enjoy all the fuss.

Yanosh doted on her. Bora would appear carrying food,

gifts, or items of clothing for them. She appreciated Bora's help but did not like it when he took Yanosh aside for long, secretive conversations. They would step outside. Bora would offer Yanosh cigarettes – he didn't normally smoke, but she saw him at times oblige his new friend – Bora would light Yanosh's cigarette and his own in a male intimacy that she found disturbing. Then two thin columns of smoke would rise from between them as they spoke.

She saw that Bora had worked some kind of charm on her husband. He would listen avidly to what Bora was telling him and would be agitated for days after his visits. A couple of times Yanosh went on trips with him for a day or two. He would tell her not to worry, as he would be back soon enough. And then she didn't hear from him until his return two days later. She worried until his return.

She tried to talk to him, to find out what was happening but he was tight-lipped. She was frightened by Bora's growing power over him and would tell him of her fears. Yanosh would laugh, tell her not to worry, but continued joining him on expeditions.

Eva suspected that they must be doing something illegal, dangerous. Why else did they need so much secrecy? He had never been this secretive in the past, even during the war in Warsaw.

As the weather improved, the sun warmed, and Eva's worries began to lift. Yanosh spent more time at home, more time with their good friends, Marek and Pawla. They planned their trip on to France, dreamt together of their new life somewhere far away – Canada, New Zealand, South America, the United States. They applied for visas to many countries, spent hours waiting in line at the offices of foreign delegations and refugee-relief organizations, such as the Joint and HIAS, enquiring, being interviewed and filling out forms.

One late afternoon, Bora visited with some news. An old friend of his from Bialystok had written to him from Australia. They'd set up an organization there of Polish Jews from Bialystok, in a city called Melbourne. They wanted to help the European refugees, bring them out to Australia, had some connections with the newly-elected Labour Party, and particularly with a politician called Arthur Caldwell, who was now Minister of immigration in the new national government. The friend had asked Bora to supply them with names of people interested in migration to Australia, preferably young people with desirable trades and skills for the Australian post-war economy. There was an economic boom there. They suffered from labour shortages. He had been asked whether he himself would be interested in coming out to Australia? He was told that there would be a job waiting for him there.

Eva had never seen Bora excited before. It was strange to see his child-like enthusiasm about Australia. She realized that Bora, who had no one left from his Polish past, whose entire family, all his school friends, his entire village had been wiped out, was talking to them as if they were his family – a surrogate family. It caught her by surprise.

"You will come too, of course," he half-asked, half-commanded.

"I will arrange visas and tickets for you too. We will build a new life there, a life without worry or fear. You will have your baby there, safe from all this European stupidity and hate. You will come to Australia won't you? You can't go on rotting here in Germany. There's no future for you here."

Bora seemed to sober a little as he waited for their response. Yanosh was obviously delighted by his friend's news, but Eva looked more hesitant.

"What's the matter, Eva?" he asked.

"I am not sure. I have to think about it. This is so sudden. Australia is so far away."

Bora smiled. A knowing smile. He winked at Yanosh.

"But, darling, that's what we have been hoping for, working towards these past weeks, and now Bora here is offering us an opportunity..."

"I know but I have to think. I can't agree so quickly."

She felt confused, overwhelmed.

"Your wife is right, Yanosh. It is a serious decision. Let her give it some thought. And while you are thinking I'll check out the possibility of helping you through my Bialystoker friend. All right?"

"Of course, Bora, of course," said Yanosh, nodding.

"All right, go ahead, Bora. Find out more and I will think about it."

"Good. Let's have a drink in honor of this splendid news!"

Bora produced a small bottle of something strong and sweet-smelling, which they passed around. It was brandy. Eva recognized the scent, but it tasted strange. She drank it slowly. Yanosh and Bora had already finished theirs. She took her time.

"You do not like the brandy, Eva? It is French. Orange-brandy, quite expensive stuff…"

"Yes, I do. It is very good," she lied, and then sipped a little more.

Yanosh seemed amused at her reaction, but soon sobered when Eva gave him an angry look. She hoped he would understand her discomfort, forgive her, but she really wanted Bora to go already, to be free of his dominating presence. She got up to collect the cups trying to hint that their little "party" was over. Yanosh took the cue:

"Bora, I think it is time you got going. It is getting late. You know … in Eva's condition she needs more rest. It has been a long day…"

"I understand. I will see you in the morning, then. Good evening, Eva."

"Good evening."

Yanosh accompanied him to the door. They exchanged a few words which she couldn't hear, and then he was finally gone.

She was relieved, wanted to talk to Yanosh without his friend's presence, and was distressed to see that Yanosh had buried himself in his notebook again. He sat there writing. Eva watched him.

"Yanosh…"

"Yes, darling…"

"Yanosh, look at me!"

Yanosh looked up, annoyed.

"What do you want? Can't you see that I'm writing?"

"I want to talk about what just happened."

"What is there to talk about?"

"I don't understand how Bora can now be planning to go to Australia after all he has been saying to people about Zionism and having to migrate to Palestine."

"Yes, I was surprised by that, too. I suppose he changed his mind, but please Eva, let me work now. We will talk about it later."

"But Yanshuk, I am worried. I must talk about something with you."

"Worried about what?"

"About our decision regarding Australia … about going there with Bora. I don't trust him. He scares me. I don't want us to be beholden to him, to owe him anything."

"Not now, darling. We will talk about it, I promise, but not just now. How about after dinner tonight?"

Her eyes flamed.

"Okay, after dinner tonight, Yanosh … but remember that you promised. Don't forget," she said. "I am going out for a stroll."

Her voice sounded shrill, but she didn't care. She walked out the door, slamming it behind her.

Yanosh was startled by his wife's anger. He stared after her at the closed door. It concerned him that she was going out into the streets of Berlin, a city she did not know, a city now infamous for its street violence and crime.

He tried at first to go back to his notebook, to do some writing. He couldn't, was distressed by Eva's angry display and worried about her. He closed the notebook, got up, went to the window and looked out. It would soon be evening, he thought.

He decided to go out after her, to placate her. He put on his jacket, checked that his revolver was there in its holster, grabbed her coat and went out to look for her.

It was now cold outside. The wind was blowing from the east; leaves swirled past him as he walked down the road. Eva was nowhere in the street. He guessed she would probably have headed for the park around the next corner. He noticed that the sun was low in the sky, and walked faster. I must get her to come home before dark, he thought.

He turned the corner. It was a long city block. As he walked towards the park, the lights went on along the way in some of the buildings. Evening was coming fast. He approached the first trees, a row of pines "standing guard." Beyond them he spotted some silhouetted figures. One of them looked like it might be her. She was standing beside a park bench talking to another woman.

He drew closer, could hear their conversation. They were speaking Yiddish. He was surprised to hear Eva speaking the language again. They had always spoken Polish amongst themselves; spoke it with other Jews who knew Polish.

Eva was still talking when he approached. Her hands were raised and waving in the air, like the hands of a conductor leading an orchestra. She looked over for a moment and saw him. Nevertheless she went on waving her hands and talking to the other woman without acknowledging his presence.

The park was pretty and well-kept. White and yellow spring flowers adorned the path on both sides. Yanosh noticed them as he waited. He was annoyed that she had ignored him. He stood beside the women, waiting, feeling awkward and impatient.

He was struck by the appearance of the woman sitting on the park bench, listening to his wife. Her long, wavy hair was brunette, but streaked with silver-grey, particularly at the sides. The features – a long, graceful neck, sharp nose, fine eyebrows, long eyelashes, smooth complexion – were almost perfectly proportioned, her movements fine. She looked aristocratic.

The lady's delicate mouth had formed a smile at him

momentarily when he arrived, then she turned her attention back to Eva. Yanosh saw that her clothes were rags. A prisoner's striped tunic, with a tear where a number had once been, revealed a white blouse which hung, over-large over her knees, overlapping a stained and patched long blue cotton dress. She wore heavy looking clogs, her stockings didn't quite match – one was dark brown, the other a lighter shade of brown.

Eva was telling her about the Warsaw ghetto uprising, as she had experienced it from their hiding place outside the ghetto. She told her new friend that the underground had supplied the ghetto fighters with some weapons and ammunition though they knew their situation was hopeless. They had tried to convince them to leave the ghetto, to fight outside, but they had refused.

"It was suicide to stay and fight the Germans in the ghetto. They were crazy to try," Eva said.

The woman shook her head in disagreement:

"You don't understand, Eva. It was Passover, the festival of freedom. The Germans were preparing to liquidate the ghetto. They wanted to save Jewish honor, to die fighting."

"It was a tragic mistake. It saved no one's honor, just added more avoidable deaths."

"Would you like to meet one of the ghetto fighters? You might see things differently after speaking to her."

"Yes, of course. I would be honored. By the way, this is my husband, Yanosh. I am sure he would be interested in meeting your friend too. Yanosh, this is Rivka Swirski."

Yanosh nodded to his wife's new friend.

"Good evening, Panne Kaminski."

"Good evening, madame."

He turned to Eva: "It's cold out here. Take your coat darling."

She smiled, put the coat on, buttoned it up.

Rivka Swirski also smiled, appreciative of the demonstrated tenderness in their relationship.

"It's getting dark," he continued, "not safe to stay here in the park at night. You should come home. Mrs. Swirski, you are welcome to join us, if you wish."

"Yes, that is a good idea. Will you join us this evening? You can spend the night," added Eva.

The older woman shook her head:

"That is very kind of you, but I must be heading back. My friends would worry. We are busy with preparations for the coming Passover festival. I have a committee meeting tomorrow morning. We will be doing a very big communal meal, with the help of various charitable organizations, particularly the American Joint. Perhaps you would like to join us for the holiday? If you do, you will meet Bronia."

"Bronia?" Eva asked.

"The woman I mentioned before. She participated in the Warsaw Ghetto uprising, survived Maydanek and Auschwitz. She is very active in the committee, and a good friend of mine. I am sure she would be interested in meeting you, too."

Eva and Yanosh looked at each other. Yanosh winked at his wife.

"We would be happy to come, Rivka," Eva said.

"I will send you an invitation. Give me your address."

Yanosh, as always, had a pencil and some pages in his jacket pocket. He wrote out the address for their new friend.

"Here is our address."

"Thank you. Give me the pencil and a piece of paper please, Panne Kaminski. I will write you my address as well."

He obliged. Her long fingers took the things from his. She scribbled out a few lines, soon handing back the page with her address on it, and the pencil. Eva and Rivka hugged farewell as if they were old friends. Yanosh shook her hand formally. It felt cold.

Walking home together, after parting with Rivka, Yanosh and Eva talked. Eva was excited about the opportunity to visit Rivka's D.P. camp and participate in a *Pesach Seder* there. She looked forward to meeting the woman who had fought in the ghetto revolt. She had, he hoped, forgotten about their previous argument. He wasn't going to remind her.

Yanosh walked beside her listening to her excited chatter. He was pleased to accompany her home safely without argument. He himself, though he appreciated Rivka's invitation to the Passover ritual meal, was not delighted to do so, had only agreed because of his wife's obvious interest in participating. He had met some of the ghetto fighters before and was not impressed with them. They had been very young, but committed Zionists, and, in his opinion, foolish. He had no desire to hear yet again the criticisms of lack of support on the part of the Polish underground. What had they expected of the underground? Miracles?

They turned the corner, leaving the lights of the boulevard behind them, as well as the lurking dangers of the park. He noticed that there were people walking along Theodore Street, where they were staying, more passersby than there had been near the park. A car drove past them, its lights blinding them for a moment. Another followed soon after, blinding them again. It was already night.

"Yanosh, look up at the sky!"

"Why, what do you see? What is it, darling?"

"Look, just look over there, above that building." She pointed towards the sky above a lone-standing wall of the building across the road.

The moon was rising. It was a half-moon of lemon-orange, a lemon-slice moon.

"Yes, I see, Eva. A beautiful moon."

"No, Yanosh. Not the moon. To the left … a little higher up. Did you see it?"

"See what?"

"It's too late now. It was a falling star. We must make a wish."

Yanosh restrained the urge to criticize her superstition this time. Domestic peace had returned.

"I wish for sanity in this world," he said.

"I wish for health, and safety."

Two weeks later they heard from Rivka again. Yanosh had forgotten about meeting her, and the invitation to the Passover event at the displaced persons' camp. He had been busy with his "business" activities; he had been spending a lot of time with Bora and his people. Eva, on the other hand, had not forgotten. She had written a postcard the next day addressed to Rivka Swirsky, Waldenburg Displaced Persons' Camp, American Zone, Berlin Area.

The days passed. She was disappointed that she had as yet received no response. She had written to her new acquaintance to remind her of her invitation and of their acceptance. The idea of participating once again in the Passover meal and in the retelling of the story of the Exodus fascinated her. It brought back happy childhood memories. When the letter from Rivka arrived she was delighted. It came on Thursday morning, along with their visas for Australia.

She was sitting in the kitchen, sketching, when she heard the postman's whistle. She glanced out the window to see him standing there, his blue cap perched on the back of his head, looking up at her. She waved to him until he saw her. He waved back. She came running down the stairs, through the green passageway and out into the front entrance where the postman was waiting for her, holding two or three envelopes.

"*Gut morgen*, Herr Schmidt!"

"*Gut morgen*, Frau Kaminski. How are you this morning?"

"I'm fine. Do you have a letter for me today?"

"What do you think? And why did I whistle if not to announce just that, that you have not just one but two. Lucky you!"

"Two letters! Let me see," she said, as he proffered the envelopes to her.

One was small and white, a little stained on one side, the other a large, official-looking brown envelope. She took both from him but before she could examine or open either of them

Herr Schmidt produced a board with a paper clamped onto it for her to sign. He gave her a pen.

"Sign here please."

She signed it.

"Thank you. Have a good day!"

"You too," she answered.

He left.

She didn't know which to open first, brought them inside with her and set them down on the kitchen table. She drank some water to calm herself a little and examined the envelopes more carefully. The big brown one was addressed to Herr and Frau Kaminski. It was from the Australian consulate. Yanosh, who was out "doing something important" with Bora, would not be back until dinnertime. She had to leave for work soon. She decided to leave off opening the official Australian envelope until dinner. It was probably yet another rejection. It would wait until evening when Yanosh would be there too. It was, after all, addressed to both of them.

The little white one, she saw again, was stained along one side. She picked it up and turned it around in her hand. Compared to the consulate letter it was light in her hand. The name on the back was hard to read, but she thought it might be "Rivka Swirsky."

"Finally!"

She opened it. Two pages of tiny writing, hard to read, like the name on the envelope, addressed to Maineh Taeireh Freunt, Chava (my dear friend, Eva) and signed Dayneh Nayeh Chavreta, Rivka (your new friend, Rivka). The pages were also a little stained on one side. I'll read this later when I have time, she said to herself, I must get to work.

She folded the two pages and put them in her handbag. She then finished drinking her water and went to get dressed. It was late, so she slipped into her blue dress, put on the new shoes Bora had brought her the day before and ran out the door.

At work later that day she read the letter. It was after hours of sitting at the sewing machine listening to her friends' chatter and gossip while trying to concentrate on what she was doing. The lunch break brought with it the usual rush outside as everyone found their way to their favorite eating spots with their meal mates. Ingrid grabbed her arm to pull her along with her in order to join Maria and Greta at their bench under the almond tree by the fence.

"No, not today, Ingrid. I have an important letter I want to read," she said, producing her two pages from her bag. "I want to find a quiet spot on my own to read it now."

"All right, Eva. I understand… What language is that?" she asked, noticing the writing on the pages Eva had shown her excitedly.

"Yiddish, Ingrid."

"You can read it?"

"Yes, why?"

"So you must be Jewish."

"Yes, I am."

Ingrid's face changed. She turned cold.

"Oh," she said, and walked away without another word.

Eva watched her walk away. She was surprised by Ingrid's reaction. In her excitement, she had not been careful enough. The sudden coldness to her because her "friend" realized she was Jewish was not a new experience. But it hurt every time it happened. That was why she was happy to follow Yanosh in his plan to leave Europe, to have their child somewhere else, somewhere not infected with anti-Semitism.

Eva looked down at the pages in her hand, which were flapping in the wind. She folded them again, and went inside. The factory was almost empty. One supervisor sat in the corner, eating his lunch. He waved hello to her. She smiled back. Neither spoke. He watched her weave her way between the sewing machines until she chose a place to sit and read. He went back to eating his sandwich. She relaxed and began to read:

March 26, 1946
My dear Eva,

It was a pleasure to meet you and your husband in the Berlin park. I enjoyed talking with you and felt we have much in common. Two weeks have passed since we met and so much has happened here in Waldenburg. I have not forgotten you. I appreciated your invitation to stay with you and was sorry that I had to refuse. Nor have I forgotten my invitation to you to participate in our communal Seder here in our camp. If you are still interested in doing so we would be delighted to have you here as our guests for the Passover holiday, which begins on Monday April 15th. Below is a map showing you how to find your way here from the Waldenburg train station.

Your friend,
Rivka

p.s. I'm afraid Bronia won't be at the Seder after all. I'll explain later.

That evening before dinner Yanosh opened the envelope from the Australian consulate. It was an invitation to an interview. They drank a lechaim in anticipation.

A few days later, on the day of the interview, another letter arrived from Rivka:

March 30, 1946
My dear Eva,

We have been hit by tragedy. My friend, Bronia, whom I wanted you to meet, is dead. She fell off a ladder while trying to fix a roof in our camp. It was a terrible accident. She fell backwards and snapped her neck in the fall. They took her to hospital. She lay there for days between life and death, before finally expiring. We are all so shocked. Everyone loved Bronia. She was such a source of inspiration to all of us. And now she is gone!

We continued planning our communal Seder, but it won't be the same without Bronia. I hope you will still join us for the festival here. There will be some very special guests – a leader of the Palestinian

*Yishuv and a former partisan commander, as well as some of the
American soldiers from the military base nearby.*

*I will meet you at the station. Please write immediately with details
of your planned arrival.*

Your friend,

Rivka Swirski

The two weeks passed.

The interview went well. Yanosh was informed that they
would be issued visas. Eva was overjoyed. They had heard
similar news from Marek and Pawla. She thought it would
be good for Yanosh to have his friend migrating to Australia
too, but felt ambivalent about Pawla. We will manage, she
reassured herself.

The days were growing warmer; trees were budding, flowers
appearing, birds sang their joy at the returning spring. The
world had become more peaceful, hopeful. Yanosh had come
home with their prized visas to Australia and had arranged
tickets for them on a ship leaving Marseilles in two months. He
had managed to contact a distant French cousin of his, Haim,
who was overjoyed that someone from his Polish family had
survived. Haim had written to them that he would be delighted
to put them up in his home in Paris for a few weeks, on their
way to Marseilles. Everything was set for their journey to a new
life in Australia. They bought train tickets for Paris and would
be leaving in another ten days. Haim would meet them at the
train station. All was arranged.

And Bora? Bora had changed his mind again. He continued
encouraging them in their plans to migrate to Australia, had
even connected them with his Bialystoker friends there, but
he himself would stay in Europe longer and would, when
the time came, continue to Palestine, there to fight for Jewish
independence. So he said.

April 6, 1946

Yesterday Bora told me that he wasn't coming to Australia after all. I wasn't surprised. His nationalist passions have got the better of him. It was to be expected.

He has been increasingly involved with the Zionists in Bricha, helping Jewish refugees cross the border, illegally, from Poland. Despite the many problems with the occupation authorities, particularly the British, they succeed in getting people out of the communist-controlled areas and into the free zone. Bora explained to me that he was needed here now, and that his military experience would be important in the coming battle for Palestine against the British and the Arabs. That might be true, but I think they are planning an act of collective suicide! After all the Jews have suffered it will be yet another tragedy. A terrible waste of the lives of those who survived.

Jewish and other refugees come here in the thousands, refusing to return to Poland or Russia. People have been crossing the border daily. Now young men and women from Palestine have arrived and have been making their presence felt in the D.P. camps here in Germany and in Austria as well. These homeless people have been used to the most miserable conditions, herded again into temporary camps they adapt. The Zionists take advantage of their misery and neediness in order to win them over to their cause and to "educate" them. They have classes, teach them modern Hebrew, agricultural skills, and have organized public meetings, protest marches against the British protesting their refusal to allow immigration to Palestine, their treatment of illegal immigrants.

Last week, a group of hotheads overturned a British jeep and set fire to it. One was killed, the others caught, incarcerated until they stand trial. They were protesting the British "White Paper" limiting immigration to Palestine. Some have joined a group called "the Irgun" and are preparing to join those attacking the British Army and police there. I have heard they are secretly training young fanatics in the use of weapons. Moniek told me Bora is involved in this too, that he is supplying them with old guns … at a price!

*If all this is true, I think many of those poor kids will pay with their
lives for this craziness, and Bora will end up in jail, or worse.*

A gradual, quiet change had come over Yanosh's wife
since her meeting with Rivka two weeks earlier, and
the subsequent correspondence. Yanosh was disturbed by it,
but had not yet said anything. She brought home some old
traditional Jewish books: a Bible, a prayer book, a *haggadah* for
Pesach. She'd bought them at a market stall.

"What are those books you are carrying?" he asked her.

"Some old Jewish books I found in the market place. Let me
put them down, then I'll show you."

"They look very old. I wonder where they came from. Why
were they being sold in the market?"

"I don't know, Yanosh. I found them amongst stacks of
second-hand books an old Hungarian woman was selling there.
She thought they weren't worth much, didn't really know what
they were. I got them very cheaply."

Yanosh picked up one book and examined it. It was a small
leather-bound prayer book. He opened it. One page was in
Hebrew, the opposite leaf in German. The print on the page
was very attractive – Gothic style letters, some tinted gold.

"Someone took very good care of this book, I think. Probably
didn't use it very much though. Maybe just once or twice a year,
like my parents," commented Yanosh.

Eva took the small book from him and began to leaf through
it herself.

"Look," she said, pointing to a stained and frayed section
where she had opened it, "the Sabbath eve service was used
regularly, probably with great devotion. These are wine stains.
Not all the German Jews were as assimilated as your parents,
Yanshuk."

"Who knows? Didn't help them much, did it? Where is the
owner now?"

He puffed some cigarette smoke upwards and pointed up
at it to make his point clear.

Eva ignored this cynical pantomime.

She put the books on the shelf next to her side of the bed, arranging them carefully by size. He continued smoking, watching her skeptically.

Every evening after that Eva would read something from one of the Hebrew books. She would sometimes read from one of them in the morning as well. Yanosh knew she read Yiddish, but was now surprised by her knowledge of Hebrew. She read psalms almost as well as she read the books of Peretz and Shalom Aleichem. She would quote verses to him, point out their wisdom or beauty. He would respond as neutrally as he could, not wanting to offend her again.

"Yanosh, listen to these words from the very first psalm in this book of psalms…"

"Eva, I'd rather not … I'm finally reading today's newspaper … it looks like the tensions between the Russians and the Americans are increasing … I'd like to read more…"

"Just for a minute, Yanshuk, you will appreciate this too, I think, just listen for a moment…"

"All right… go ahead…"

Eva recited to him:

> *Happy is the man who has not followed the counsel of the wicked…*

> *He is like a tree planted beside streams of water,*
> *Which yields its fruit in season,*
> *Whose foliage never fades.*

> *Not so the wicked;*
> *Rather, they are like chaff, which blows away in the wind,*
> *Therefore the wicked will not survive judgment*

"Aren't these wonderful metaphors for good and evil? Righteousness, kindness are nourishing growing things like a beautiful tree. Evil, on the other hand, is dry, ephemeral, blows away in the wind. I like that. It reads true to me," Eva said.

"Eva, the poem is... er... expresses a beautiful sentiment, I agree, but it is wishful thinking. The world is not like that, you know that. There are ex-Nazis who are prospering, doing business with the Americans. Where is their judgment? Please... don't be naive!"

"Oh, Yanshuk, you don't understand..."

"I understand quite well. Eva, please, let me get back to the article I was reading."

Her new-found interest in religion disturbed him. It somehow challenged his secular, humanist beliefs, beliefs he thought he shared with her. Eva noticed his disquiet, explained that she was just feeling nostalgic for the old Jewish culture since meeting Rivka, that she was preparing for the coming Pesach celebration – the *Seder*.

Yanosh nodded to indicate his understanding, but he did not understand at all. He did the best he could to appear appeased. Eva seemed relieved, went back to her Jewish books. But, then, just before their trip to Waldenburg, the Friday night before, she set up two candles on their dinner table, waved her hands in front of them, covered her eyes and whispered something – the traditional blessing. Yanosh was shocked. Was this his Eva, his atheist, the woman with whom he had spent so many years critically discussing religion and its dangers, talking of it as a medieval relic? He looked up at his wife again in astonishment. She was in tears.

"Yanshuk, come here. Stand with me by the candles," she said.

He got up reluctantly and stood beside her. She put her hand on his shoulder.

"Yanosh, look. They are pretty aren't they?"

She looked up at him, waiting for his response.

"Yes, they are, I agree."

"So why did it upset you so to see me light them tonight?"

"You know why, Eva. We have talked about it often. Perhaps too often."

"No, Yanosh, you don't understand. I am expecting ... We are expecting. We will have a child. I want that child to grow up in a Jewish home. I am not religious, Yanosh. I don't believe in God, or, at least not in the traditional understanding of that word, but Shabbes candles ... they make a meal on Friday night something special ... more than an ordinary meal."

"Yes, they turn it into a religious ritual! They make us live a lie. How can you say the blessing over the candles in which you mention the God you don't believe in, the God of the 'chosen people'?"

"I just can. I just feel the need to do it. Can't you accept that, Yanosh? Does it have to be a theological issue? Do we have to argue over this?"

"Listen, Eva, I'm not able to participate in Jewish religious rituals, certainly not in my own home, not after what happened in Poland during the war! No, not just in Poland – all over Europe. How can one believe in a God after that? How can such a deity be praised or blessed? Your entire family was murdered and you can bless Him!?"

Eva began to cry again. She looked at Yanosh beseechingly.

"Why can't you understand? Why can't you just give a little, for my sake?"

Yanosh remained silent, stone-faced. Eva continued to cry.

"I'm going out for a walk," he said. He was at the door already, hand on the doorknob.

"Yanshuk, please ... please. It's Shabbes. Dinner is still warm. Yanosh, please try, for my sake, for your child's sake!"

He let go of the door and turned towards her. She is pregnant, he thought. Perhaps that's why she is behaving so strangely. He took her hand, but she pushed it away.

"Eva, I'm sorry. I didn't want to hurt your feelings. It's just that seeing you lighting candles on a Friday night and making a blessing like that makes me see red. You can light candles if you want, if it makes you feel good, just don't expect me to say amen or make a blessing over wine for you. That I won't do."

One day Yanosh discussed his wife's new interest in religion with Bora, sharing his worry with him, hoping for some good advice on how to deal with the issue.

Bora seemed amused.

"Yanosh, you must understand your wife. She is looking to feather her nest before giving birth. Religious practices are a kind of decoration in the home. They add something, community, continuity. You should be happy about this development. She is a good woman, and homemaker, and will be a fine mother. A little tradition in the home is a good thing."

"I suppose you are right, Bora."

"I am sure I am right. You will see."

But, of course, Yanosh was not placated by his friend's words.

As the day of the *Seder* grew closer, Yanosh's nervousness at Eva's newfound interest in religion increased. He did the best he could to remain calm and understanding, but it was not easy. She had started cleaning the house very thoroughly, scrubbing the kitchen over and over again.

"What are you doing?" he asked her one evening, after suspiciously watching her cleaning out kitchen cabinets for a while.

"What do you mean, Yanosh? You can see what I am doing, can't you? I'm cleaning our kitchen. Spring cleaning."

"Eva, it is not just an innocent spring cleaning! I remember my grandmother doing this every year before Passover. Jews all over Warsaw would do the same during the weeks before the *Seder*, scrubbing, cleaning, preparing. It's another ritual! It's because of what's written in the Torah, forbidding unleavened bread in the home. I know what you are doing. Did all their devotion to the rituals and rules of the Torah save them from the gas chambers, from starvation in the ghetto?"

"Yanosh, please. Let's not argue about this again. I'm just cleaning the kitchen, that's all."

"Ah ha ... so why do it just before the Passover?"

"Yanosh, please..."

"Will you not be eating bread, only matzo this year?"

"Yes, I was thinking I might do that."

"Why, Eva? Why do you have to do this?"

"I don't know. I don't know. I just feel that that's what I want to do."

"And are you expecting me not to eat bread for the week of Passover as well? To only eat that cardboard-like flat bread, that tasteless, burnt stuff?"

"No, Yanosh. I don't expect you to do anything, just to respect my need to do it, that's all. Just that, nothing more."

"All right, Eva, but I still don't understand why you are practicing a religion you don't believe in."

"I don't understand, either, Yanosh, but that's what I want to do."

There were no tears this time, just quiet determination.

The day before the *Seder* she had the apartment cleaner than he had ever seen it. She washed the windows, the floors, scrubbed the kitchen surfaces and the walls. Their home smelt of soap, and it glowed.

He was in and out of the house that Sunday morning, busy though he was with Bora business. Every time he popped in she was still cleaning and tidying, cheerfully singing to herself as she worked. The mood was infectious and by afternoon he had rolled up his sleeves and found himself helping her, forgetting that he was in fact participating in an ancient religious rite to which he objected. There was something refreshing, liberating, about all this cleaning. Not such a bad thing to be doing after all.

Yanosh and Eva went for a stroll towards evening. He saw a flower seller on a nearby corner, led them in that direction, and bought some roses which he handed to her, saying: "In honor of the spring festival, my love."

Eva laughed. "This is romantic silliness!" she said, but she accepted the flowers. "Yanshuk, thank you. They are very pretty. They will adorn our dinner table tonight."

As they walked home he took her arm and admitted that he had been caught up in the pre-Pesach excitement created by all her cleaning, that he looked forward to participating in the festive meal the next evening in Waldenburg with Rivka.

"You know, Eva, I haven't participated in a *Seder* since I was a boy. I always managed to avoid the occasion after I turned 16 and became active in the Polish Socialist Youth group. My parents would go to my grandfather's Pesach *Seder* and make excuses for me there. I know it saddened my mother's parents every year that I didn't come, but I didn't care. I think my mother understood, so she let it go. I wish she hadn't. I am willing to join in this time."

"Many missing loved ones will not be at the *Seder* table with us when we sit there, tomorrow, Yanosh. It will not be easy."

"I know, but it is a good thing to do. They would have appreciated it."

"Yes, I am sure they would have."

7

The Seder

Eva and Yanosh followed Rivka, their host, into a large hall. It looked like it might once have been a warehouse or factory building. Six long trestle tables arranged into a kind of semi-circle filled about half the space. Each table was covered with a white tablecloth, in the center of which there was a vase of sorts – an empty soda bottle, specially painted for the occasion – containing a paper flower or two, which caught the eye. Yanosh thought there were places set for about 150 people, maybe 200.

There was a poster hanging over the head table. It read: "From Slavery to Freedom" in Yiddish, flanked by two big Zionist flags in blue and white, with a large Star of David in the center. Some smaller American flags had been hung beside them. Around the walls were sheets of paper with slogans in Yiddish and Hebrew. Artistic talent was evident in the illustrations that accompanied them, depicting imaginary scenes of ancient and modern agriculture in the Land of Israel.

"It's beautiful, Rivka!" Eva exclaimed. "Must have been a lot of work to prepare all of this."

"It was a *zkhus* (an honor) to be involved in planning and preparing this year's *Seder*," replied Rivka. "We had a wonderful committee that worked hard taking care of all the details. I only hope the participants are as appreciative as you are. We Jews are not easy people at the best of times, as it says: *am kashei oref* (a stiff-necked people). We are quick to criticize, and find it easy to find fault, as you know. I am just sad that Bronya, may her memory be blessed, didn't live to see the result of all her devoted work. We all miss her."

"Yes, we know, Rivka, we know," said Yanosh.

"I am sorry," said Eva, touching Rivka's arm to express her sympathy. Rivka dried her eyes as they continued talking.

As they spoke and walked by the tables, people began to arrive through the entrances at either end of the hall. There were women who, like Eva, were pregnant. Some small children came in, following their parents into the room, rowdy and excited. A group of American soldiers arrived, led by an officer, who handed them white skullcaps as they filed into the hall. One of them began to give out chocolates to the children and was soon surrounded by most of the youngsters in the room.

Suddenly an irate bearded older man jumped up to stop the distribution of chocolates, yelling:

"Hametz! hametz! Tur nisht essen! Kinder! Ess es nisht kusher! – Don't eat them, they're not kosher."

"No, you can't do that!" a burly Zionist official called out as he intervened, grabbing the man's shoulders, trying to protect the stunned soldier from the man's flailing hands.

Some chocolates, fell to the floor. They were swooped up by eager hands, accompanied by the wail of the deprived victim.

The soldier protested: "They are kosher chocolates; they were given out yesterday by the Joint Distribution Committee."

He showed the man the wrapper. Yanosh could see Hebrew writing. A modicum of decorum was restored, faces were wiped of chocolate smears and children seated, some on soldiers' laps.

The room began to fill with excited babble as more and more Jews entered. Smells of fried onions, potatoes, and chicken schmaltz merged with human smells. Legs and arms, many with a blue number tattooed on them, moved around the tables in a scramble for places near friends, some tripping. The other people dodged the stumblers as they made their way.

Yanosh was surprised to see that there were a few family groups, young couples with small children. Here and there an older person came into the room, supported by someone younger. He wondered if these were remnants of families. There was even a group of identical twins, two pairs of them.

"Look Rivka, twins," Eva exclaimed, pointing at the corner table where these dazed children had located themselves.

"Mengele's twins, Eva. Have you not heard of his 'experiments' at Auschwitz?"

Eva nodded, sadly remembering what she had heard about the sufferings of these children.

Yanosh was relieved that the subject was not pursued further. He didn't want Eva's *Seder*, which she had awaited with such excitement, spoiled by the atrocity stories. He remembered his own horror when first told of Mengele's evil work.

Rivka steered them to a place near the head table. Taking a seat beside them, she leaned the chair on her other side onto the table. She then turned her long graceful neck this way and that, looking around the room.

"What are you doing?" Yanosh asked.

"I'm looking to see if a friend has arrived."

"Someone from the organizing committee?"

"No, it's someone special, a friend of Bronya's, may she rest in peace, a man who participated in resistance actions during the war; a partisan hero. I'm sure he will be here soon. We also have a special guest this evening, one of the leaders of the *yishuv*. He'll be sitting at the head table together with Rabbi Adler and Colonel Cohen."

"Sounds like this is an important event."

"It's the first Jewish public event here in Waldenburg since 1935 – you could call it an historic occasion, I suppose."

Yanosh watched as the table filled. Some of the people were still wearing the striped pajama-like clothes of the concentration camps – a year after the end of the war. Most were better dressed than these but, with few exceptions, they seemed to be wearing ill-fitting clothes or strange combinations of colors. Yanosh noticed a woman sitting at one of the tables in what looked like a once fine evening gown of white satin or silk, with a broad blue sash across the front of it. Her shoes and the yellow shawl she had around her shoulders were incongruous.

The shoes were heavy, black army boots; the shawl tattered and much-repaired.

Could that old shawl be a remnant of a former life, which had been destroyed during the war, he wondered?

Rivka rose. She turned to her new friends from Berlin, saying: "I must go to greet our special guests now, but I will be back soon. I will introduce you to the great man in person, when he joins us here."

Yanosh watched the woman's graceful movement as she left the room. She might have been a ballet dancer, he thought, but she's much too tall.

Eva said, "Yanosh, look. They have prepared a special *haggadah* for the participants."

She picked up a small, illustrated booklet and started to leaf through it.

"This is not a traditional service," she commented.

"Look at this illustration," she said a moment later, holding it up to show Yanosh.

Yanosh looked at the black and white image on the page. He saw a blur at first, until he straightened his glasses and managed to focus. He grabbed Eva's hand to steady it, and looked again. He saw a drawing of what must have been meant to look like a concentration camp: a barbed wire fence, little skeleton-like figures in prison garb, big Nazi guards with exaggerated swastika armbands, a dead prisoner hanging from a gallows, and, in the far corner, a chimney bellowing smoke. The word *slavery* headed the page. Above that, in Yiddish, there was a line, barely perceptible, which Yanosh didn't understand.

"It's a pretty good drawing…"

"What?"

"I said the illustrator is very skilled."

"But, Yanshuk, do you understand what it says here in the corner?"

"No, Eva. You know I don't read Yiddish very well, especially handwriting."

"He's written 'No one hears!' It's a bitter joke, a play on the verse in the Exodus story, which reads: 'And He heard their cries...'"

"A clever artist … He's right. There was no one to hear their prayers."

Eva whispered, "Yanosh, don't speak so loudly. This is a *Seder*, you might offend people. It's a religious occasion, a celebration of freedom … sha!"

"What kind of freedom, Eva? Millions murdered, the survivors destitute and neglected refugees, many of them still behind barbed wire, like those who live here, like those the British have imprisoned in Cyprus. You expect them to feel grateful to the Deity?"

"Maybe you are right, but there are religious people here. Now is not the time to be saying such things."

"What? Not state the truth."

Just then they saw Rivka returning from one of the two entrances. She was accompanied by a group of well-dressed people. The babble all around them continued but people began to rise as Rivka's little group approached the table. Yanosh remembered seeing people stand to show respect to rabbis in the past, but this was not a religious man, nor was he dressed in formal attire. He was wearing khaki pants and an open-necked white shirt, and his head was bare.

The Jews' eyes were riveted on this short, stocky man, walking beside Rivka. He looked very familiar, bald, apart from two curly tufts of disheveled white hair on the sides. He had a round, suntanned face, bicycle-spoke wrinkles around the corners of the eyes. His eyes twinkled mischievously. Where had Yanosh seen this man before? His memory failed him at first. Eva whispered to him:

"Yanosh, do you not recognize him?"

"Not sure … Maybe."

"It's Bar Giora, the Zionist leader, the one making all the problems for the British! I had heard he was visiting the refugee camps this week. That's him. I've seen him in the newspapers."

"Really. For a moment I thought it was Bora. They do look similar, don't they?"

"I suppose so, but Bora is younger, and he is taller than that. Bar Giora isn't more than five feet, at the most! Rivka towers over him."

"Shh … They are coming closer."

Rivka came over to them and they were introduced.

"Mr. Bar Giora, these are my friends – Yanosh and Eva Kaminski."

"Nice to meet you!"

The man's grip was powerful, as he squeezed Yanosh's hand. He did not look like Bora from close-up. He was much older, his face craggy and deeply wrinkled whilst Bora's face was smooth and youthful.

Rivka escorted him to the head table where he sat down between the bearded, black-hatted Rabbi Adler and the American officer. Colonel Sam Cohen was a redheaded man with a long, pointed nose and beady blue eyes. He was wearing a small white yarmulke, and was dressed in a well-pressed dress uniform with gold buttons, the silver eagle insignia at his collar and gold epaulettes on the shoulders. He was the senior American Jewish officer in the area but looked nervous and out of place, shaking his head disapprovingly, drumming fingers on the table. An impatient man, Yanosh thought. Rivka had told them that he was not very popular with the refugees, that he was antagonistic to their nationalist aspirations.

When the old *Yishuv* leader finally sat down, the other participants did so as well. The rabbi passed him a black yarmulke, which he carefully placed on the plate in front of him. The rabbi frowned, but said nothing. Around the room people muttered their comments. Some looked shocked, others approving, even delighted at his defiance of religion. Yanosh thought he could appreciate this man.

He heard one woman comment on this nearby: "He isn't intimidated by the rabbi!" she said.

Rivka soon rejoined them, a little breathless with excitement.

The chair beside her was still waiting for its occupant. She saw that Yanosh was looking at the empty space.

"He will come soon, don't worry."

"I'm not worried, Rivka, but you seem to be," commented Yanosh.

Eva poked him under the table.

"Yanosh!" she whispered.

"It's a great honor to have Mr. Bar Giora here with us this evening," Rivka said.

"He is one of the leading figures in the Palestinian Jewish community today, isn't he?" asked Eva.

"Yes, but not very respectful of Jewish tradition, I think," commented Yanosh.

"I didn't think you were so concerned about such things."

"Well, I am wearing a yarmulke, unlike him!"

Rivka smiled. Eva frowned.

The yarmulke felt like it was burning a hole into Yanosh's head. He was jealous of the old Zionist leader who appeared to be so free of religious convention.

Rabbi Adler picked up a silver goblet and stood up, holding it unsteadily, spilling wine over its sides as he did so. He gently balanced it on the palm of his tobacco-stained right hand, and spoke to the crowd:

"Ladies and gentlemen please fill your cups for the first blessing over the wine," he said.

He was swaying, as he waited for their response, eyes closed in concentration.

Chaos had meanwhile broken out. People stood, chairs screeched, their hands reached out for bottles of wine to fill their cups, and those of family members. Cups were knocked over, spilling their contents onto the tables.

The rabbi stood swaying, seemingly oblivious to it all. He was being ignored by most of those present. Yanosh found their behavior shocking.

It was Bar Giora who soon restored order. His booming,

bass voice surprised Yanosh. Such a small man with such a big voice!

"*HavEYrim, havEYrim*! A little quiet, please. We are celebrating the festival of freedom this evening! Tonight our people all over the world, and especially our *chalutzim* in *Eretz Yisrael* are telling the story of our exodus from Egyptian bondage. It would be a terrible *shandeh* if we do not do so here tonight. Let us fill our cups and give our full attention to the proceedings. Rabbi, please continue."

The cups were picked up, tables were wiped down, plates were straightened, children scolded.

Rabbi Adler opened his eyes, stared at Bar Giora for a moment, blinking at his bare, bald head and then continued with the blessing over the wine:

"*Baruch atah* ... our Lord, our G-d, Sovereign of the Universe, creator of the fruit of the vine..."

And continued with the blessing for the festival:

"*Baruch atah* ... our Lord, our G-d, Sovereign of the Universe for granting us life, for sustaining us and for helping us reach this day..."

Yanosh heard some sobbing at one of the other tables. Something in the words of this blessing had set it off. Soon others were weeping as well. For a moment he regretted that he knew no Hebrew. He did not understand what this was all about.

The rabbi slowly took a sip of wine, eyes closed. He opened them and looked around the room at the motley crowd of camp survivors, returnees from the Soviet captivity, those who had come out of hiding, the few resistance fighters, the cripples, the children, Mengele's twins, the sprinkling of American soldiers, the visitors from the land of Israel. The room had grown silent, in expectation, anticipation, but words failed him. He wiped the tears from his eyes, and said:

"Please be seated again, and enjoy your first cup of wine tonight, the first of the four our sages have commanded us to drink as free Jews."

His voice was strained, the word "free" barely audible as he spoke.

The enchantment of the moment ended, the near-riot was renewed. More wine was spilled and children cried. People began eating the *matzoh* and other foods on the table, while others told them off for their offensive, sacrilegious behavior, telling them to wait for the rabbi. The hum of a few whispered voices turned into a buzz of talking, chairs squeaking and tables creaking. Hands waved, people changed places in search of illusive community, or to escape annoying neighbors.

Yanosh had poured wine into Eva's and Rivka's cups, as well as his own, and now sat between them sipping the red, sweet drink with distaste. A man entered the room as they sat down, drinking. He strode over to their table. Yanosh sat there, his cup held half-way up to his mouth, frozen in mid-movement. There was no mistaking him. It was Yosef Borowski.

Rivka lit up the moment she saw him.

"My friend Bora is here at last!" she cried out in delight, her cheeks flushing as she rose and invited him to join them.

"We invite the children up to the head table now to sing the *ma nishtana*," announced the red-headed colonel, in as loud and authoritative a voice as he could summon. Rabbi Adler's coal-black eyes glowed, burning, under his bushy white eyebrows.

Bar Giora stood up, smiling broadly, stepped back and walked around to the front of the table. He opened short, muscular arms wide, and in a warm, deep voice invited the children to come forward: "*Kim, kinder, kim ahere, tayereh Yiddishe meydalach und yingalech!*"

And a few children did begin to get up from around the tables to join the old man in front of everyone. Some were pushed out by adults, others rushed forward of their own accord. Some came up holding hands, supporting each other, as they walked straight ahead, avoiding the eyes watching them. Rivka and Bora both got up and each took the hands of the shy ones leading them up to the front to join the others and Bar Giora.

Yanosh counted about a dozen children standing there with Bar Giora. Two were blond kindergarten-age boys, wearing German-style knickerbockers and long white socks. A redhead, rosy-cheeked girl, who looked perhaps twelve, her puberty budding, stood next to the twins, blushing, holding hands with a lanky, defiant-looking teenage boy. The other children stood behind them, huddled in their oversized rags of adult clothes, half-smiling, half-crying. Dark heads of hair and black eyes in thin pale faces turned to stare up at the legendary Zionist leader. Bar Giora's round, tanned, old face beamed above them with pleasure.

The room filled with the bittersweet voices of these children, accompanied by some of the adults. As they sang the beloved old tune, many sitting there found themselves wiping away tears. Yanosh listened to their singing and remembered, despite himself, his own family with whom he had sat at the *Seder* table before the war, remembering the moment Yantek, the youngest, had been cued to sing this song. He saw again his proud parents in their finery for the festival, his brothers and sister. All of them were gone, torn away forever. It was only after the song's rendition was completed that Rivka and Bora rejoined them at their table, both drying their red eyes.

"Eva and Yanosh, I would like you to meet…," Rivka began to say.

"Bora! How are you? I haven't seen you in so long … not since the day before yesterday," Yanosh said, laughing as he proffered his hand to his friend.

"*Gut yontef!*"

"*Gut yontef*, Yanosh, *Gut yontef*, Eva."

Eva smiled, bowing slightly.

"You know each other?" Rivka asked, surprised.

"Yes," answered Bora, "the Kaminskis lived near me in Berlin. We have known each other for some time now. We met in Poland, in Silesia."

"Please be seated, and talk more quietly!"

The American officer at the head table glared at them, looking annoyed. Yanosh regretted sitting so near him.

"You are disturbing everyone with your loud conversation." They sat down.

The rabbi was leading the ritual reading of the *haggadah*.

"*Avadim hayinu…* we were slaves to Pharaoh in Egypt, now we are free," he chanted.

Rabbi Adler was chanting aloud in Hebrew, then translating into Yiddish. He swayed to and fro, as he read the passages, translating them in the same high-pitched Talmudic singsong. One hairy hand was entwined in his thick, graying beard; the other was resting on the page. Yanosh was impressed with his intensity. It frightened him a little.

"That's not what we have here in our *haggadah*," he said to Rivka.

"No, you're right. The rabbi is reading from a traditional text. He would not appreciate the *haggadah* we gave out."

"Isn't that dishonest?" asked Eva, surprised.

"That's the religious for you! Always hiding from the truth, or being protected from it by others." Yanosh commented.

"Yanosh!"

"No, I don't think it is dishonest. I am happy to give Rabbi Adler a copy of what we prepared some other time, but I don't want to upset him this evening. We really appreciate his willingness to lead our *Seder* tonight. I am sure it is not easy being here with such an irreligious crowd."

Yanosh looked around the room, appreciating the truth of Rivka's statement. Rabbi Adler is faced with a difficult task, he thought. Rivka is probably right that he is making a sacrifice being here with us tonight.

Some people were chanting along with the rabbi, others were sitting in stony silence. Many were talking with their neighbors, ignoring the proceedings. Most were eating and drinking, apart from the white-yarmulked American soldiers and one or two pious old people. Everyone at the head table, on the other hand, seemed to be fascinated with the swaying rabbi.

Rivka, too, was absorbed in the rabbi's chant, singing along quietly to herself. Next to her Bora had taken out a small notebook filled with Yiddish handwriting, which he was reading to himself.

"This is like a circus."

"Yanosh, please ... don't start again!"

"But, Eva, you can see that most people here aren't really interested in what the rabbi is doing. They are just waiting to get more to eat. They've finished almost everything on the tables. If there wasn't more food to come, I think most of them would just get up and leave!"

"Yanosh, you must be more understanding. Consider what they have been through these past seven years."

"Eva, I understand what you are saying, but even so I would have expected better behavior tonight."

"Look at Rivka!" Eva whispered to him.

"And look at Bar Giora now," she added, lifting her eyes in that direction.

Yanosh looked over to see that Bar Giora had now placed the black yarmulke on his head, that he was also swaying to and fro, and chanting. For Yanosh himself the yarmulke still felt like molten lead, heavy and burning. He took it off, placing it next to his plate as Bar Giora had done before. He felt relieved. No one had noticed. No one said anything, yet. Eva was now talking to Rivka, no longer looking his way at all.

He had expected something else – more religiosity and decorum, not this noisy, marketplace scene. He didn't understand why the old Zionist leader and Eva and her friend Rivka seemed enraptured. His friend, Bora, who was a welcome guest here, was as uninterested in the proceedings as any of the most apathetic or bored participants. He just sat there reading his notes, adding penciled comments or corrections here and there, sometimes singing a tune or eating a little *matzoh*, or *chrein*, then going back to his papers.

"Yanosh… why did you take off the yarmulke? Come on… Even Bar Giora is now wearing one. Don't embarrass us in front of our friends."

"I am not comfortable wearing it, Eva. It indicates belief in God. I can't do that…"

Bora looked up from his papers and laughed at the little tiff his friends were having.

Rivka remained silent, but looked at him with understanding. She squeezed Eva's arm. Eva let the issue drop, rather than make a scene, but Bora then placed a cap on his head.

"A sign of respect," he explained, "not a statement of faith. I recommend you do the same, Yanosh, at least for your wife's sake."

Rivka and Eva smiled at Bora in appreciation, as Yanosh reluctantly donned the black yarmulke again.

The rabbi was now talking about the four sons mentioned in the *haggadah*, explaining how they were construed from different verses from the Torah. There were verses for the wise one, the wicked one, the simple one, and the one who did not know what to ask. All of this was new to Yanosh, but only of moderate interest.

"We are all here this evening," the rabbi said, "the wise, the wicked, the fools, and the silent ones, the remnant of the Jewish masses of Europe, to celebrate *Pesach*, our festival of freedom, according to our Holy Torah. Many of you know that the last and some of the worst camps in Germany were liberated at *Pesach* time last year, and that since then we have been involved in a desperate struggle for our national freedom. We must rise up out of the ashes and insist on our return to *Eretz Yisrael*. With the help of *ribbono shel olam*, we shall succeed. Nothing will stop us!"

He had raised his voice, and was almost screaming, when he suddenly stopped and looked with fiery eyes out at the crowd. Many of them were chewing, looking vacantly at him, seemingly impervious to his passion. Others went on talking, but those nearby had fallen into shocked silence, were watching and listening to the man.

Until that moment Rabbi Adler had gently conducted the *Pesach Seder* as he might have in any religious Jewish home at any time since the days of the ancient sages. The rabbi now pounded on the table, yelling at the crowd: "Brothers, sisters we are free now, free!"

Yanosh was stunned. He found himself standing with everyone else, applauding enthusiastically. He looked around the room. Everyone was indeed standing, even the American Jewish soldiers, the twins, the cripples and his socialist wife. They were all, at least for that moment, *farbrenteh* Zionists – nationalist fanatics.

"What am I doing?" Yanosh asked himself, surprised at his own behavior, "I don't want to go to Palestine," he reminded himself.

He stopped applauding, and sat down. Soon others were sitting too, but the majority stood there for some time, chanting Zionist slogans:

"Never Again!"

"Bevin is a murderer!"

"*Am Yisrael chai!*"

"Let My People Go!"

It was frightening. He thought for a moment of the Polish fascists, the communist youth groups and their political rallies in Poland before the war, their jingoistic slogans and sheep-like chanting. He hated the phenomenon then and it disturbed him to see it amongst the Jews now.

After the tumult died down, Rabbi Adler spoke up again. He had calmed himself and was speaking in his normal alto tone. The shriek was gone, but not the urgency and pain:

"Our return to *Eretz Yisrael* is our most important *mitzvah* today. To migrate to America or any of the British colonies far away is to choose to continue our exile, or, even worse, to end our existence as a separate people, God's people. Those working to open the gates of the land to us, to overcome the British treachery in preventing our return are doing God's work. They are to be blessed for their holy work."

Yanosh saw that the rabbi had again lost the attention of many of the participants, who were eating, chewing food and words. But he was filled with eager anticipation when he heard the next words spoken:

"One such a person is our guest tonight, Mr. Dov Bar Giora, a leader of the *Yishuv*, who has devoted himself to saving the remnant of European Jewry, by breaking the British blockade through so-called 'illegal' immigration. Another is our friend Yosef Borowski, a hero of Jewish resistance in Lithuania, whom we all know for his tireless efforts in the *Bricha* and his help for his fellow Jews here in the German refugee camps. I invite them each to say a few words to us, before we continue with the *haggadah*, and then begin our much-awaited meal."

Bar Giora rose, standing in the center of the head table facing the other table. The crowd seemed to hush, to quieten, though there were some negative comments made just behind them. Yanosh heard a loud sigh, and someone snicker. He picked up some of what was being whispered nearby: "Those Zionists again with their long speeches."

"*Yoh, Avider Zeh Hakt mein in Chanick yetz!*"

"Doesn't matter what he says, I am going to Canada. I have had enough war for a lifetime!"

Bora slowly got up to join Bar Giora at the head table in response to his invitation. They hugged and turned to the participants, smiling, arm-in-arm. Colonel Cohen watched them like an angry owl. Then Bar Giora began to speak, his bass voice booming out into the room's furthest corners: *HavEYrim* and *havEYrot*, during these six terrible years of war, we never forgot you for a single day."

"Sure, sure," a wrinkled young man said, winking at Yanosh, "tell us another one Bar Giora!" The man's wife or girlfriend poked him to shut him up. He obliged, first laughing, but then falling silent.

"We have been working to build up our land so that you may

come there to live as decent human beings among your own people and where you will never fear again. It is time for you to come home, to join us in *Eretz Yisrael.* You will need much courage and determination to do that.

"The British have decided to prevent the return of more than a paltry few survivors with immigration certificates; the rest they expect to resettle in the countries of Europe. They want to appease their Arab friends, whose oil they need. Considering the years of Hitlerite genocide, the silence of the rest of the world as millions of our people were murdered, and the continuing anti-semitism in Europe since the war ended, it is clear that a Jew cannot trust the *goyim.* That is why, despite all you have been through these past years, despite the temptation to migrate to other more comfortable places, you must choose to come home to *Eretz Yisrael.* You need us to feel free and fully human again. We need you to become a majority in our own land, to declare our independence at last in our own Jewish state. Together we will succeed. *Chazak, chazak venitchazek!*"

At first there was silence; stillness.

The wrinkled young man could be heard making strange noises into his chin, saying something about wanting to live not die for the Zionist cause. He was again silenced by his wife. A number of people at his table nodded in agreement.

There were also shouts of support. Applause. Slogan-chanting. Colonel Cohen's beady blue eyes showed his discomfort. Bar Giora standing there waiting, lifted his arms to appeal for quiet.

"Many of you already know my friend, Yosef Borowski, a former partisan commander in the Naroch forests of White Russia, activist of the *Bricha* and a partner in the current activities of the Zionist movement here in this accursed country. His message is crucial and relevant to all of us today in our struggle for our own country's independence and for the future of the Jewish people. Mr. Borowski, please…"

Bora stepped forward to speak, pulled out his notes from his jacket pocket, cleared his throat, and waited. After a while the crowd understood. They responded to his patient presence and grew quieter.

"My dear friends, I want to wish you all a wonderful *Pesach* holiday! As we have just read in the *haggadah* this year we are still not free here in Germany, but next year we will be free again. We will only be *bnei chorin* if we stand up for our rights. As we read at the end of the service every *Pesach*..."

Someone in the crowd loudly completed his statement: *"leshana haba'ah biyrushalayim!"*

Many cries of support were heard in the hall:

"Next year in Jerusalem! Next year in Jerusalem!"

Then some people started to sing the words to a Hassidic tune, others joining the lilt until their fervor was stopped by Bar Giora's deep voice asking for quiet again:

"Silence! Our guest has the floor now! Let us hear what he has to say."

Bora waited a moment, then spoke again:

"During the three years I spent fighting the Nazis in the forests of Byelorussia, there was one dream which kept me going, a hope which accompanied our efforts for the *Bricha* over the past two years, the hope to again be free as a Jew, to live amongst my own people. The time has come to realize that dream, to stop only hoping, to stop waiting for the Messiah to come and save us from our sufferings in exile, to end the 2000-year-old exile before the exile finishes us off."

Silence. Then shouts of support. Applause. Bora started to walk back to his seat again, folding his papers and putting them back in his coat pocket. Suddenly three shots were heard, fired from outside. The three explosions followed in quick succession, with the whistle of bullets flying past Bora's head as he ducked behind the nearest table. The sound of tearing wood on the far side of the hall ... the smell of gunpowder and then ... screams.

People dived to the ground. Bora pulled out a gun, opened fire in the direction of the shots, and then began running forward towards the source of the shooting. Yanosh was stunned but also impressed with his friend's quick reflex. It was the opposite of his. He had grabbed Eva and moved to cover as fast as he could, under a table from where he continued watching what was happening.

Sirens soon sounded. Running boot-steps. The hall was full of American soldiers, who rushed in from both sides of the hall looking for the assassin. A couple of them had jumped Bora and were pinning him to the ground.

Yanosh and Eva got up from under the table to see Bora being led away by a couple of soldiers. They had confiscated his weapon. He had been handcuffed. They were soon out of sight, but Bora's voice could be heard yelling: "*Am Yisroel chai!*" (The People of Israel live!). They heard him repeat it a number of times. Then he was gone.

The tall American colonel stood in the center of the room calling for quiet. After a while he managed to get something of a lull in the excited chatter of the shocked crowd. Bar Giora was inspecting the far wall, examining the three bullet holes, accompanied by some of the curious children. Colonel Cohen glared back at his guest from Palestine, and then began to speak:

"Please, ladies and gentlemen, we must restore calm here. I understand that the gunfire, the apparent assassination attempt is very upsetting, but we are all, unfortunately, well-acquainted with violence and hate, especially at *Pesach* time. We must not let this incident disturb us. We must remember that tonight is *Seder* night. As we Americans say: "The show must go on!" Please return to your seats and we shall continue our reading of the *haggadah*, and enjoy our festive meal. The American forces here will take care of our security. They have orders to protect religious freedom here in Germany and they will do so to the best of their ability. Please be seated once more! It is *yontef...*"

Some people returned to their seats. Others continued sitting on the ground, looking dazed. A few had gathered at the far wall to inspect the bullet holes. One old woman was laughing strangely, hysterically. A frightened couple were still huddled under a table. Yanosh watched as Bar Giora came up to speak to the American officer when he had finished speaking. He could hear every word of the ensuing conversation:

"Colonel Cohen, I would like to have a word with you."

"Go ahead, Mr. Bar Giora. I am listening."

"Release the man your soldiers have just arrested."

"You mean Borowski?"

"Yes, Yosef Borowski. As a fellow Jew I am sure you are aware of the importance of a former partisan commander to the survivor community. It is a matter of morale. They see him as a hero, a defender of their rights."

"I understand all that, Mr. Bar Giora. I am well acquainted with Borowski. He has been something of a troublemaker here in the past. A little time to cool off his passions would do him good, perhaps even keep him alive a little longer. A live hero might be more useful to his fellow Jews than a dead one, don't you think Mr. Bar Giora?"

"I think he can take care of himself. It is Passover. If you release him quickly you will win over a lot of people here tonight."

"I will consider what you have said, sir, but there has just been a shooting incident, which must be investigated, and Borowski was, I think, the target of an assassination attempt, apart from himself brandishing and using an unauthorized weapon. It is *Pesach* and we should go on with the *Seder*, sir. The people here seem to respect and listen to you. I would appreciate your help restoring order so we can get on with the proceedings."

As they spoke people were leaving the room. Rabbi Adler, visibly upset, appealed to them to stay but many continued fleeing the scene, having overcome their initial shock. The laughing woman left. Then the shivering couple and a small crowd of children, holding hands. Bar Giora and the colonel saw what was happening and joined the rabbi in his efforts, leaving their conversation unfinished.

"*Yidden*, wait! Stay! You mustn't leave! We have a *Seder* to finish." Bar Giora begged them, but to no avail.

The rabbi stood there in tears, as the American officer gently placed his hand on his shoulder:

"I am sorry rabbi," he said.

It was Rivka who then spoke up.

"Come," she said to the assembled remaining few, "let us get on with the *Seder* and not let these events distract us. Be brave! Let's do so in Bronya's memory. She would have expected no less, I am sure."

Her rallying call had some impact on some of her friends. They soon found themselves sitting around the same table, ready to continue. Yanosh was surprised at her resolve and even more surprised at Eva's response. She grabbed his hand and pulled him to the table as well.

Rabbi Adler, wiping his eyes, turned to those sitting with him at the table now:

"Our people's story has been one of the *she'erit hapleta* who continued our journey of faith through history despite the massive odds against us. Looking at you here with me now at this table I know we shall prevail. You are that faithful remnant."

Yanosh fought off a powerful feeling of belonging, reminding himself that this was only a religious ceremony, but did not quite succeed in feeling totally alienated. Something still stirred inside.

The rabbi restarted the service, leading them in chanting the blessing over the *maror*, bitter herbs, joined by the deep gruff voice of Bar Giora, the sweet tunefulness of Rivka and Eva, and a determined-looking Colonel Cohen's high-pitched tenor. Others soon joined, even some of the soldiers, but Yanosh continued sitting there in silence. He could still smell the burnt gunpowder.

Yanosh looked over at Eva, saw her shining eyes, then looked down at her belly which was beginning to show. There was a growing baby inside. He thought of their future as a family, the world into which they were bringing this new life.

They were now singing "Next year in Jerusalem!"

"Should we go to Palestine after all or have we had enough of this? More struggle and tears, or safety for our child?" he asked himself.

8

Bora: In Captivity

Bora knew that this had been an attempt to kill him. It wasn't the first time, and there would probably be more. That was why he had attended the *Seder* armed. He had no choice but to shoot. He was sorry that the party had been disrupted, that others might have been hurt, but felt that one had to respond quickly. It was shoot or be shot. He had learned that basic truth during the war.

He was outraged by the loss of his weapon. How dare they disarm him! What right did they have to take his gun from him!? How could they stop him from defending himself!

Bora attempted to grab it back, only to be met with a blow to the solar plexus. When he straightened up, and got his breath back, he saw that they had clamped handcuffs on him. Since his run-in with the French police the year before he had not felt as impotent, as vulnerable as he did now.

Why were his friends just standing there! Why didn't they do something to help him? Why didn't they protest? They celebrate their supposed freedom, but behave still like slaves! He must do something to move them, to wake them up, to stir them into action.

He began to yell: *"Am Yisrael chai!"*, "Let my people go!" and similar slogans.

He had hoped to arouse Bar Giora and his people to do something, to intervene with their American Jewish friends. It was his only hope to regain his freedom, but they just stood there confused, looking blankly at him.

As they dragged him away, he turned around to see Bar Giora talking to an American officer, the one who had participated in the *Seder* with them. Another twist of his arm sent a sharp stab of pain through his body.

"What are you looking at, Jew! You won't be seeing your friends for a long time. Now, turn around," the soldier ordered.

Bora's English was limited, but the tone of the soldier's comment was clear, and his hand movements indicated that he turn his head forwards, which he did. He didn't relish the possibility of another twist of his arm.

They led him forward and out into the night. It was chilly outside, drizzling lightly. More soldiers joined them on the way, cursing the cold and the need to go out into it. He could understand their complaints. Their English was simple.

"What did this guy do?" he heard one ask his escorts.

"Top military secret."

"Come off it! What did he do?"

"Mind your own fucking business!"

They went inside, walked along a long corridor, tracking in mud behind them. They came to a desk, behind which sat a pudgy, bespectacled soldier. There was a ledger open in front of him.

"What's this? You are messing up the floor! What do you guys want at this hour anyway?"

"Another Zionist troublemaker... He was carrying a gun, Sarge! Colonel Cohen told us to bring him in for 'babysitting' until he figures what to do with him."

The black soldier tossed Bora's revolver onto the counter.

"Here, a present for you! Evidence for the court."

"Wow! That is a nice piece ... an automatic pistol. Where did you get that?"

Bora remained silent. He didn't know what the man was saying, but understood that they were admiring his weapon. He smiled, regaining his composure a little.

The desk sergeant picked up a pen.

"Name? *Nomme?*"

"Yosef Borowski." This information was recorded in the ledger.

"Address?"

Bora gave him an address in Berlin. The pen noted that too.

"*Du Farshteist Anglish?*"

"*Nein.*"

"Tomorrow morning we'll have someone here who can translate for us. Come on, let's show him to his hotel room."

The sergeant led them around a corner, and along another corridor, until they came to a row of iron doors. He pulled out a ring of keys and examined them, counted a few cells along the right side and opened one slowly. The place reeked of urine. A black soldier took off Bora's handcuffs and pushed him in roughly. The door closed behind him.

There was one window, high up in the opposite wall, through which some light shone into the room. It was too high to see anything outside. He shoved the metal bed over to the window and climbed onto it. Still too high. He saw a snitch of night sky, part of a cloud, the edge of a pole, from which a strong light shone. Nothing else.

Bora sat down to think. He heard voices on the other side of the wall ... speaking German, he thought. It was hard to hear what they were saying. After a while the voices died down. Quiet descended on the cell block. An occasional clank of metal disturbed the silence, echoing on into the long corridor along which he had been escorted-dragged earlier.

After a while he began to doze off. He had not slept a full night in days and, though he was usually a light sleeper, he could not keep his eyelids from closing. He soon found himself asleep sitting on the bed, head bobbing up and down. So, he gave in to his need to rest and lay down on the hard mattress, pulled the single, dusty blanket over himself.

The chirping of birds woke him. He stretched his body, looked over at the window of his cell and saw that it was morning. How long had he slept? Where was he?

He heard the distant sound of footsteps. They grew louder. Voices. English. These must be Americans, he thought, not

French. He began to remember the night before, the Pesach celebration, the shots, his arrest. His arm ached.

Keys clinking at the cell door. The door opened. Two American soldiers entered his cell. One was tall, bespectacled, seemed friendly. The other, shorter, one looked familiar. From last night? He had a hooked nose, sharp brown eyes, jutting red jaw and angry look. The tall one came in first and spoke:

"Mr. Borowski?"

"Yes, that is my name."

"Colonel Cohen would like to talk to you. Follow us, please."

"Cohen? His name is Cohen?"

"Yes, sir."

"I see."

"Yes, you will see, sir."

The conversation with the friendly soldier ended abruptly when the other glared at his mate and ordered him to stop talking.

"Don't talk with the prisoner, McKlellan! Time to go. Come on."

Bora followed them out of his cell and along the corridor. It was a corridor of metal doors, each with a small grate in the bottom half for passing in food, which was the only break in the metal sheeting. Otherwise the walls, which were off-white, the plaster peeling in places, revealed a light green under, or former, coat.

They had handcuffed him again. One of them held the door at the end of the hall for him while the other escorted him through.

"Why don't you take these off me?" he asked, in his rudimentary English, holding up his arms towards the older of the two, "it would be easier."

"Sorry, we can't do that. Orders."

"What's your name, soldier?"

"Sorry. I can't tell you. Orders."

"Where are you taking me?"

"You'll soon see."

"McKlellan, shut up!" yelled the hooked-nose, as they stepped out into the courtyard.

Bora was blinded by the sudden exposure to sunlight. When his eyes grew accustomed to it, he saw that he was in a small yard, perhaps 20 by 10 meters, surrounded by a two-meter high wall, topped with broken glass and a roll of barbed wire around the outside. Across the courtyard was a padlocked gate, somewhat rusted, with remnants of green paint in places.

His escort led him to the gate. The hooked-nosed soldier brought out a number of keys on a chain with which he wrestled for a while until he found the right one. He opened the lock, then the gate. It creaked in protest. They went through into a small garden: two fruit trees, a flowering lemon tree and a just budding pear or apple tree were its main occupants. It was tucked into the space between two office buildings and the barbed wire coil which had been laid around them. He was led across the garden to a bright green door. Bora's English was good enough to manage the name on it: "Colonel Samuel Cohen," he read.

The hooked-nosed soldier knocked.

"Come in!" came the high-pitched voice from within.

McKlellan opened the door for his prisoner, smiling sympathetically at him. Bora appreciated his sympathy, but not what happened next. Hook-nose gave him a sharp shove from behind, whispering *"bloody Jew!"* as he did so.

Bora tripped and crashed to the floor, landing in the center of the office. Colonel Cohen rose from his desk, and came forward. He bent down and helped Bora up. Hook-nose left the scene of his crime, McKlellan stood at the door, stunned.

"What happened to you?" Colonel Cohen asked Bora in Yiddish.

Bora understood, despite the man's strong American accent.

"I tripped," he answered.

The Colonel passed him a handkerchief. Bora began to daub

his bleeding nose. The handcuffs hindered him. The American officer took the bloodied cloth from him and put it to his nose for him. He ordered McKlellan, who still stood alone on the doorstep to come in and help out.

"Uncuff him, soldier," he said.

"Yes, sir."

"Is this how we treat our prisoners?"

"What do you mean, sir?" McKlellan asked, as he uncuffed Bora, who shook his hand free and then took the handkerchief back to stop the bleeding.

"He didn't just trip, did he?"

"No, sir ... I mean yes, sir."

"What happened, Borowski?"

"I fell, that's all."

"Come sit here, Mr. Borowski."

"McKlellan, go bring the man a glass of water."

"Yes, sir."

McKlellan left. Bora sat down. He studied the room, then looked down at the handkerchief. The bleeding had stopped. He looked up at the American and examined him.

"I know you," he said.

"Yes, we met at the Passover meal."

"Colonel Cohen?"

"Yes, Sam Cohen. You remember well. And you are Yosef Borowski, the former partisan and well-known smuggler," he said, offering him his hand.

"I see. You have heard of me?"

"I have heard too much about you, Bora. You see I know your nickname as well. I have heard there is a saying in the Jewish refugee community, 'if you have a problem, Bora will take care of it for you – for a price.'"

"I am impressed with your intelligence, Sam, but you have the saying wrong. They say..."

A knock. McKlellan, with a glass of water.

"Thank you, corporal. You may retire for now."

"Yes, sir. Thank you, sir."

The soldier saluted and exited, smiling to himself.

"Okay, let's cut the small talk. Bora, you are a constant source of trouble for me. You have a lot of chutzpa. Coming into the U.S. military zone, carrying a weapon is a serious offense. Using your gun in a crowded room was irresponsible. Luckily you didn't hit anyone."

"Colonel Cohen, I…"

"No, let me finish what I have to say first, Borowski. I could have locked you away for a long time, put you on trial and had you jailed for a couple of years, I'm sure. There would have been protests, but they would eventually subside. They would forget you in the flow of events, of life, but I'm letting you go, despite all I have against you. I am doing you a favor."

Bora smiled for the first time during their meeting.

"Don't smile so fast. Listen to me. I am releasing you, but there is a condition."

"I'm listening."

"You will have to leave Germany as soon as possible."

"Why? So I'll cause you less trouble?"

"Yes. But that is not the only reason. I don't want your death on my conscience. Last night's bullets were meant for you. There will be more, I'm sure. Sitting with us in jail here will not keep you safe, I am afraid. You are likely to endanger innocent people as well. You must disappear and fast. I will do whatever I can to help you get out of the country, but I won't let you out of the clink without a commitment from you that you will leave. Do I have it?"

"Yes, you do. I value my freedom as you know. Give me a week and I will be over the German border. I won't come back this time."

"How do I know I can trust you, Bora? I have heard of previous agreements you have made with the British, which you didn't keep. You told them you would clear out, but did not keep your word."

Bora pulled a dollar note out of his pocket. He tore it in half, handed one half to Colonel Cohen.

"You have my word. When I cross the border I will send you the other half. Okay?"

"Borowski, I am not impressed. We know your tricks. Keep your money."

Colonel Cohen passed back the torn half-note.

Bora's smile faded.

"Sorry to hear that you don't trust me. We Jews should at least trust each other, don't you think?"

"We are first and foremost human beings, Borowski. Some men can be trusted, others cannot. I tend to think of you as being in the second category. Whatever the case, I am taking no chances. You will be escorted to the French border from your Berlin apartment tomorrow morning. I have arranged a ride for you to Berlin this afternoon at 2:00 p.m."

Bora didn't respond. He got up and walked across the room, stopping at the window on the far side. He heard Colonel Cohen breathing behind him at his desk. Beyond the barbed-wire fence of the military compound he saw green fields, spotted with yellow and white wild flowers, a blue spring sky, streaked with feathery clouds.

"What do you say, Borowski?" he heard the Colonel ask him.

"Do I have a choice?" he asked without looking back behind him.

"No, not really, but you could be more or less cooperative. It is in your own interest, you know."

Bora saw some birds fly past. Dark little birds ... sparrows?

Bora pointed at them.

"Do you see those birds? They are free to move where they want, but me? You want to kick me out of Germany. How will I be able to help Jews if I'm not here where my fellow survivors have congregated?"

Colonel Cohen did not respond.

He turned back to the Colonel: "All right. I will cooperate."

Bora was returned to his cell. His lunch was brought to him. He then had time to think, to come up with a plan. He picked at his food. Some potatoes, peas, a small piece of red meat, barely warm, a couple of slices of rough bread, a little margarine and some jam. He set aside the bread.

He appreciated the sweet tea, drank some more, then reached for the bread and jam. He imagined his father's disapproval, seeing that it was Pesach, but the years in the forest with the Russian partisans had toughened him. He could not afford to be sentimental. I have turned into a goy, he thought, as he took a bite.

He heard the delivery of lunch to the nearby cells. The opening and closing of food grates one after the other along one side of the corridor and then along the other. He heard the shuffling of feet along the prison corridor. Probably prisoners being led somewhere, he thought. The prison seemed to be buzzing with life as he sat there trying to think. He would be without his gun when they let him out ... without a weapon!

Being weaponless made him angry. He valued that Walther P38 pistol. He had not come by it easily and was sad to part with it, it felt good by his side, was a powerful friend. An automatic – German craftsmanship – the *mamzeyrim,* the bastards, knew how to make weapons!

They were not likely to return it. He would have to get a new gun. He would go to Moniek or Fima before he left the country, leave them instructions. Moniek was a better bet – he had more access to weapons because of his job. But, then, Fima was more circumspect, more careful about what he said and to whom. No, he would go to Moniek, he had little time. Moniek was more accessible and owed him. He would be good for a new weapon.

Should he cooperate with them and let them throw him out of the country tomorrow morning without a fight? He could take advantage of the one evening in Berlin to disappear, stay where he was needed, but then he would become a fugitive, be under constant danger of arrest by the Americans, not only the British and Russians. It would only be a matter of time until someone got him, until he lost his freedom again, or worse.

Better to cross into France, as the Americans wanted him to do, perhaps try to stay involved in the *Bricha* work and settle accounts with the S.S. men from afar. *Shaysa!* That wouldn't be the same – he would no longer have the pleasure of watching them die, having them beg him for mercy.

No, it was time to move on, time to let go, put the past behind him. There were others who would continue what he had started.

Lo aleicha hamelacha ligmor – It is not for you to complete the work, the Talmud says.

Moniek, Fima, Yankev – they were good men who knew what to do and did it well. Pity about Yanosh, he had the potential too, but he had a pregnant wife. She was ... interfering, suspicious ... his wife. It was good to help them with their immigration plans, the child would be better off in Australia. Anyway, one always wondered about Yanosh's Jewish loyalties. He had non-Jewish friends, did not espouse much nationalistic feeling in conversations, often made critical comments.

The door opened. Hook-nose and another guard, a tall black soldier, stood there.

"Give me the tray," the black soldier said.

"Get up, Borowski," added hook-nose, "it's time to go. They are waiting for you at the fucking prison gate."

Bora got up slowly. They can wait, he thought, there's no hurry.

"Hurry up, we haven't got all day," hook-nose said, irritated.

Bora kept his calm, moved slowly, smiling.

"I am happy to see you are in such a good mood this morning, my friend," he responded, irritating the man still more.

It was with great effort that the soldier managed not to strike Bora, who enjoyed his obvious discomfort.

The black soldier waited placidly at the door.

They led him out, the black soldier towering over them as they walked down the prison corridor and across the courtyard to the outer gate. He hummed to himself as he went, further irritating hook-nose. The gate creaked open slowly. Freedom! Freed at last! He walked through, smiling and breathing deeply.

As they left the prison gate and walked towards the waiting army truck, Bora remembered another departure, years before.

"Please climb in, Mr. Borowski," a voice disturbed his memories.

Bora looked up to see McKlellan's familiar face. The man's hand was outstretched to help him up.

Bora climbed up into the back of the truck and sat down on the wooden bench opposite him.

"So they let you out, sir?"

"Yes, they did, and I am happy to be out of there."

"Colonel Cohen is a tough one. You are lucky he let you out."

"I am aware of that."

"He has no special sentiments for his fellow Jews. If anything he is tougher with them than with others. There have been unpleasant run-ins between him and the Zionists here a number of times in the past."

"Is that so?"

"Yep. And I know for a fact that he doesn't like you either."

"I thought as much."

"I guess he let you go in order to get rid of you. Probably thought that you would be a trouble-maker in the jail as well."

"Something like that."

"He asked me to accompany you to your flat in Berlin, spend the night with you and make sure you caught the morning train to Paris."

"I see. Well, I am happy it is you, Corporal McKlellan. You seem to be a good person. I remember your kindnesses yesterday and this morning."

"Thank you, sir. You can call me Joe."

"Ah, really! My name is Joseph too."

"Is that so? My, what a coincidence."

"What's that word, Joe? I don't know it. Co-insi-dens?"

"Coincidence, sir, is when two people have something in common, and you don't expect them to."

"Like our having the same first name?"

"That's right. That's it."

The truck rumbled on towards Berlin, increasing its speed as the road improved. Bora could see the green German countryside whizzing past them as they moved fast along the road westwards. The sun had begun its descent, he supposed. It could no longer be seen above them through the truck's flapping tarpaulin cover.

McKlellan and Bora gripped the metal bar to which the cloth cover was attached to prevent themselves falling out the back of the vehicle. The wooden crates with which they shared the space were tied with ropes, and though they slid backwards and forwards, danced a little, they were well secured. The human cargo was a lot more fragile and not given the same careful attention. McKlellan slid along the bench towards the driver's cabin, getting as close as he could.

"Hey! Slow down! You want to get us all killed, you crazy bastard!" he yelled.

"It is no use, McKlellan. He can't hear you!" Bora yelled after him.

They fell silent and thoughtful. Conversation was now impossible, anyway.

Bora noticed that McKlellan had laid his rifle down on the truck floor, jammed between the nearest crate and the bench. After a while he began to nod off. Bora was amazed to see this soldier sleeping in the noisy, moving truck, his head bobbing up and down, eyes drooping and opening, drooping and opening. Markov would have had him shot on the spot in the forests, he thought to himself. He remembered more than one such execution, had once almost been caught dozing himself.

He considered the possibility of trying to grab his rifle and jumping out of the moving vehicle. Not a realistic option, he thought. The truck is moving too fast to risk the jump. Anyway, his foot is resting on the rifle butt. Shouldn't underestimate the man and what he might do. His good will was not to be wasted, either.

Bora thought about his plans for the future, sifting through a mental list of things to do: people to contact, instructions to be given before his departure for France the next day. The next day. Tomorrow! It was little time to do so much. He would have to be disciplined, would not be able to sleep much that night.

Having finished his personal inventory and having planned his next moves, he relaxed again, aware that despite the circumstances, this was his best opportunity to release the tension of the past couple of days. He focused on his breathing, consciously slowing it down, relaxed his ankles, while still gripping the metal bar behind him. He poked McKlellan to wake him, concerned that he was loosening his grip and might fall. The soldier smiled in appreciation, but he soon nodded off again, head nodding as before.

Bora returned to his apartment to find it in disarray. Clothes were scattered across the bed and floor. Papers were spread out across the kitchen table. The drawers were all open. There were things everywhere, but at least nothing was broken.

McKlellan expressed sympathy, but Bora was livid and not to be appeased easily. Who had been here? Had anything been stolen? He started organizing his things again with McKlellan's help. There seemed to be nothing missing, which surprised him.

He asked McKlellan to wait in the kitchen a moment while he got changed, and packed a few things. He escorted him there, poured him a beer.

"I'll be out in a minute, Joe. Enjoy the beer."

"What about you? Don't you want a drink too?"

"Sure I do. Don't finish the bottle. Leave me some. I'll be back soon."

"Okay Joseph. I'm waiting."

Bora returned to his room. Picked out some new clothes, which he put on quickly. He then went over to the rug beside his bed and pulled it up. He lifted a floorboard there and pulled out a small black metal box, which he unlocked. He took out some money and papers, and a small handgun, which he loaded and slipped into his inner jacket pocket. Smiling to himself, he returned to the kitchen to rejoin McKlellan.

"It took you awhile. Here I saved you some of your beer."

"Thank you. I just checked that nothing valuable was missing."

"And?"

"It's okay. Whoever it was didn't take anything."

"Who do you think it was?"

"Hard to say ... there are so many people after me – Russians, ex-Nazis, the British. Could have been anyone."

"You are a popular fellow."

"Fellow?"

"Man ... a popular man!"

"Yes, you could say that. It is probably good that your officer is making me move on."

"I think so. Someone tried to kill you. They'll be trying again, I would guess."

"Maybe ... there's another bottle here in the fridge somewhere. Have another drink... Here's to your health, Joe!"

"To your health Joseph, what is it you Jews say? Ah... le... Lechaim!"

"I'll drink to that. Lechaim!"

"I will be keeping my eyes open tonight. My orders are to protect you until you leave the country tomorrow."

"Let's go out to get something to eat, McKlellan. I am hungry."

"Sounds good. Okay. Let's go."

The next morning Bora was up early. He packed a few things, taking special care to conceal his weapon in a holster under his shirt. He scribbled a note to Moniek with an explanation of what had happened and instructions for continuing their work. He taped it to the mirror in his room, knowing that Moniek would let himself into the flat, as he regularly did, and would see it there. Then he woke McKlellan.

They left for the station.

He boarded the train after a two-hour wait with his convivial guard. They shook hands, wishing each other all the best in a warm farewell. Bora climbed into the carriage and found himself a seat, his eyes following McKlellan's back as the man walked away. He was surprised to see Moniek running through the station gate. He called out to him but was not heard or seen. It was too late, the train was already moving, but he knew at least that his friend Moniek had read his note, that he would now know his destination and when he had left. As the train pulled out, Moniek finally spotted him as well. He waved, Bora waved back, and then he left Berlin behind.

9
The Wedding

It was not long after the *Seder* that Eva turned to Yanosh one evening with a strange request. She had, much to his relief, lost her intense interest in religion. She had gone on to reading other books, moved the religious books aside onto a shelf where she occasionally dusted them. She did continue lighting candles on Friday nights, but Yanosh learned to live with that. He appreciated the fact that she lit them after dark when they sat down to eat and not according to Jewish law before nightfall. He still cringed when she made the blessing over them, but had to admit that the candle light gave a special feel to their Friday night meals. They had reached a modus vivendi in their life as a couple: a little tradition, but no specific demands. So it took him by surprise when she came up with her new request.

It was a Sunday evening. They'd returned home from a very pleasant outing with Marek and Pawla into the flowering spring countryside. It had been a sunny day and Pawla's idea that they organize a picnic was readily accepted by all. They'd grown tired of talking about Bora's sudden disappearance after the *Seder*. Two weeks of intense rumors had left them just as ignorant about his fate as they'd been the day after the *Seder*, when Colonel Cohen had informed a delegation of refugees that he had been released by the U.S. Army and that they had no idea as to his whereabouts since.

They sat there, the two of them, tired after their Sunday outing, drinking tea.

"It was a lovely day, Yanshuk."

"Yes, it was."

"Renting a horse and buggy for the day instead of schlepping out into the country by train was a brilliant idea."

"You enjoyed that?"

"Yes, I did. It was fun being able to choose where to go and not being limited by train schedules and routes. We saw more of the countryside."

"I enjoyed the greater mobility too. It did cost us a lot more, but I think it was worth it."

"Would you like some more tea?"

"Yes, thank you."

"The bloody Germans have a beautiful country. Why did they need to invade their neighbors and start wars with them? Could they not have been satisfied with what they had already?"

"They were crazed with power. Hitler had them mesmerized, fed into their sense of superiority. You know, *Deutschland Uber Alles*, all that lethal, crazed rubbish…"

"Yes, I know, and now the Zionists are trying to whip up some of the same nationalist shit amongst the Jewish survivors of the Germans' madness. They want us all to migrate to Palestine, that arid little country, surrounded by hordes of hating Arabs."

"It's not the same, Yanosh. It's not the same at all."

"Well, maybe they are not fascist racists, but they are crazy. What they want to do is impossible and irresponsible."

"I'm not so sure. That Bar Giora is not only a visionary. He is a very practical man… Perhaps they will succeed.

"I doubt it. They will just lead the Jews to another tragedy!"

"You are sometimes so cynical, so negative."

"Realistic, my dear wife, just realistic."

"Yanosh! Do you have to smoke? I think Pawla has been a bad influence on you."

He put out his cigarette, commenting: "I'm not addicted to it like she is. I just enjoy an occasional smoke, that's all."

"Yanshuk … there's something I've been wanting to ask you for a while now…"

"Go ahead. I am all ears…"

Yanosh pushed his big ears forward in an attempt to make a joke of this, but Eva's response was sharp. She obviously didn't find it funny.

"Yanosh!"

"Okay, okay. I'm listening. What is it?"

"I've been thinking that we ought to get married."

"You what! Get married? But Eva we are married. I have a wedding photo to prove it. What are you talking about? What do you mean?"

"You know, Yanshuk." She gently touched his arm. He pulled his arm away.

"No, I don't understand."

"Well, we were married, but it was a civil wedding. We never had a *huppah* (wedding canopy). We were never married according to Jewish tradition."

"What, more of this religious rubbish again! I thought you had finished with that. No, I'm not interested in doing a religious ceremony. I will not have some bearded old man recite some Hebrew mumbo-jumbo over a glass of wine in a tent in order to be "kosher." We are already married!"

"Yanosh, please. Don't get so upset. Let me explain…"

"What do you need to explain? I understand very well what you want. I'm sorry, I will not do it. I can't. You are asking too much of me this time, Eva."

"Yanosh, I know your feelings about religion. We talked about it so many times, but I am asking you to do what everyone does, even some of our Communist friends. It would make me so happy, and be meaningful. It would be an assertion of Jewish life and continuity after all we have been through."

Yanosh shook his head as she spoke, but he was weakening.

"Your mother wanted us to do a Jewish wedding, not only a civil one. You do remember her reaction when we told her that there would be no *huppah*, don't you?"

Eva looked at him beseechingly, waiting for his response.

Yanosh was moved, but held back his feelings.

"How could I forget?" he said, as she gently put her arm through his.

"So, Yanosh, if you won't do it for my sake alone, think of it as honoring your mother's memory. I will agree to wear your mother's ring, if you do."

This was too much for Yanosh. He rose angrily, letting her arm drop behind him and began to pace the room to calm himself.

"What are you doing?"

"Walking … thinking."

"Look at me, Yanosh."

He looked and saw that she was crying. He sat beside her again, awkwardly.

"We are expecting a child!"

He took her arm.

"Do you still love me?"

"You know the answer to that!" he said, caressing her neck as soothingly as he could. He put his arms around her.

"I'll think about it, Eva. Maybe I can do it, maybe. Give me some more time to think about it, that's all."

She smiled, wiping her reddened eyes.

That night was nevertheless stormy in bed. Eva would not let Yanosh touch her or come near her. She lay silent on the far side of the bed, curled into herself, until she slept. Her breathing irritated him. Yanosh could not fall asleep.

He rose, got out of bed and wandered into the living room-kitchen space. He made himself a cup of tea and sat thinking about Eva's request while sipping it. He remembered the ring, his mother's ring, which he had held onto since it was found in Warsaw. After Eva had refused to wear it he had considered selling it when they had needed money. He had twice taken it to be valued, once negotiated to sell it to a jeweler in his Berlin store. The man had started counting out the money to buy it, but Yanosh had bowed out of the deal at the last moment. The jeweler had yelled at Yanosh as he left the store still holding the precious ring. Yanosh could still hear his shrill voice and the sudden silence when the shop door, which slammed behind him, suddenly blocked it out.

He got up from his empty cup and musings, went back into the bedroom, where Eva was snoring quietly and looked for the ring again. He found the tiny, felt ring box Bora had procured for him and took it back to the kitchen to look at the ring. He had had it polished in order to sell it, and when he opened the little maroon box, it reflected the light of the lamp.

He looked at it a long time in the kitchen light, reflecting on what it represented to him. Could he go through with the religious ceremony she wanted? Would that not be hypocritical of him? What would his mother have wanted him to do? He didn't know, couldn't know… Ah, but Eva was right, his mother had wanted a public wedding, had been upset when he had refused. But where would all these demands lead, what would happen when they had to educate a child? He could not decide, needed more time to think this through for himself.

Yanosh went back to bed, dreamt of his mother and the many others who had disappeared under the Nazis. He slept poorly that night.

May 18, 1946
Wedding Day; Lag BaOmer

They stood there in a line in the yard of the Waldenburg camp, three little wedding crowds. The smoke from the nearby factory hung in the air over the camp. Rabbi Adler arrived, accompanied by the American Colonel Cohen and his skinny chaplain Freiberg, some representatives of the Joint Distribution committee, who had supplied much of what was needed for the festivities, and, of course, the Reform rabbi, Theodore Bick, who was to perform their ceremony. Three crowds, each around its own couple to be married, waited impatiently.

A row of men, soon organized the place for their *huppot*, the symbolic homes under which these three couples were to be married. Tables were arranged nearby for each of the wedding parties and all was ready for the proceedings. The three weddings were to be celebrated one after the other, since there were camp residents invited to all three, but they would be in close succession. The camp officials, the wine, the cup and the *huppah* itself were all to be shared. It was clear that Yanosh and Eva's Reform ceremony was to be boycotted by the Hassidim. The whole thing had become a rather delicate affair.

Rabbi Adler soon led his contingent of officials over to the crowd of Hassidim and their friends, carrying the special white and black awning, which was to serve as the wedding canopy. The Hassidim refused its use, stretching a prayer shawl out instead, and insisting that their own "rebbe" conduct the ceremony. Yanosh and Eva and their little entourage watched from afar, dared not approach for fear of conflict. Rabbi Bick stood with them, explaining what they heard and saw in his low, gentle voice. Soon the final breaking of a glass, the reciting of the words "*Im Eshkahech Yerushalyim* – If I forget Thee O Jerusalem..." was accompanied by loud wails and sobbing, not only joyous song. The sad little group of Hassidim led the bride and groom into a nearby barracks to consummate their marriage and then waited, around a trestle table, for their return.

The second wedding commenced after Rabbi Adler had organized the chaplain's assistants in stretching out the official Joint-donated wedding canopy. The ritual fringes blew in the wind, the men holding the heavy canopy struggled to keep it erect and taught. This was a larger crowd of fairly irreligious camp survivors and other refugees for whom the love affair, which had led to this wedding had been a source of much gossip and curiosity. It was quite crowded and rowdy around the *huppah* as people struggled to find a good spot to stand and see the proceedings. Rabbi Bick, Yanosh and Eva and their friends could see nothing, but they soon heard the shouts of "mazel tov!, mazel tov!" They knew that they were to be next.

The bridegroom, Yankel, who was well-known as an "organizer" had many connections throughout the camp population. He could have chosen any of a number of eligible young women as a bride but had brought his bride-to-be, a dark silent beauty with blue eyes, back to the camp from one of his escapades in Berlin. No one knew anything about her, and she would tell them nothing of her past. He led his bride and singing friends towards a couple of well-laden tables on the far side of the camp yard, as Rabbi Adler left the scene demonstratively to join his beloved Hassidim. The chaplain and Colonel Cohen then marched towards the Reform gathering, followed by a few curious camp residents.

They soon had the wedding canopy standing again, and handed the bottle of wine and ritual cup for the blessings to the Reform rabbi.

"You may begin the ceremony, Rabbi Bick," the chaplain said, stepping aside to watch the ceremony from a safe distance.

"Thank you for your kind permission," Rabbi Bick responded with a touch of sarcasm, while pouring some red wine into the heavy silver cup.

The bride and groom were then led towards the *huppah* by their friends, while others hummed the tune of a popular wedding march. Pawla and Rivka walked on either side of Eva, and Marek and Moniek flanked Yanosh. Soon the two were standing side by side in the center of the space under the canopy.

Eva wore a blue dress she had inherited from a friend who had died of typhus, and a blue felt hat with white lacing. Her bulging belly could be clearly seen under the dress, but everyone knew she had already been civilly married to Yanosh before the war, and that she was expecting. She loved the dress, and Rivka and Pawla could not convince her to wear anything else.

Yanosh's attire was a pair of black trousers, a white shirt, and a fine navy jacket (a little too large), which Moniek had procured for him. He wore a yarmulke, which reminded him of how he had felt wearing one at the *Pesach Seder*, as if it might burn a hole in his head. This time, however, he had been careful to pick a white one, not the black that the religious Jews wore.

He felt nervous, could find nowhere to put his hands. Eva was smiling from ear to ear. Statuesque at the bride's side, Rivka, who had "matched" the rabbi with the young couple and had taken charge of many of the other arrangements, was beaming with pleasure.

Rabbi Bick's presence was soothing, calming. He was a tall man, slightly stooped, whose smooth skin made him seem younger than he was. His small white goatee wiggled as his spoke. His eyes twinkled with good-humour and kindliness.

"Just as you have shared this wine, may God bless you both with many, many joyful years together sharing the wine of life," Rabbi Bick said, with some pathos.

Yanosh winced at this sentimental statement.

"Do you have the ring, Yanosh?"

Yanosh started searching his jacket pockets for the ring, but there was nothing there. Eva looked at him, concerned.

"I have it. I have it!"

It was Marek. Yanosh had asked him to be his "*shoshvin*," his best man, whose main task was to carry and produce the ring at the appropriate moment.

"Here it is," he said, showing it to the rabbi as he gave it to Yanosh. The gold ring caught the afternoon sun's light as it was handed over. Eva smiled again. The rabbi relaxed.

"Is it your ring, Yanosh?"

"Yes, it is."

"You bought it with your own money?"

"No, sir. I was left it by my mother."

"It was your mother's wedding ring?"

"Yes," Yanosh answered stiffly, repressing his anger. "It was my mother's wedding ring."

Eva smiled at the interchange. She remembered how she had refused to wear the ring when Yanosh had first offered it to her. Only when he agreed to stand under a *huppah* with a rabbi had she consented to using his mother's ring.

"Please hold up your hand, young lady ... the index finger..."

All eyes followed the movement of Eva's right hand as she extended it towards Yanosh.

"Repeat after me: *Harei at mekoodeshet li betabat zoo kedaat Moshe ve Yisrael.*"

Yanosh repeated the words as best he could, knowing no Hebrew. He placed the ring on Eva's index finger as instructed by the rabbi. His hand shook as he did so.

Rabbi Bick then unrolled the parchment scroll he had been holding, quickly read its contents to the couple, translating the Aramaic into Yiddish and German for those listening, handed it to Yanosh and said: "This is your wedding contract, your *kesuba.* You should give it to your bride and say, after me: *Hinei kesubaseych.*"

Yanosh took the document from him and repeated the words as best he could, as he passed it over to his bride.

Eva took it, looked at it briefly and in turn passed the parchment scroll on to Rivka, who stood beside her, acting as her "surrogate mother."

Eva glanced over at Rivka , appreciatively. Rivka had been by her side throughout the day, helping her with the preparations for the wedding. There was no one more appropriate as her *shoshvinit* on this wonderful day.

Eva thought of the other two couples who had just been married. All the brides and grooms were orphans, just as she and Yanosh were. They had all been accompanied by a few close friends, who themselves were orphans as well. She thought of the children these marriages would probably produce. None of these children would know their grandparents, would have living grandparents or aunts or uncles, she thought. Yanosh seemed to have relaxed besides her now, but she was silently weeping. He looked at her lovingly, took her hand as the rabbi continued with the ceremony. He was talking about the sanctity of marriage, about the week's Torah portion, but they were not really listening, their souls, flooded with memories of family and loved ones, were not open for what the rabbi was saying.

"...so, Moses was not able to come into the Promised Land

after leading his people through the wilderness," he was saying, "all that generation that had known slavery died out, but their children inherited the land. So, perhaps, we will not live to see *Eretz Yisrael* free again, see the final ingathering of the exiles, the *sheerit hapleta*, the coming of the long-awaited Messiah, but certainly our children will. Let us break the glass in memory of *Yerushalayim*, raise her above our greatest joy," he said, looking directly at each of the young people standing before him as he spoke.

Yanosh did not follow the rabbi's words or remember what he must say, but he knew it was time to break the glass and end the ceremony, and he did. He did so with a forceful, angry stomp of his right foot. The glass shattered.

"Mazel tov! Mazel tov!"

"You may now kiss the bride!" someone called out.

And he did. They stood there under the wedding canopy, embracing, kissing and momentarily forgetting everyone and everything that had happened. Momentarily.

The rabbi stood by looking patriarchal and approving. The small crowd formed a circle and began to dance a *hora* joyfully, Rivka leading. Marek looked awkward and gangly, but Pawla picked up the steps quickly.

The other two wedding parties were still celebrating as well. You could hear the Hebrew words of wedding songs coming from them: In the words of Jeremiah, "*Od yishama Beharei Yehuda* – Again the joyful voices of bride and groom will be heard in the hills of Judea, a promise not yet fulfilled."

And more recent songs such as: *Hava Nagila* – Let us be joyful and *Kol Dodi* – The voice of my beloved.

It was not long until the two neighboring wedding parties joined, men and women dancing together in a swirl of skirts and shirts, sweating arms and sensual movement. Rabbi Bick joined them in their dance. He was surprisingly lythe and lively for a man his age. The other rabbis stood looking on. They did not seem to approve of the proceedings, looked uncomfortable.

On the far side of the yard the Hassidim had congregated

around some tables – boards propped up on boxes – on which some food and drink had been laid out. The men and women stood by different tables, for their *seudas mitzvo* – the ritual feast. The Hassidim had always been known for their love of song and dance, as well as their greater piety. But they did not dance like the other Jews, nor did they sing. They were listening to their rebbe speak as they stood there eating.

Eva and Yanosh and their wedding party passed them on the way to their own wedding "feast." Yanosh noticed the intensity with which these people listened to their spiritual leader. He was not a particularly impressive figure: a shriveled little man with a high-pitched voice and no beard. Some of the people listening to him were swaying. Others looked mesmerized or in a trance. As they entered the "wedding hall," the former Wehrmacht barracks where Rivka and her friends had prepared their repast, Yanosh heard the Hassidim beginning to sing again. This time it was a haunting tune without words, a *niggun*. He wondered how they could celebrate a wedding with such sad music.

Inside there was a long table, spread with a white tablecloth, on which were laid various delicacies. Yanosh was delighted to see a full bottle of vodka beside the flowers at the head of the table. He looked forward to a drink to help him relax. Eva's eyes focused on the flower-decorated seats there.

"Seats of honor for the *hassan* and *kallah*!" announced Rivka, pointing to the two chairs at the head of the table for the groom and his bride.

Rabbi Bick lowered himself down onto a chair at the other end of the table. Rivka sat beside him, everyone else arranging themselves along the sides. Eva and Yanosh sat in their flowery seats of honor.

"Lechaim!"

"To the young couple!"

"May you have many happy years together."

"Lechaim!"

"Lechaim!"

Rivka remembered weddings before the war, the joy of the family occasion, the good food, the music playing in the background, crowded rooms full of guests. Here they sat: a small group around the one table. No family. No family at all. Eva and Yanosh were both orphans. Everyone sitting here with them had no family. They were alone in the world, only had each other.

And the food? She had tried so hard to arrange a good wedding feast, but it was so simple a repast. No challah. No wine. A bottle of vodka, some cans of sardines, a plate of boiled potatoes, some hard-boiled eggs, pickles, a loaf of rough camp bread, a little jam, a bottle of water, and a plain cake she had baked. That was all.

Rivka had decorated the cake with raisins, which she had arranged to make the Hebrew words "Mazel Tov!" Yanosh might not be able to read it, but she knew that Eva could. She would tell him what it said. It was such a pity that an intelligent, educated man like Yanosh knew so little about his own people's culture, was so negative about the Jewish religion. Eva was much more open than he was, had more of a Jewish *neshomah*, even if she was not religious.

She was happy to be participating in her friend's wedding. She looked around the room. Across the table sat Moniek, Bora's friend. He was a big man, maybe six-feet-two tall, broad-shouldered with a head of dark tight curls. Even while sitting, he seemed to tower over those around him.

He had been a football player in Warsaw before the war, had played for the Hakoach Club. His strength, his muscular body, which had gotten him through the ghetto and concentration camps, had not been altogether lost despite years of deprivation and malnutrition, had been revived again after the war. His every movement seemed powerful, yet graceful.

He now played football again, was something of a star on the field, but talking to him was frustrating. He had little to say, and when he did speak, you needed endless patience to hear him out. He would stutter in a low voice, get caught on consonants unable to complete them. Rivka found it painful to hear him struggle with his words. He would lapse into embarrassed silence in mid-sentence, the words and thoughts caught inside like a stone stuck in the spokes of a carriage-wheel, bringing everything to a stop, unable to move on. You could pull a stone out, but with Moniek you just waited.

Moniek sat silently at the wedding table, brooding as everyone chattered away. Jadzwa passed him a plate of food, poked him gently and said: "Eat, Moniek, eat. This is better food than usual. Have a drink of vodka!"

Rivka laughed to herself, watching the woman mother the huge man. He picked up his fork and began to jab at his food a little, put it down, and poured some vodka into his cup, took a big swig.

"To the *hassan* and *kallah!*" someone called out, lifting up a cup.

"To the *hassan* and *kallah!*"

Moniek lifted his refilled cup, too, and drank yet again. Rivka was impressed with the quantity he put away so fast. The drink had loosened his tongue and he began to speak: "That was the... the... the... the rebbe from Soda... daa... daagora."

"What, Moniek?" Eva asked.

"That was the... the... the... the rebbe from Soda... daa... daagora."

"The rebbe of Sadagora?" Rivka repeated his words as a question.

"Uh... ha," he responded, nodding his head.

"You know him, Moniek?" the rabbi joined the conversation.

"Yes. Yes, he gave me a be... be... be... blessing before the war, buh... buh... but he looks de... de... de... different now. No be... be... be... beard."

Rivka had heard of the rebbe, knew he had been an important figure before the war, had become a legendary saint during the war. She was surprised to hear of Moniek's connection. All eyes had turned to him. He now had everyone's attention. They all waited for him to tell them more, had stopped eating.

"Go on, Moniek, go on," Pawla said.

Everyone could see Moniek's discomfort, gave him encouraging looks.

"A ge... ge... ge... ge... reat man. A tzeh... tzeh... tz... adik," he said. "He stayed with his ha... ha... Hasidim. He didn't aba... ba... ba.... bandon them like the other ones de... de... did."

10
Bora In Paris

Bora's first weeks in Paris were difficult. It took time to acclimatize, to begin to learn the language, to adjust to the French temperament, to renew his contacts with the migrant Jewish circle there. He found a room in a small apartment in the Marais Quarter, in a lane off the Rue de Rosiers, which he shared with the Kuhns, Sylvia and Yancheko, a couple from Hungary.

They were assimilated Jews who spoke no Yiddish, only a little French and German. They managed to communicate somehow, sharing, as they did, a former Communist commitment, partisan activity during the war, and a deep disillusionment with Stalin who had destroyed their utopian dreams of youth. Sylvia was an attractive blonde, slim and cheerful, not Jewish in appearance. Yancheko, though he was tall, muscular, athletic-looking, looked like many of the Jewish lads who had been in the forests with him, had curly dark hair, a Semitic nose. His morose presence, and dark, brooding eyes disturbed Bora. He understood that the man had been tortured by the Gestapo, had managed to escape, to return to find his Sylvia in the arms of another man. He'd killed him, and taken his woman back, but was always jealous of her. It was strange that he had agreed to take in a lodger who was male, but he had. Economic necessity.

Bora's French improved, just as his English had in Berlin, dealing with the British, and the Americans. He had a talent for languages. Already knew Yiddish, Hebrew, Polish and Russian from his younger years. He had since learned German as well. Now he was learning French, practicing it on the Parisian ladies, kissing hands and, sweeping them off their feet and into bed.

Bora planned a short trip to Germany. He had crossed

borders in the past without being caught. No reason to suppose it would be different this time, but it was wise to be cautious. He would make sure that his friends, Sutzker and Kaginski would know about it, but without telling them too much. They would know to contact Moniek if there were any problems. He knew them from their underground days together.

He now had a new pistol, an old Luger. Though on the heavy side, it was a reliable and accurate weapon. Moniek had met his expectations. He had supplied him with this gun, and had remained devoted to their Berlin "projects." As he oiled it in preparation for his trip, Bora's mind skirted back to other guns he had owned.

He remembered the feel of each of them: the rifle supplied by the Polish government in 1939, the Kalashnikov he'd been issued when he became an officer in the Red Army, the German hand-gun, a battle souvenir he'd had at his side for years, until the Americans confiscated it. But more than all of these he remembered the old Czech rifle thanks to which he had first been accepted into Colonel Markov's partisan unit in the forest of Naroch. You could not join a partisan group in the forests unless you came to them armed, in those early days of 1942. That rifle had saved his life many times, but the thing had smelled for a long time after he had first dug it out of the mass grave, near Vieleka. The local peasants near the town had told him about it, had pointed out the place where the Soviets had buried the Polish officers they had murdered in 1939.

As he dug into the mound the stench increased. He began to unearth an arm, twisted in a strange way, sergeant's stripes on the inside sleeve. A hand rolled out of the earth and the arm straightened out, the hand dangling at its end. A silent protest at being disturbed… Long tobacco-stained fingers, not yet eaten away, but smelling putrid, which held nothing anymore, hung stiffly below the bones which had once been a wrist and palm.

Bora found it hard to continue any further. He knew he was transgressing a very basic, ancient and universal taboo for Jews. One does not disturb the dead. He knew that.

But he also knew that these men, Polish officers, had been buried with their weapons. He was surprised at that information when the peasant had told him. He had dug along the edge of something hard, wooden. Perhaps it was a rifle butt! He needed a weapon. So he continued digging…

Bora finished oiling his Luger and put it down. There was a knock at the door. He slid the gun into his jacket pocket and went over to the door, lifted the latch to see who was outside, but could see no one. With his other hand gripping the gun inside his jacket, he opened the door. A boy stood there, perhaps ten years old, holding a cap, and nervously playing with it.

"Excuse me, Monsieur," he said.

"What do you want?"

"I was sent up here to call you down to the cafe. You have a phone call."

"Thank you. I'm coming down right away."

Bora gave the young lad a half-franc piece. The boy took the coin examined it, placed it in his pocket, put his cap on and scampered off. As an afterthought he called back: "Merci, monsieur. Merci beaucoup!" as his cap disappeared from view down the stairs.

Bora locked his door and came down the stairs to the cafe, wondering who would be calling. He entered through the frosted glass double door to find the proprietor waiting for him, phone in hand.

"It is for you, monsieur… I sent my son, Jean-Alaine, to call you."

"Yes, thank you. He was rewarded for his trouble."

Bora took the receiver to hear heavy breathing on the other end: "Hello …hello…"

No one answered, the breathing continued for a while.

Then he heard a deep voice, speaking Yiddish:

Borowski, Bora, the avenger, you are doing very important, holy, work.

"Yes. I know."

"God bless you."

"Thank you. Who are you?"

"A friend. *Amcha*. Be careful. You are being stalked. You must leave Paris."

The phone then went dead.

Bora was disturbed by the call, knowing that very few people knew where he was, or about his activities. He was planning to leave Paris, but had told no one of these plans. Perhaps he needed to speed up his schedule, to heed this warning, but not before he went back to Berlin to settle one more account with a certain Mueller, who had alluded him until now. He would move on only after that *mamzer* was underground, not before. But whose voice had he just heard? It did not sound familiar at all.

He walked on thinking about this but also keeping himself alert to his surroundings. Nothing looked suspicious. French people carrying shopping home. A bicyclist passed him, whistling to himself. A grey Parisian afternoon like the others before it. He turned into the Rue de Rosiers, glancing behind to see if he was being followed, but no one was behind him. Soon he would reach his favorite cafe to meet his friends.

Bora had found a community of Yiddish writers in Paris, a group of intellectuals who gathered regularly at the Cafe Royale in the Rue de Rosiers. The place was run down, could do with a new coat of paint, some of the chairs creaked loudly, the tables were worn and old, but the coffee was cheap and the proprietor, Jacques Lefreque, was friendly.

Lefreque had been active in the resistance during the war, was known as someone who had hidden and helped Jews, who had married a Jewish woman after the war. No one had ever seen his wife, but the rumor was that she was stunningly beautiful. Lefreque was a good-natured sort, who knew a few words of Yiddish, remembered all his customers by name and was amenable to helping out customers in need in various ways. There were people who came to him for loans, for hand-outs of food, who had not paid for their coffee and cake in weeks.

Bora wondered how he could manage a business considering

his unbusiness-like behavior. The truth was that this was his fourth establishment, that he had gone into deep debt many times, that he had closed down in the past because of his excessive generosity, but he enjoyed what he did so much that he kept reopening new cafes. Yanchiko had told Bora about the place and its popular owner. It wasn't long until Bora became a regular there.

Bora walked down the Rue de Rosiers until he reached the Cafe Royale entrance. He heard the muffled sounds of conversations inside as he approached. The glass doors swung open. A couple emerged, arm-in-arm. The woman had inaccurately painted red lips and long eyelashes. The man wore a black beret, cockily placed to one side of his rather bald head. Both were smoking.

"Ah, Borowski!" said the man, "How are you today?"

Bora smiled and silently passed by them on into the smoke-filled cafe and the din of conversations in French, Yiddish and English. He walked across the room to his usual spot, feeling his Luger by his side as he sat down and ordered a coffee. It wasn't long until he was joined at his table by two of his friends.

Abraham Skutzer was a tall, thin, lanky man, whose face and arms were particularly bony and angular. Shmirke Kaginski, on the other hand, was short and stocky. Even in these difficult times he managed to carry around a respectable paunch and a double-chin. Skutzer was a silent listener most of the time, staring intensely at his fellows when he wasn't brooding. Kaginski was loquacious and outgoing, telling stories and jokes, entertaining and charming all who came in contact with him. Bora enjoyed their company and was happy to see the two of them again.

"Shmirke! Avrum! Nice to see you. Come sit with me here. We'll schmooze awhile before I have to go."

"Go! We just saw you come in. We were sitting over there, but you didn't see us. What do you mean threatening to leave so soon? Go where? You just got here, Borowski!"

"Just sit down, Shmirke. I will explain. You too, Avrum! Here... here's a chair for you."

Bora shoved two chairs away from the table for his friends to join him and produced a small bottle from his jacket pocket.

"Will you gentlemen please join me for a little Lechaim?" he said, proffering the bottle.

"What's the occasion, Bora?"

Bora pulled out a paper from his inside pocket, unfolded it, as they passed around the bottle, each taking generous swigs of its contents. He read the following to them:

My dear Yosef,

I want to inform you of your friend Yanosh Kaminski's upcoming wedding on...18th May, 1946 in Landsberg D.P. camp. He doesn't know that I am writing to you. In fact, he doesn't know where you are. I have been careful to keep your whereabouts secret, as you instructed. I am sure that he and Eva would be delighted to see you at the wedding if you are able to come.

Your friend,
Moniek

"So you are going to your friend's wedding, Bora?"

"Of course not, Shmirke. It is too dangerous. My enemies are waiting for just such an opportunity to put a bullet in my head. Anyway, Yanosh and Eva are already married, in fact. They have been married four or five years already. It is just Eva's mishegas that they need a kosher Jewish wedding now. Yanosh complained to me about it. I told him to humour her. But it is an excuse for a little drink, my friends. So, lechaim!"

"Lehaim!"

"Lechaim!"

Bora looked at his watch. His friends looked at him in anticipation.

"So then, my friends, its wonderful to see you again, and looking so well! But I have to go now, can't stay any longer. I have important business elsewhere..."

They finished their drinks, and waited, but no further explanation was forthcoming. Finally it was Skutzer who asked:

"Well, then, you said you would explain. We are listening, Yosef!"

Bora fingered his hidden Luger as he considered his response to Skutzer's question. They waited. They knew their enigmatic former commander and his wily ways.

"Follow me," he said, beckoning to the door.

"Garcon, the bill please!"

They exited the smokey cafe. Kaginski paid, shrugging off their protests that they could pay for their own coffee with his usual bonhomie.

Walking down the Rue de Rosiers towards St. Paul's station, Bora turned into a little entrance hall, his friends behind him. He looked around to see that no one else was within earshot and then spoke softly.

"I am going back to Germany."

"Why?" asked Skutzer.

"When?" asked Kaginski.

"I am headed for the train station now to catch the Berlin train at ten-thirty."

"But why?" asked Skutzer.

"But you are carrying no luggage!" protested Kaginski.

"I am carrying an important item of luggage," Bora retorted, showing them his Luger, "this is all the luggage I need."

"Bora, you are looking for trouble again."

"Perhaps... I have some business to finish in Berlin. Something you both would approve of, I am sure. I can't tell you more now. If I'm successful you will hear about it."

"Be careful, Yosef."

"When will you return?"

"I'll be back in two weeks' time. I have enjoyed your company here in Paris. I will look for you here at the cafe Royale when I am back. Go back the other way. I will go on walking down the road to the station."

He walked down the road without looking back, though he could feel their eyes still staring at him. They had surprised him. He had not expected them to look so shocked at his weapon or the news of his trip back to Germany. After all they had been in the same partisan unit, had seen action together, had roughed it in the forest together, had survived. But they seemed to have grown soft since the war, had become sentimental and anxiety-ridden. Could he still trust them, he wondered, as he turned into the train station. He looked back to see the two of them walking back towards the cafe arm-in-arm, talking.

11
Goodbye Rivka

Not long after the wedding, Eva received a letter from her friend. It was full of excited words about a big change in her circumstances that she wanted to share with them. She invited Eva and Yanosh to visit her again and promised then to share her special news. She wrote that on the fifth of June there would be a celebration of the *Shavuot* holiday, and that would be a wonderful opportunity to spend time together. After conferring with Yanosh, Eva wrote back saying that they would be happy to come, and would be happy to bring some offering from the Berlin market.

Rivka asked for apples.

Two weeks later, on the fourth of June, Yanosh and Eva arrived at Waldenburg station carrying stay-over bags and a large bag of apples.

"Rivka, it is good to see you again. You are looking well."

"Thank you."

"And we are dying to know what your news is, that you were hinting at in your last letters."

"Yes, I knew you would ask right away. Let me get you settled and then I will tell you everything, I promise."

Rivka led them to a waiting truck, in which some newly-arrived refugees were huddled, waiting to finally leave the station. They clambered up with their things, being careful to protect the apples from damage, and seated themselves amongst the silent, staring others and their parcels and bags. After a short but bumpy ride they arrived at the camp, where they went through the now familiar wire gate, barely noticing the barbed wire that had so disturbed them on their previous visits. They were soon set-up for the night in one of the barracks.

In the morning, over breakfast, Rivka told them her news.

"I am leaving for Palestine."

"When? Why?"

"I will be travelling to Italy in three weeks time. That's when. About why, well I am surprised you ask. After all you know I am a Zionist. I have always dreamt of going to *Eretz Yisrael*."

"But Rivka there is fighting. People are being killed there every day. And the British are limiting the number of immigrants."

"I know all that."

"Do you have a certificate? They are so hard to get. How did you do it?"

"I don't have a certificate."

"You are going illegally?"

"Yes, that's right. I will be going on a boat called "Shoshana." By the way, this is confidential. You are to tell no one. That's why I couldn't tell you in my letters. We don't want them to stop us sailing."

"But Rivka, why go now?"

Because I have the opportunity. Why not? If I don't go now I might find myself, God forbid, settling down here in Germany. I have made up my mind."

Parting from Rivka was difficult. Both Yanosh and Eva had grown to value her friendship. They appreciated that she had organized their wedding celebration. She came to the train station in Berlin to bid them farewell when they left for Paris. Yanosh had to forcefully separate Eva and Rivka, both of whom were weeping, to board the train. He doubted that the heartfelt promises to stay in contact, to correspond would be kept. Life had its own powerful dynamic. Rivka was headed for Palestine, was planning to join friends there, to challenge the British blockade on one of the illegal immigrant boats. He and Eva had chosen to migrate to Australia. They would be tossed by history's waves on their different journeys. Would they reach their alternate destinations safely? And if they did, would not the currents of events there not submerge them in other relationships, other stories?

Yanosh remembered his initial scepticism about the woman and his doubts about Eva's relationship with her. He had changed his mind. Although he found her gentle religiosity annoying, he did like her deep tolerance of different opinions, her sensitivity and love of literature. He wondered how someone with her sensitive personality would cope with the brutal reality people like Bora were creating in Palestine, the cycles of violence, revenge and nationalist extremism?

He had been happy about her support in his disagreements with Eva about Bora. She was an old friend of Yosef's (she never called him Bora) from before the war, and had often told them about the urbane Borowski family, particularly about Bora's older sister, Faigeh. Faigeh had been accepted to law school at Vilna University. As a Jewish woman that in itself was an achievement, but she had gone on to be one of the top students there while remaining loyal to Jewish observances such as the Sabbath. It was through Faigeh that Rivka had met Bora. As the librarian at the university, she was impressed by the man's voracious appetite for literature. Faigeh was always borrowing books for him.

June 7, 1946

Talking to Rivka these last days has led me to realize that there is another side to Bora, another personality hidden under his tough exterior. She told me that as a young man he had been something of a poet, had published some poetry in the Vilna YIVO journal. She said that his poems were primarily concerned with nature, but also related to the dream of renewal of the Jewish soul through return to the Holy Land. They had been well received. One of them even won a prize from the "Yunger Vilner" club.

I suspect there may have been a romantic episode in Rivka's relationship with him. The way she talks about him, the look in her eyes as she does. These Litvaks are hard to understand, they don't like to share emotions. She and Bora are similar in that sense. Of course they both would deny any such suspicion. I will respect their privacy, of course.

It is sad to part with Rivka. She is a fine woman, and became a good friend. Who knows what will become of her over there in Palestine? She might not get there at all and end up going instead to the British detention camp in Cyprus. I did not succeed in convincing her of her mistake in trying to go to Palestine illegally.

12
Bora Back on Board

The train pulled into the Paris station and came to a loud stop, giving forth a last billow of steam. Bora boarded when the whistles blew, along with the human throng, soon finding himself in a crowded passageway. He weaved along until he found a non-smoking compartment, opened the heavy wooden sliding door, and sat down beside a window. He looked around to see who else was nearby. Across from him sat two nuns, looking like two penguins in their white aprons and brown habits. They sat there stiffly, looking at nothing in particular. One was an older woman whose face was wrinkled and prune-like; the other had a younger face, highlighted by a row of reddish-brown freckles, which bridged over her puggish nose. Both had pale-blue eyes. Blank eyes. There was no one else in the compartment, which could comfortably seat six. The passageway, on the other hand was still crowded.

Bora could hear babble in a number of languages: French, of course, but also German, English, Italian, Slavic languages. He heard no Yiddish.

A whistle blew. The doors slammed shut and people began to look for seats in the compartments, as the train began to move. A tall, thin man stooped down and peered in through the glass window in the compartment door. He was bearded, and wearing a black hat. A battered fedora with a white feather stuck in its band on one side. Bora wondered whether he might be a fellow Jew. A Yiddish-speaker would make the trip more interesting, he thought. The nuns didn't look promising as traveling companions. He hoped the man would come in to join him. He smiled at him through the little window to encourage him. The man smiled back, opened the door and came in.

He was carrying a black valise, had a long dark, woolen coat draped over his arm and seemed to limp slightly.

"Is there room in here? May I join you?" he asked in French.

There was no trace of another accent, as far as Bora could tell. Maybe he didn't speak Yiddish after all.

The nuns didn't respond.

"Of course, you are welcome," Bora said, indicating the seat beside him and across from him as possible seating options for him to consider.

The man placed his bag on the seat next to the window opposite Bora. He carefully folded his coat and lifted it up into the rack above the valise, which he then picked up and placed on top of the coat. He then sat down below his things, with an awkward movement. Once wounded on his left side, Bora thought, as he watched him. They smiled at each other after he sat down, said a few polite words of introductory pleasantries, but nothing of consequence.

The train went through a long tunnel. When it emerged, the two nuns were asleep, the younger leaning on the older's shoulder, while she, the older woman, slept upright, her head resting on her chest. The man and Bora began to talk a little more.

"Mr. Borowski..."

"Yes, monsieur."

"Tell me a little about yourself. I am curious. Where are you from? To where are you travelling? Where were you during the war? What did you do? What became of your family?"

"So many questions!"

"Well, as I said, I am curious."

"I am happy to respond, but it is a long journey. We have time... You know a Jew answers another Jew with a question. What about you? Tell a little about yourself first, then I will be happy to oblige, too."

"All right. I have nothing or no one to fear anymore. I am Alphonse De La Pergule. I was born in Marseille, but moved to Paris when still a young man, studied architecture at the Sorbonne…"

He learned that the man was a French Sephardi Jew, who had fled across the Pyrenees into the Iberian Peninsula during the war, found refuge from the Germans in Franco's neutral fascist country. No Yiddish, unfortunately. They spoke French, with occasional references to German when Bora lacked a word or appropriate phrase.

"What happened to your leg? I noticed that you have a limp on that side," Bora asked.

"A minor wound during the war. I will tell you more about that some other time, Joseph. It is time you told me something about yourself. I am still curious."

Bora told him a little about his war years fighting the Germans in Byelorussia, about his family, all of whom had been killed by the S.S. Einsaztgruppen, murdered in mass shootings, forced to dig their own graves. He told him about his sister, Shaina, the doctor, who had worked in the hospital in the Vilna ghetto, which the S.S. had burned to the ground, shooting all those trying to escape the flames. He told him about his own war wound, the piece of shrapnel still lodged in his right foot, how he had been transferred to a "softer" partisan unit while he recovered. About meeting Shaina in the forest again when she escaped the Vilna ghetto in 1943, with the other 250 partisan fighters, only to lose her again when Jacob Glazman led a group of them into a German ambush, returning to camp with only two other partisan survivors of the battle. How he wanted to kill the man, but Markov beat him to it, had him shot.

Alphonse listened to Bora's narrative. Bora felt his sympathetic listening, its intensity, and something inside him opened up, allowing him to feel things long frozen inside. The tears were rolling down his cheeks as he finished speaking. They sat some time, facing each other. Alphonse reached across the aisle, placed his hand on his shoulder and said: "That's all over now, Borowski. The war has ended. It is time to move on.

"You are right, Alphonse."

The rattling train soon had both of them snoozing as well. This was an express, there were to be few stops on the way, so it was easy to sleep undisturbed if one wanted to do so.

Bora woke sweating. He looked around him. He saw his fellow passengers staring at him, and remembered where he was. He took out a handkerchief, wiped his brow, and recovered his composure.

The two nuns each took out little black books, opened them and began to read, ignoring him. They looked like the pious old ladies in his shtetl before the war, who were always reading psalms. They were all dead now. These nuns were very much alive.

Bora wiped the cold perspiration off the back of his neck.

"What happened to you?" Alphonse asked him.

"What do you mean?"

"You startled all of us. You started yelling in your sleep. In Russian..."

"I was yelling in Russian?"

"Yes, and clapping your hands, like this."

The man began clapping his long, thin hands in a slow rhythm.

The nuns looked up over their books, obviously amused.

"Clapping my hands?"

The two women whispered to each other and giggled behind their books.

"Yes, you were clapping. It was strange. I wonder what you were dreaming of. Was it a nightmare of some sort?"

"I don't remember anything at all. Sorry if I disturbed or woke you. Let us all drop the subject now, all right."

"Okay."

Bora got up, left the compartment, sliding the heavy wooden door back into place behind him. He walked along the passageway with difficulty. The train was speeding around a curve as he walked towards the lavatory. He felt nauseated. He still heard the two nuns giggling, saw Alphonse clapping, and struggled to repress the memory. There was another, more deeply repressed memory floating up into consciousness, one he dreaded.

He reached the toilet door. No one else was there, no one inside. He went in, closed the door and sat down. It was hard to breathe so he opened his collar, freeing his neck and upper chest. He loosened his belt as well, but the nausea continued to bother him. There was a sink in the cubicle. Perhaps a little water will help me, he thought. He got up and bent down at the sink to drink.

The train lurched forward, and suddenly, in a screech of brakes, stopped. He was hurtled backwards, banged his head on the tap as he fell. He sat down on the toilet seat, stunned… saw stars. The nausea was gone now, his throbbing head replacing it as the locus of his attention.

After awhile he got up again, drank some water, straightened out his clothes and started walking back towards the compartment. The train was moving again. The wind was blowing in at him from the open windows he passed as he continued moving towards the wooden door. He reached it just as the train was pulling into a station. The name on the sign read Alsace.

The two nuns got up, collected their bags, and left the compartment, barely looking at him as they passed. Alphonse smiled upon his return, over the newspaper he was reading. People passed along the passageway in both directions, carrying bags, holding children's hands, talking excitedly. They were all speaking French, as far as Bora could tell.

A little later the train prepared to pull out of the station again. The station master blew his whistle, a voice yelled out a loud, gruff warning, wooden doors slammed shut and, after a tremendous whooshing emission of steam, the wheels began to turn and the locomotive surged forward.

An older man looked in through the window, assessing the space inside. His ruddy face, which was framed by a close-cropped white beard, looked friendly enough. His large bald pate which shone in the pink glow of the early morning sunlight coming through the window behind him, gave him the ludicrous appearance of an overripe red cabbage or a beetroot. He opened the door and asked:

"Are there seats here for my family?"

"How many of you are there, Monsieur?" Alphonse asked him.

"My wife, myself, and two children, sir."

Alphonse looked across at Bora, questioningly.

Bora nodded.

"There is no problem. You are welcome."

"Thank you. I will be back soon. I'm leaving my bag here until I return. Please hold the places for us."

He placed a large grey duffel bag down on one of the seats and left.

The man soon returned, followed by his short, kerchiefed wife and two red-haired children – a boy and a girl holding hands on either side of their mother. They appeared to be country folk, probably farmers. Their clothes were rough and simple. Not long after they had settled in, all four of them fell asleep. The man snored loudly, reminiscent of the locomotive pulling them along the tracks to Berlin. The woman, whose sharp nostrils produced an occasional whistling sound, slept, leaning on her husband's shoulder, her two young ones curled together, like red-haired puppies, on her lap.

Alphonse folded his newspaper and put it down beside him. He looked over at Bora with an expression of concern.

"You don't look well, Mr. Borowski."

"I'm fine."

"I would recommend a coffee. You look pale. Some coffee would do you good. Why don't we walk down to the cafe to get some?"

"That's all right, Alphonse, I'd rather stay here for the time being, but thank you."

"May I bring you some coffee when I return?"

"If you insist..."

"I will then. See you later on."

"*Au revoire.*"

Alphonse got up and limped towards the door. He looked back at Bora, but saw that he was preoccupied. He seemed to be in a kind of trance. His eyes had a glazed look about them. His breathing was shallow. De La Pergule left the compartment perturbed, puzzled by his new friend's strange behavior.

He returned some time later, carrying a steaming cup. Bora had fallen asleep. He woke him.

"Here is your coffee."

"Thank you."

"You know I admire you for your courage and resourcefulness during the war years."

"Alphonse. You don't understand. I had no choice. A lot happened that was just luck. Many others, more resourceful and courageous than I, perished."

When Alphonse and Bora parted in Berlin, they swapped addresses, phone numbers, promised faithfully to stay in contact.

They walked along the platform together talking until they reached the ticket-collector. They shook hands and walked their separate ways. Bora stood there watching his train-friend limp away. The man took with him many secrets that Bora was not going to share with anyone again.

Moniek was waiting at the station for him. His dark, curly head could be seen towering over the waiting crowd beyond the ticket-collector's cubicle. He was peering over people's heads looking for Bora. Bora ignored him until he had parted with Alphonse. He then stole over to him from behind. He poked him in the back, and quickly stepped aside as the giant swung around suddenly.

"Looking for someone?" he asked, smiling that thin, toothless smile of his.

"Be... be... b... Bora!"

"Sha...shhh," Bora responded, "not so loud, Moniek!"

"I am ha... ha... happy to see you, Yosef."

"I am happy to see you, too, Moniek, but there are some

people here in Berlin I would not like to see, and I don't want to be seen by them, either. Let's get out of here."

"You have no lu... lu... lu... luggage?"

"No, it is only a brief visit. I just have one account to settle, and then I will return to Paris, long before my friends, the Americans, ever notice I have been visiting."

They strode out of the station together, Bora keeping up with Moniek's long strides with difficulty. The odd-looking pair walked along the main road a few steps and then turned into a side street.

Bora noticed, or, rather, sensed a fleeting presence, a shadow, turning the corner with them. He looked back, but saw nothing. Nevertheless, he grabbed Moniek's arm and pulled him into an entrance hall. They waited there, Bora with his Luger readied for action, pointing to the entrance door, Moniek with his own pistol pulled out waiting for a sign from his former commander. He had clicked a clip of bullets in and had opened the safety latch.

They heard footsteps approaching and passing by the entranceway. Bora looked out through a crack in the door. He saw a suspicious-looking little fellow, wearing a dark green overcoat, a balaclava rolled up above his eyes and carrying a brown paper package. He saw the green coat and brown bag continue down the street.

"He has gone," he told Moniek, "but he is probably waiting for us around the next corner."

"Le... le... let's go back to the station, they won't be lo... lo... looking for you there anymore," Moniek suggested.

After a while Moniek and Bora put their weapons away and cautiously stepped out into the street. They turned back towards the railway station, and walked away from the corner around which the green-coated man had followed them.

Bora spied a taxi stand across from the station as they approached. He hailed the first taxi that appeared.

It was a grey Volkswagen. Bora noted that the driver was wearing a green coat; he saw a balaclava stashed in the corner of the dashboard. On the seat beside him sat a familiar-looking, mousey man wrapped in a brown overcoat. This man got out of his car and opened the back car door for them to get in.

Bora then saw the brown paper bag on the floor of the car where this man had been sitting. He pulled out his Luger and pointed it at him: "Who are you?" he asked.

"*Amcha* – a friend," was the answer, "Put that gun away. You don't need it."

Bora studied the person standing opposite him. Brown eyes, sharp small nose, thin tight lips, and a heavy beard-shadow... There was something familiar about the face, but he couldn't place it. It was only when he looked down to see the man's right hand or, rather, where there should have been a hand that he realized.

"Haimke Luz!"

"Yes, it is me, Borowski. You didn't recognize me?"

"No, I admit it. I didn't. You have changed a lot and your behavior was suspicious, but now that I see it is you, Haimke..."

He pocketed his gun. They hugged. Bora remembered his loyal lackey who was standing by, looking awkward.

"Moniek, ah Moniek... Let me introduce you. This is my friend, Haim Luz. We were in the same partisan unit years ago near Vilna. Haimke is quite a hero, succeeded in derailing many German trains during the war."

Luz nodded his agreement, looked pleased with the description.

"And this is Moniek Rothberg. A good man ... faithful, trustworthy, strong as an ox and a good shot, too. Moniek participated in the sonder commando rebellion in Birkenau, one of the only witnesses to survive to tell the story."

Moniek and Haimke Luz shook hands. Luz noticed him looking down at the metal hook which had replaced his right hand.

"A work accident when laying an explosive on the rails for

the German cargo trains... I was lucky to survive that. Bora here saved my life."

"Let's not stand here babbling away in the street like this. Never know who is looking. We should move on."

The three got into the Volkswagen and Luz's taxi-driver friend, whom he introduced as Shmulik, started the engine again. They drove off.

"So how did you know I was coming back to Germany. It was a well-kept secret?"

Moniek nodded.

"Bora, can I trust your friend here?"

"Yes."

"Okay then, they are watching you ... all the time. They know you are here and they know your plans. You are in danger and I came here to warn you about it."

"Who are 'they' Haimke? And you still haven't answered my question. How did you know I was arriving here today?"

"Listen carefully to me. 'They' are called Odessa, an organization of former S.S. men, not well known yet but with powerful connections and money. They know that you have been behind the revenge killings of their people here in Germany. They are planning to stop you, to kill you. I can't tell you how I know, but I can tell you that you have some well-placed friends in the *Yishuv*. It was they who have sent me to meet you here to encourage you to stay away from Germany, in fact to 'disappear' for a few years.

"Bora, we need your help overseas for a while. We want you to go to Australia, where you have some connections. There are some good friends of our cause there, wealthy people who are willing to help us in our struggle for independence from the British and the coming war with the Arabs in Palestine."

"Australia? That is so far away! My place is with the *hevreh*, not half way around the world!"

"It's an order. You are not being asked."

Haimke stopped the car. They were back at the station.

"Bora, you must go, get on the next train to Paris. From there you have to travel on to Marseilles. Here are some tickets for you for a British ship, the Aurora, which is picking up passengers for Australia there, some money and a letter of instructions. Good luck."

"Okay, Haimke. I will follow these instructions, but first there is one thing I must do here in Berlin."

"Be careful."

"Of course."

13

Marseilles

Eva and Yanosh arrived at the Marseilles central station at midnight. Yanosh saw the name flash past on the wall as the train approached the terminal. Marek and Pawla were waiting for them on the station platform as their train pulled in. It had been raining. They were standing there in dripping rain gear, each in a pool of water. It was hard to see them through the steamy windows as the train approached.

Yanosh rubbed his window with his sleeve to see more clearly. There weren't many people waiting on the platform, but he did see their two friends standing there. He turned to call Eva to look as well, but found her asleep again. He decided not to disturb her. It was some time until a shrill whistle sounded declaring "all clear."

Yanosh waved at Pawla and Marek through the glass. They could not see him. They were eyeing the carriage, looking right at him. They did not respond to his calls or waves. He tried to open the window. It would not budge. He tapped on the window. Then the train's whistle shrieked and the rush of disembarking began, drowning out his tapping noise... Marek and Pawla disappeared from view. He woke Eva, who stretched up, cat-like beside him.

"We have arrived! Pawla and Marek are out there. I saw them," he told her.

Eva yawned, sighed, and got up to join Yanosh, rubbing her eyes.

"You saw them? They are out there waiting for us?" she asked.

"Yes, yes ... they are both out there waiting. Let's get going."

Eva stretched her limbs and smiled at him, her eyes lifting

to their baggage above. Yanosh reached up into the rack and pulled down their bags. Eva took her bag from him, despite his offer to carry it. They started walking along the passageway towards the doors, each carrying their bag.

Yanosh led the way, pushing his way through for the two of them. He used his suitcase as a shield and battering ram. Eva looked down at the old, battered brown case and remembered that first time she had seen it in Warsaw. It seemed long ago, much had happened since. This suitcase had been with them, through it all.

She wondered if Yanosh clung to it because it reminded him of his mother. She wished he would replace it with something else, something less disturbing, less reminiscent of the horrors of Poland. But she knew he wouldn't let it go, however much he said that he wanted to leave the past behind.

The crush at the doors was terrible. Bags were being swung. There were flailing arms. All were trying to squeeze through that narrow space. Refugees from throughout central and eastern Europe were arriving on that train. There had been many such trains before, fleeing the Nazi past and Stalinist present. All eyes were focused on the platform in search of friends and family. Few found anyone there waiting for them, offering them the assistance and encouragement they needed.

Eva knew how lucky they were. So many had not a soul in the world, were totally alone. Once they managed to step down through the doors and escape the human crush there, they saw their waiting friends, both of them smiling broadly, coming towards them.

Eva and Pawla hugged. So did Yanosh and Marek. Then they swapped, exchanging kisses. They looked at each other, making comments about how much everyone had changed.

Pawla made a fuss over Eva's pregnancy. Eva knew that her friend had waited long for a child herself, with no success. She and Yanosh had postponed starting a family because of the war and their involvement in underground activity in Warsaw. Pawla and Marek had made no such decision, they had just been unlucky, or lucky, depending on how you looked at it. The tensions of the period had effected her menstrual cycle adversely. She hoped that in a more peaceful environment they might become more fertile, but that had not happened ... yet.

It was with a mixture of joy and pride in her own pregnancy, but also sadness at her friend's barrenness, that she greeted them. The situation was embarrassing, awkward. Her face had become flushed, both cheeks must now be bright red, she imagined. Her body felt good, ripe, as she hugged Pawla. Pawla's envious look distressed her. Yanosh's good humor salved her, calmed her soul.

"Eva, you look so pregnant now! You look wonderful. I think this pregnancy has been good for your complexion, too."

"Pawla, please ... don't embarrass me in front of the men."

Eva was blushing again.

Yanosh chuckled, as Marek slapped him on the back: "A father soon, eh ... Praise the Lord! Who would have believed it!"

"We are very happy about it, but let's talk about practicalities now."

"We have arranged a place for you to stay tonight. Our ship, the Aurora, sails the day after tomorrow," Marek told them.

"I wish you could stay with us," Pawla added, "but there just isn't enough room."

"That's all right," answered Eva, "we will be spending plenty of time together on the ship. We have what to talk about, but now I would like to get some sleep. I couldn't sleep in the train at all."

Yanosh smiled. He remembered how he had sat in the train next to his sleeping wife.

Marek took Eva's bag. She gave it to him willingly. She felt exhausted. Pawla took her arm and led the way. The two men carrying the bags followed them. They went out through the station gate, an ornate piece of ironwork, which looked more like a palace or church gate than that of a train station.

That afternoon, after they had rested, refreshed themselves, and taken in the sights of the town center, Yanosh and Marek went off for a walk together, leaving the two women to spend time catching up over tea.

As they walked along the beach, Yanosh's imagination carried him out to sea, and filled him with thoughts of the coming journey and what awaited them beyond. Marek walked silently beside him, enjoying the view.

Yanosh's eye caught the glint of the afternoon sun on an object hanging from Marek's neck. Ah, yes, his cross! Marek's religious faith was unfathomable to him, as deep as the sea before him, but also sometimes shining like the gold on his chest.

He decided to ask him about his beliefs, something he had never done before. It was Marek's belief in God, he thought, that had seen him through their years of struggle against their common enemy, those years of murder and revenge, hate and war. He knew that Marek felt impelled by his God to resist evil, to protect and save those weaker and more vulnerable than he. That much he had heard from him in past conversations.

Marek had risked his life often in saving him and Eva. He had taken risks to save many other Jews as well, people he had not known before, whom he had smuggled out of the ghetto, as he had them. It was not, he was sure, only about personal friendship. The man was driven by his faith. And he wanted to understand that, felt baffled by it, especially since he knew many devout Polish Catholics to have been vigorously, profoundly anti-semitic.

"Marek, tell me," Yanosh opened the conversation, "why are you different? How were you able to be a believing Christian and yet help Jews during the war? You did not blame them for their own fate as others did, nor justify their suffering as divine punishment for rejecting Jesus. Why not? And faced with the terrible suffering of the Polish people, the deaths and torture of millions during the war was your faith in God not weakened at all? How can you continue believing in His goodness and grace? I don't understand how that is possible."

Marek did not stop walking at hearing Yanosh's questions. He kept striding along at the same pace as before, Yanosh straining to keep up with him. He seemed to be struggling to find words with which to answer.

"Yanosh, you ask me so many questions, difficult ones, at that! I am not a theologian or a philosopher, but I do know that your questions on theodicy are not new. They are as old as the Bible. The book of Job was only one in a series of struggles with that issue, and many have thought and written about it since, as I am sure you know. What happened in Poland does not change the basic issue. It boils down to a simple question – do you have faith in the ultimate triumph of good over evil or not, and do you believe that is God's will or not? I do. I can't answer the theological question adequately I suppose, but I do go on believing."

"But what about the Jews, their fate? And why did you devote yourself to saving Jews?"

"That's easier for me to answer, my friend. I believe that the Jews are God's chosen people, that through them our redemption and Jesus' second coming will be fulfilled. My Lord Jesus was a Jew, and just as he suffered for our sins, so did the Jews suffer for our sins. It is through their terrible and seemingly incomprehensible tragedy that the fulfillment of the ancient prophecies will take place. We will, I believe, see the dawning of a new, peaceful age for humanity."

Yanosh was baffled by what he heard, did not know how to respond, and decided to change the subject rather than pursue it further.

"Marek, What you are saying is in a sense a justification of all that suffering and tragedy. I can't accept that. I think I understand what you believe, but I don't agree. I can't. For me there is no God. This world we know is all there is, and the human race in it, and in humanity, or rather in human beings I no longer have any faith. Let's change the subject, all right?"

"Sure. As you wish. I don't like to talk about my faith. It is a private, intimate matter. And your oft declared Atheism pains me, especially because you are of a Jewish family. I see this is upsetting you."

Yanosh's face was now red, but he kept his feelings to himself, said no more and no further discussion ensued. They walked on silently together, until they returned to the hotel.

As they parted, Marek surprised Yanosh with one more confidence: "Yanosh, did I ever tell you that my grandmother, my mother's mother, was Jewish?"

"No."

"Well, she was."

"What happened to her?"

"She died before the war, thank God."

The next morning Yanosh woke early. He looked over at Eva. She was sleeping peacefully. Her nostrils moving gently with each breath, the little hill formed by the blanket around her pregnant belly rose with each breath. It had been so exciting for her to share the movement of the baby with him the previous night, despite her exhaustion. He had fallen asleep with his hand resting on the spot, until she had turned to curl up next to him. He looked at his watch, saw it was five in the morning. It was still dark outside.

He got out of bed and went over to the window. The floor was cold. It was a tiny room, two strides and he was at the window. They were on the fourth floor. It had been difficult going up the narrow wooden stairs with his pregnant wife and the luggage, both of them dripping wet and tired. Their wet clothes were there still on a chair by the window. He pulled the dirty curtain aside. The road below was lined with lights, silent sentries in the dark. Most of the buildings outside were shadowy, gloomy, the familiar strangeness of a new place in the night. A light on, in the house opposite. He could see a bare light bulb. There was some movement in the room, for a moment the light was blocked by a human body going past. Someone else had woken early, and was moving around over there.

His eyes moved down along the lit streets, tracing the route they had taken from the train station. He recognized the station about a block away, its clock tower was unmistakable. Those were the trees around which they had turned. Birds were chirping in them now. From there they had turned into the main road below. It felt so different from what he had known in Poland or Germany. One could smell the sea.

He considered possible escape routes: out the window, across to that balcony, down to the next one, and then to slide down that pipe. Would Eva be able to make it too?, he worried. But this is not Poland. The war is over, he reminded himself. The communists can't get you now. We are in France, he remembered Marek saying the night before, in response to his expressed anxiety.

Yanosh felt the tension in his throat and hands. He loosened the grip on the window and relaxed his hands, massaging his neck as he watched a paperboy make his way down the road from building to building. The boy wore a dark beret and a red scarf that waved behind him as he walked briskly along the pavement. He was whistling, joining the birds in their morning song.

Eva stirred behind him. He turned to see her rolling over to her side. She opened her eyes, rubbed them, asked why he was up so early and fell asleep again before he could answer.

Yanosh got dressed as quietly and quickly as he could and headed for the door.

"Where are you going, Yanshuk?"

"Just going for a morning stroll. I will be back soon. Go back to sleep. I didn't mean to wake you," he said, blowing her a kiss as he went out.

He knew she wouldn't remember their conversation later, that she was talking in her sleep.

His eye caught a movement in the window across the way. A blind was being pulled down. He saw a person looking down at him. The man was short, stocky and bald, apart from two tufts of curly hair on each side of his head. He looked vaguely familiar, but it was hard to be sure, since he was standing against the light. Beside him stood a tall woman, her right hand resting on his shoulder. Yanosh stared hard at them. That man, didn't he know him? Was there something strapped across his other shoulder?

A gun? ... a holster? Could it be him? Borowski? It looked like Bora. But how could that be? The blind went down. He could see him no more. Eva groaned in her sleep and turned away from the window. He left the room, his mind preoccupied with what he had just seen in that window. Who was he? Could it be Bora?

He descended the stairs to the ground floor, his mind also was spiraling around, just like the stairs. At the bottom landing he found the night porter snoring, his bald head down on the reception counter. He didn't leave the hotel room's key as was customary, putting it into his coat pocket instead.

He stepped out into the wet street. It had stopped raining. Everything glimmered in the first light of the rising sun. The trees looked as if they had been decorated for a special occasion. The rays of the sun caught the drops on the leaves, which sparkled in the light. Perhaps this would be a sunny, spring day?

In his mind he replayed his late night conversation with Eva, as he walked along.

"Australia. We are leaving for Australia in two days. Can you believe it?"

"I am scared. What will our lives be like there? It is so far away. How will we manage?"

"We will be all right. We will learn the language. We have friends coming with us. We will help each other."

"It is so far away."

"So far away from where? From Poland? From Germany?"

"Yanosh, I am expecting a child. I am frightened..."

He walked into a park, realized he was walking through the same one they had passed the night before. He was enveloped in the chirping of birds. A man lay on a park bench rolled up in newspapers, snoring. His graying hair was long, covering his eyes and nose. Thick protruding lips reverberated with each snore. As he passed him he smelled alcohol on his breath. It reminded him of the drunks of Warsaw. They were all gone, probably dead. This man, this derelict, who had more chance of surviving in the warmer Marseilles weather, would not be disposed of by Nazis or Communists with drastic social laws.

Were there drunks like this in Australia? It was warm there, he thought, warmer than here. There in Australia they probably didn't freeze to death in the morning the way drunks did in Poland.

Bora!? It couldn't be him. He was dead. Just looked like him. A man with a gun ... not such an unusual sight these days, he tried to reassure himself.

Yanosh headed back to the apartment, having been out walking for perhaps half an hour. He had hoped to find a spot to do a little writing, but had found nowhere to do so. He was too distracted to write anyway. It was time to return, Eva might wake up and worry about him.

He found the building easily, recognizing the red shutters, the brick wall, the neoclassical style entrance with its columns and decorated arch. Must have been a fancy hotel before the war...

Eva was up, had been tidying the little room, looked annoyed at his absence: "Where have you been? I was worried about you. I was awakened by awful shouting from that building over there. Heard shots ... you weren't here ... I was scared."

"Shots? There's been shooting? I didn't hear anything. I wasn't very far away."

"Yes, there was shooting. The police came, then it was quiet again. I was worried about you..."

"You needn't have worried. I was just out for a morning stroll."

"That's really reassuring, Yanosh! It could have been you that was shot while out walking. How could I know otherwise until you reappeared? I was worried about you. You shouldn't just disappear on me like that!"

"My bad luck that something happened this morning. I have been out early for a walk in the past and have often gotten back before you woke."

"I know you love to go out early in the morning ... to explore new places. I know, but I was so worried, scared something had happened to you."

"Let's go find ourselves some breakfast."

"Yes, that's a good idea. I am hungry. Some coffee would be great, too."

Eva got dressed while Yanosh waited, still with his coat on, and then they went out together. They went down into the hotel lobby. This time a different porter was there. This one was awake. The porter beckoned them over to him. His substantial, black whiskers were impressive.

"You have a message, Monsieur. Please wait a moment."

Whiskers wiggling, he turned to a small cubicle behind him and produced a folded piece of paper, which he handed to them. Yanosh noticed that his little fingernail was quite long, unlike his otherwise well-manicured hand. He wondered why he had not cut that nail as well, but quickly focused on the paper in his hand.

It was a note from Marek. He recognized the handwriting with its distinctive long pen strokes. It read: "Pick you up here at 8:00 a.m. Ship leaves this afternoon. Marek."

He gave the note to his wife to read. The whiskers followed the passing paper. Yanosh looked at his watch.

"It's 7:00 a.m. now," he told her, "which doesn't give us very long. I saw a little cafe not far from here. Let's head there quickly so we can get back with enough time to pack and meet Marek."

The whiskers moved with Yanosh's waving hands up and down.

"Are you sure there is enough time?" Eva asked, a little incredulous.

The whiskers turned back from Eva towards Yanosh, who nodded.

"No, Yanosh. I don't agree. Let's go back up and pack first. Then if there is time we can go out for coffee."

Yanosh didn't like to argue. He followed Eva back up the stairs. The whiskers followed their ascent until they were out of sight, and then returned to their former repose beneath the bulbous nose of the swarthy porter.

Half an hour later the two descended again, carrying their bags. Marek was sitting there waiting for them, reading a magazine. He looked up and smiled.

"Good morning! Let's go," he said. "We must be at the port by midday. The ship sails at three."

"Do we have time for some breakfast before we set out?" asked Eva, looking over at her husband and winking.

"Yes, I saw a nice little cafe just down the road," Yanosh added.

"Sure. I am ahead of you! Pawla is already waiting there for us, creating her usual fog of smoke at the table. I asked her to wait there and order us some breakfast. Let's go, shouldn't keep her waiting any longer."

The cafe was tiny. Two tables, draped in dark green, each adorned with a small vase of red poppies, and a row of stools at an espresso bar. Pawla sat there smoking. She looked up from her book when they came in, the tinkling of a bell attached to the door announced their arrival. The sleepy proprietor appeared, scratching his head. They joined Pawla, who had ordered coffee and croissants. Marek explained again that the ship was leaving at 3:00 p.m. that afternoon. They would have to be on board by 1 p.m., but could board from 10:00 a.m. They would go back to the hotel to collect their bags right after breakfast.

"So we can go straight there," said Eva, sipping her steaming coffee.

"That's the plan," said Marek, waiting for his to cool a little.

"Someone you know will be traveling with us on the same ship," added Pawla.

"Who?"

Yanosh looked up from sniffing his coffee. He loved the rich aroma.

"Bora. Borowski will be on board too."

Yanosh put his cup down, spilling some onto his still untouched croissant.

"Bora?"

"Bora. That's what I said. Are you hard of hearing these days, Yanosh?"

"Bora... but I thought he'd been killed!"

"Why should you think that? Rumors. Just rumors."

"No, Marek. I saw him go into a building in Berlin. There was an explosion. He never returned. I never heard from him again. That was more than three months ago. Someone was looking to assassinate him, had tried before. I was there, heard the explosion. He could not have survived it."

"Well, he did. He was very badly hurt, spent a couple of months in hospital, under another name. He chose to disappear from view for obvious reasons when he was released ... moved back to Paris. I met him there in a coffee shop. He had been at a Yiddish literary gathering in the Marais Quarter, across the road, in a cafe, Royale I think it was called. When the group came into the cafe I recognized him. He looked different, his face badly scarred on one side. He was a little drunk. He told me he was going to Palestine."

"So why is he boarding the Aurora? I thought he was a Zionist."

No one answered. They sat there silently, mystified.

Yanosh looked over at his wife. She was hugging herself as she listened to the conversation. He knew what that meant.

"What's the matter, Eva? You seem nervous."

"Of course I am. I don't like that man, Bora. If he is on board we can expect trouble."

14
Boarding The Aurora

They boarded the Aurora at 2:00 p.m. The British ship, a passenger liner before the war, had been converted into a troop carrier and had now been revamped to serve again as a passenger ship, this time as a refugee carrier. One deck was designated for first-class passengers.

Despite the new paint – the glistening white walls and black trimmings – the ship was not new. There were dents in the metal. Yanosh spotted bullet holes near the prow – a row of them. Were they from a sea battle she had survived? She sat in the waters of Marseilles Harbour, like a battered old bird among the sleeker and healthier looking vessels on either side.

They walked up the boarding ramp carrying their few things, accompanied by Marek and Pawla. Yanosh was overwhelmed by emotion. They were surrounded by refugees from all over Europe: Ukrainians, Poles, Italians, Bulgarians, French, and Greeks. A veritable tower of Babel reassembled to journey to Oceania, speaking a mix of European languages.

Eyes filled with hope lifted up towards the battered old ship, eyes which saw in her their salvation, the ark which would carry them away from Europe to a new, better life in a continent far away. No one knew very much about Australia, few knew what to expect there, but all hoped that they would find a livelihood, and peace.

Yanosh thought he saw Bora standing on deck, looking down at the people boarding the ship. It was hard to be sure; the man's face was shadowed by a brown cap with a prominent peak. Marek and Eva waved at him as they walked up the grey ramp. He didn't respond. He couldn't see them. Yanosh felt the warming sun on his back. It must be shining in the man's eyes he thought. He turned back to see the lines of passengers climbing the ramp and the afternoon sun emerging from between the clouds and the buildings on the wharf. The sun's glare was blinding. Looking ahead of him again he saw that the man was gone.

"Did you see him?"

"Yes, of course I did."

"I don't think he saw us."

"No, I guess not."

Eva moved her bag from her right to left hand and took her husband's free hand.

"Let's forget about Bora for now, Yanosh. We will see him again on board. You will find him if you really want to."

"Strange. It's very strange," he said to himself as much as to his wife.

She looked at him with concern. She hoped she would not see "Bora" again, but felt she would.

Yanosh was still carrying his mother's brown suitcase.

"We are leaving Europe, Yanshuk."

"Yes, we are, darling and I am happy that we are.

"But Australia is so far away."

"Far away from where, Eva?"

She nodded her understanding.

"You are bringing the past with us?!" she added protesting, pointing to the suitcase.

Yanosh smiled, but didn't answer.

They reached the ship's deck and walked on past the stiff and severe-looking British sailors. One of them, a ruddy, pug-nosed redhead, with insignia on his shoulders and an important-looking cap, said something to them. Yanosh couldn't understand his English. The man spoke too fast, swallowed his words. Eva looked like she understood something but Yanosh just nodded, feigning understanding.

They followed the crowd to the right, which was where this head sailor or captain was pointing. Pawla and Marek followed them, whispering as they walked, a small cloud of smoke from Pawla's cigarette trailing behind them. He heard them mention the name Borowski a few times, but couldn't quite hear what they were saying. He saw in astonishment that Marek's eyes were red. Pawla's chin jutted forward resolutely as they advanced.

They were escorted down metal stairs, which curled around into the bowels of the ship. The rhythmic sound of feet clanging down stairs accompanied the solo of the ship's horn, belting out its farewell to the port of Marseilles. The refugees going down the stairs were prodded by crew, like a herd of cattle. People pushed each other as they went down. Some stumbled. Men were sweating, many were breathing heavily, burdened with bags and bundles, and their heavy memories.

Eva leaned on Yanosh for physical support, as they went deeper into the depths of the ship, sweating profusely from the heat in the confined space. They passed the hot metal wall of the engine room. The churning inside drowned out everything else. It smelled of petrol and oil. Finally they reached the bottom – a big open, poorly-lit space, with dirty old mattresses lined up around the walls, each bedecked with a couple of folded, coarse grey blankets.

Yanosh saw that Eva could not help herself any longer, that despite the relief of being able to finally put down her belongings, stretch and rest, she was starting to cry. He stood beside her feeling helpless, and annoyed. Around them others sat, stood, or lay down exhausted.

It was Marek who first spoke up:

"We are today starting a special journey, leaving our past behind and starting anew. This is a reason for celebration, not sadness. Why don't you all join me for a little drink?"

He produced a small bottle from his coat pocket, held it up to the light of the flickering lamp above and said loudly:

"As you Jews say when you drink, Lechaim – To Life!"

Pawla took the bottle from him, drank a little and passed it on to Eva, who took the smallest of sips before handing it over to Yanosh.

"Protecting the baby," she explained, apologetically.

"And may God protect us all on the journey!" Marek added.

Yanosh let the alcohol help him relax, but was angered by Marek's comment.

"Leave God out of this! To the baby, too."

He took another swig.

15

The Voyage

The first days of the sea voyage were difficult. Eva couldn't keep her food down. And she wasn't the only one having trouble. Seasickness affected many passengers, though after a few days it subsided as they got more used to the constant rocking and rolling of the ship.

One of the sailors commented that the Mediterranean was easy compared to what awaited them beyond Suez on the open sea. Yanosh tried to distract Eva, but she had heard the comment and began to worry about it. Efforts were made to keep the overcrowded cabins and the steerage area clean. People were constantly washing floors and the toilets to prevent epidemics and get rid of the smell of vomit.

Yanosh wondered when he would see "Bora" again. He looked for him, asked about him, but no one knew him or anything about him. Marek said he had seen him twice since they had boarded but hadn't spoken to him. It seemed as if he was avoiding them. Strange. The man had played such an important part in their lives, had helped them escape the N.K.V.D. They were traveling to Australia because of him. Yanosh would have been more than happy to spend time with him again, to catch up with him, to learn the secret of his survival. How had he survived the murder attempt in Berlin? It was frustrating to keep seeing glimpses of him, with no real contact, to know nothing. Was he angry at them because Eva had convinced Yanosh to back out of his business plans with him? He had no answers to his questions.

They made new friends on board the Aurora. The days on board were monotonous, the food unchanging, lacking variety. The boredom was becoming increasingly oppressive. It led Eva to look for interesting people to converse with, with whom to share stories. There were problems of language, but she somehow managed to communicate despite them. Yanosh, on the other hand, hated the lack of privacy.

Eva befriended a woman from Lodz. Her name was Ostelle. They'd met once before at the Lodz train station. That was years ago, but now they still recognized each other. Ostelle had also been involved in the Communist youth movement before the war, but her wartime experiences had changed her outlook on life. She no longer trusted ideological movements or political organizations, not even the Zionists. She had survived the ghetto. In 1944, it was the last existing ghetto in Poland, still had 70,000 remaining inmates long after the others had been destroyed.

She had succeeded in jumping from the train taking the last Lodz Jews to Auschwitz, had dodged the bullets, and found refuge with a local farmer who had kept her alive in his barn until the liberation. She told her that the infamous Rumkowski, head of the Judenrat, had been on the train, and that she had heard that he had been killed by his own enraged people before the Germans could do it.

Ostelle had no one left after the war, no reason to stay in Poland. In the D.P. camp in Austria she had met a man, Artur, who was planning to leave Europe for America, to make a new life. They had boarded the Aurora, mistakenly thinking they were sailing to America, the "golden medina." It was only later that they understood their mistake. Their visas were for Australia, so they were shepherded onto a ship headed there. They knew nothing at all about the country but, since they were headed there, they began to ask.

Eva was a font of knowledge about the southern island-continent. She had read about Australia in a Polish magazine years before, during the war, and so had become one of the ship's experts on the subject amongst the refugees.

Ostelle was fascinated by Eva's stories of the war years, particularly her involvement in the Polish underground, the fact that she had been part of the resistance to the Nazi barbarity, had carried a weapon. Eva did not like to talk about those years, but Ostelle was always dwelling on her experiences in the ghetto until her escape, reliving traumatic moments like the "aktsia," the action in which she had lost her family on the train to Auschwitz. She shuddered when she mentioned that dreaded name. She often launched into a trance-like description of ghetto life, of starvation and slave-labour, and the selections and "aktsiot." Eva would try to change the subject. Only two things made that possible: answering Ostelle's questions about her years in the resistance or telling her what she knew about Australia.

"Is it true that all the animals there carry their young in pockets?" Ostelle once asked her.

"Yes, they are called marsupials. They have pockets but they don't wear coats! The pouch is built into the mother's body."

"That sounds so strange. How do they fit into the mother's pocket?"

"They crawl there just after birth, when they are quite tiny. There are teats inside from which they nurse. When they are bigger they begin to explore the world, returning to sleep in the pouch. Eventually they are too big and the mother expels them."

"Where is this pouch?"

"The kangaroo has it in the front, on her belly. Most marsupials are like that, but there are some who carry their young on their backs."

"Amazing. Nature's ways are fascinating. It is a pity that human beings came on the scene. They have brought so much destruction and hatred into the world!"

"I've been told that Australians are, on the whole, nicer than Europeans."

"I hope you are right, but I don't really believe that. Human beings are pigs, or, rather, crazy apes."

Eva laughed. It was hard not to agree. Bitter humour, it was.

When the intensity of Eva's new friendship with Ostelle got

to be too much for him, when he could no longer stand Artur's sullen, heavy presence, Yanosh would go for a walk. Walking the deck of the ship was not as satisfying as a walk in the streets of Warsaw, Berlin or Marseilles. No interesting buildings, no trees, no fields or flowers. No variety of scenery to distract him. The water was constantly changing color and form, but it was always water. It was soothing to look out at it, to study the clouds, feel the sun's warmth, notice again the salt smell, the squawking of the seagulls. In the city he could get away from people to meditate. It was so much harder to do that on board the ship. Even when he looked out at the sea, or up at the sky, human voices and smells were always present. People would interrupt his thoughts to make conversation, when he desperately needed some solitude and silence.

He would observe the first-class area on his walks. They seemed so much more relaxed up there. They sat on their deck-chairs looking out at the sea, drinking tea. People up there played deck-quoits or volley-ball with happy shouts of victory or cries of support or disappointment. Well-dressed couples strolled their deck contentedly sharing pleasantries. Music wafted down from their section: waltzes, jazz, livelier swing music. He saw them dancing or partying during their evening parties. Did they suffer from seasickness too? Were they haunted by terrible memories? Could they find the solitude they needed in their first-class paradise? Or were they also feeling cramped and crowded, tired of the sea, irritable and claustrophobic?

One day he spotted Bora up there again. His bald head and round face were unmistakable. He called out to him. The man turned around, revealing a badly scared left side, a damaged-looking eye. He had seen him, he was sure. He called out to him again, and Bora called back:

"Yanosh! How are you?"

"Hello Bora, hello! I ... what happened to you? How did you survive the bombing in Berlin? Your face ... Why haven't we heard from you?"

Bora answered something, but his voice was lost in the wind. He waved, and was gone. What was going on? How could a fellow refugee afford to be up there with all those rich British people? he wondered. And why was he here on the boat to Australia, and not on his way to Palestine? But he was gone, and with him went the answers to his questions.

Eva was alone when he returned from his walk that day. Pawla and Marek were not there. Artur and Ostelle were not either. He was happy to see her alone and to see that she looked more relaxed than she had been before his walk. He knew she disliked Artur, he didn't like him much himself but, if she wanted her special friendship with Ostelle, then Artur came attached. She'd explained how she felt to Yanosh but didn't seem to want to make the effort with Artur. So they lived with the tensions of this new friendship of hers. People could be so complex, he thought! She smiled a gentle welcome to him. He sat beside her, feeling comfortable and at home at her side.

"Feel," she said, putting his hand on her now bigger stomach, "Do you feel that movement, Yanshuk?"

"Uh ha," he responded, giving her a caressing kiss on the neck.

"That's our baby moving inside my womb. Isn't it exciting!"

"Uh ha," Yanosh said, smiling too.

"Yanosh, are you aware of what's happening? We will be parents soon. Only six weeks until I am due to have the baby. That's just when we are supposed to arrive in Australia."

"I know. You have told me that before. That's what the doctor said too. He also mentioned that most first births are late."

"Will he be born on this ship, or will we already be in Australia when he is born?"

"Hopefully already in Australia. I don't like the idea of you having the baby here on the ship. It is so crowded and dirty here. Not a good place for a birth."

"I spoke to one of the sailors. He arranged for me to meet the ship's bosun. I want you to come with me. On Monday morning, in the first-class passengers' area – there's a doctor there who'll examine me after we meet him. He explained to me that if the baby is born on board, he will have British citizenship. The mother will be allowed into the infirmary in the first-class section."

"Sounds good, but I would rather my son..."

"Or daughter!"

"...or daughter is born in Australia."

"So would I, Yanosh, but just to be sure that you know what to do if I give birth early, you should go to the meeting tomorrow."

"Of course, my sweet, of course. We'll have to start thinking about a name," he said, yawning.

She hugged him.

"I saw Bora again," Yanosh said.

"Bora? Did you talk to him? What's the story?"

"No, I couldn't talk to him. He was up in the first-class area, but I did call out to him and he responded. His face looked strange, as if he had been badly hurt in an accident. It surprised me to see him up there. Where did he get enough money to travel as a first-class passenger? Do you know how much that must cost? A small fortune!"

"It's very strange – a Polish refugee with enough money to be up there amongst all those rich British people. He knows we are down here and now he knows we know he is here. I'm sure we'll be hearing from him. I don't know if I'm so happy about that. Bora makes me nervous."

"I know what you mean, darling, but he did save our lives. We owe him so much. He has helped a lot of other people too. I find him fascinating. Maybe I'll make contact with him on Monday when we are up there in the first-class section."

"Do you have to? Why don't you just wait for him to contact you? What's the hurry?"

Pawla and Marek appeared while they were talking, carrying a loaf of bread, and some soup in a large tin container.

"Dinner time?" Yanosh asked.

"We're not carrying this stuff here from the food distribution point to play with it!" Pawla said, catching her breath.

"It is time to eat! Let's start eating before the soup gets cold."

"Pass me some bread, Yanosh."

"Here, take it all, Marek. Take a piece and then pass it on."

Yanosh handed him the brown rye bread, having ripped off a piece for himself.

"The bread is stale, but with a little soup it isn't bad," he explained, half complaining.

Yanosh heard with half an ear. He was listening to the sound of the sea washing against the hull as they ate. He thought of meals he and Marek had shared in the past in even worse circumstances. Who would have imagined that they would now be sharing a meal on a ship so far from home. Poland? No, it was no longer his home; he understood that now. But Marek? How was he, such a Polish patriot able to do this? He wondered whether his friend was not making a terrible mistake traveling half way around the world. It was a heavy price to pay for their friendship, he thought. Australia sounded like such a rough and uncivilized place for a religious Polish intellectual to migrate to.

Marek produced a small bottle of vodka, which they handed around.

"To wash the food down."

They all laughed. They soon cleaned up and retired for another restless night aboard ship.

Yanosh did hear rumors about Bora from other passengers during the voyage. These pricked his consciousness and concern about the man. Marek told him that he had heard that there was an organization of former Nazis called "Odessa," which, apart from protecting those accused of war crimes, settled accounts with people like Bora. Perhaps his secrecy and disappearance, the bomb incident they had heard about, might be linked to them. Marek thought it likely that he was escaping them.

To faraway Australia? Yanosh was skeptical about this

explanation. This strengthened his desire to make contact with the man and discover the truth.

Monday morning came. They went up on to the first-class area, reached the infirmary. Yanosh had gone up with Eva to see the doctor, as he promised he would. It was to be a check-up, an opportunity to ask some questions about the pregnancy and the impending birth. Eva was nervously doodling on a sheet of paper. Yanosh sat there wondering how he would make contact with Bora.

He watched people pass outside, looked to see if he might see Bora. A group went by the door and on down the deck. One of them might have been him, had the right stature. He got a good look at the man only after he had passed by. The bald head with two curly tufts on the sides looked like his.

Eva looked up, stopped drawing: "What's the matter, Yanshuk?"

"I think it was him! Bora. That man who just walked by..."

Eva glared at him.

"I know. Of course," he mumbled, but he couldn't help himself. He was, he knew, obsessed with Bora, but this was an opportunity he could not ignore.

"Yanosh! Forget about him. We are here for a reason, remember."

Yanosh shook his head, saying: "I can't, Eva... I must know if it is him."

He got up, turned to reassure his spouse, and then darted out the door. The man's walk was definitely familiar. A powerful, silent movement of legs and arms. He drew closer to him, called out:

"Bora, please! Stop! Wait. I want to talk to you."

The man turned around, smiling. It wasn't Bora.

"You are mistaken, sir. That is not my name."

Yanosh apologized and turned to go, disappointed, when he heard the man continue: "But I do know the man you are looking for. He does look a little like me I've been told."

"You do?"

"Yes."

"And could you tell me where I could find him?"

"Well, I suppose I could take you to his cabin."

"That would be great. I would appreciate it."

"Follow me, then."

Yanosh followed the man around the upper deck, and soon was standing outside a cabin door.

"Try in there," he said, and started to leave.

"Thank you."

"No trouble, but be careful," he said, walking back the way they had come, whistling to himself.

Yanosh knocked on the cabin door, but no one answered. He opened the door and entered. There was no one there. He wondered whether he should wait longer.

Eva must be upset, he thought. I shouldn't leave her alone any longer. I will come back here as soon as I can, now that I know where to find him. He scribbled a note to Bora: "Please contact me. Urgent. Yanosh." He turned to go, but remembered to add the date and to underline the word urgent. Then he left.

As he walked away he did a mental inventory of what he had seen in the room: a bed, a small cabinet piled with books, some papers, a sharp metal object which was probably a letter opener beside them, a bed lamp, pajamas neatly folded on the bed, a chair. Nothing unusual there. Most of the books were Yiddish – not surprising, but the one on the top of the pile looked different than the others, looked like a religious book, perhaps a Bible. That seemed strange. He knew Bora was not a religious man.

He made his way back to Eva, wondering when his next opportunity to look for Bora would provide itself. She was next in line, so the recriminations about his sudden departure were brief. The doctor was polite, but stiff and formal in a very British way. He checked Eva and informed them that everything was all right, that the baby had not yet descended. The birth was not imminent, he told them. They were both relieved at that news, but Yanosh could not keep his mind off the presence of Bora's cabin nearby. He could not focus on what Eva was saying as they walked back out into the salty spray of the sea evening.

"Yanshuk, you aren't listening to me!"

"Of course I am. I heard every word. You said that you are happy to hear that there is still more time before the baby's birth, even though it is getting harder for you with that big stomach."

"But Yanshuk you are just repeating what I said!"

"I guess you are right. I am sorry, Eva. I am preoccupied with having almost met Bora. I know where his cabin is now!"

"I don't care about Bora or where his cabin is, just about our baby. We came up here to see the doctor, not Bora. Yanosh you are impossible."

Yanosh smiled, took her arm, and they continued down the stairs talking about their future life in Australia.

The ship heaved and rolled through the night. People moaned, people sighed. A baby cried. A woman led a young curly-headed child across the room, hushing him as they went towards the passageway which led to the lavatory. A weak light came flickering down the stairwell from above, seeming to be dancing to the rhythm of the ship's engines.

The ship's movements had woken Eva again, but Yanosh was still sleeping. She lay there waiting for him to wake as well. She felt the baby moving inside her, wanting to share it with him. His chest rose and fell rhythmically under the grey blanket. Watching and hearing him sleeping next to her calmed her. She soon fell asleep again.

In the early morning, Yanosh stirred beside her, turned over and curled into himself beneath the blanket, pulling it partially off her as he did.

She yanked it back. He woke, startled.

"What's the matter?" he asked.

"You pulled the blanket off me."

"I'm sorry, darling. It was in my sleep."

"I know, but I was cold."

"Uh... uh..."

Yanosh rubbed his eyes. Eva took his hand.

"You know, Yanosh, it is time we talked again about a name for our child."

"Again!"

"Yanosh, don't look at me like that! You're going to tease me again! I know we've already talked about it but we didn't decide anything."

"I'm sorry, darling, it's just that I'm not ready for this conversation now. I just opened my eyes."

"Yanshuk, you're always finding excuses for not talking about this. It's time we did. You don't want the baby to be born without a name, do you?"

"We could call him baby Dura, couldn't we? ... until we figure something out."

"Stop it! It's not funny. Yanosh, please stop. If it's a boy we need a real name, for the *bris*. That's only eight days after the birth."

"And if it's a girl?

"I suppose we could wait longer without a name, but why should we? I want my daughter to have a name, just like any boy who was just born."

"No, no you didn't understand me! If it's a girl we could do like the Bedouin Arabs do..."

"Stop Yanosh! I don't care what anyone else would do. I just want us to decide on a name. I want the name to reflect what's happened to us and our choice to restart our lives. I want our child to know that his or her birth gave us hope for a better future."

They were interrupted by the protests of their neighbors.

"You two are making too much noise. I can't sleep."

"Shut up!"

"*Sha, Ich vil shluffen!*"

Someone threw a hat at them. Yanosh caught and tossed it back.

"Eva, come on, let's go for a walk on deck. We'll continue the conversation up there."

"All right, but only if you promise to be reasonable and not to tease."

"I promise."

They walked the deck talking about names for a long time without resolving the issue. Eva suggested naming the child after his or her deceased parents, according to the Jewish custom. Yanosh objected. He didn't want to burden their child with the past.

"What about an English name like Tom or John?" he asked.

"We could do that, but I want the child to have a Jewish name too."

"To continue carrying the curse!"

"Yanshuk, it's not a curse. It is an honor to carry a Jewish name, to continue our ancient tradition."

"Don't start with that again! Next you'll start talking to me about teaching him medieval superstitions as well."

Yanosh lit a cigarette and looked out at the ocean waves, which soothed his turbulent soul.

"All right, Eva, we will give him a Jewish name as well."

Yanosh heard the squawking seagulls circling above, the ship's engines. He felt like screaming with the birds.

Eva took his arm and broke the silence.

"Thank you. I knew you would be reasonable in the end."

"Yes, you always have your way in these things," he said, holding down the emotional storm within.

During the long days of the sea journey, Yanosh managed to find some peace of mind. For the first time in years his writing began to flow. He wrote a number of poems and a short story, apart from writing down his memories of the Polish resistance movement under German occupation. About his own personal losses, his mother, brother and sisters, the multitudes of murdered Jews he found it difficult and painful to write, but here and there some of that crept into his writing as well.

He found himself a hidden corner on deck, where he could not be seen by friends. Eva knew where he would often sit, but kept his secret. She knew how important his writing was to him. His more cheerful demeanor now that he had begun writing again was some reward for her efforts to protect him, to let him write.

She did complain to him that she felt abandoned at times, that his "new girlfriend" kept him away from her a lot, that she expected him to be a more devoted father than he had been a husband lately. Yanosh understood this to be said jokingly, but wasn't sure. He would sigh, promise to be a better husband, and that, of course he would be a good father. He looked forward to playing with his little boy.

"It might be a girl, Yanshuk!" repeating yet again her correction to his fixation on male offspring.

"I'll play with my daughter, then."

She would smile or laugh delightedly.

They eventually did return to the issue of a name for the child. Eva wanted a daughter to be named after her mother, Shulamit, a son after her father, Mordecai. Yanosh didn't care to give his child a Jewish name, nor did he want it named after his dead in-laws. He had not come up with any suggestions of his own, so he ended the conversation with a request for more time to think about it. Eva found this behavior frustrating, but she bade her time, waiting for the right circumstances to bring the name issue up again. She worried about it, knowing how stubborn Yanosh could be.

Eva would sometimes take out the sketchpad Yanosh had bought her months before for her birthday. There weren't many sketches in it yet. She had been so preoccupied with the travails of her pregnancy, the uncertainties of their travels across Europe, the distraction of Yanosh's nervousness that she had not found the energy to do much sketching. Now that he had gone back to writing, she felt inspired to return to her own creativity. So she began to sketch again.

She sketched her husband sitting in his corner on deck, hunched over his writing. The pencil drawings showed his wrinkled, broad forehead, long legs folded under him, trousers rolled up to reveal hairy legs, his big protruding ears like two wings carrying him off into his imagination or memories.

She sketched the people on board with them: the ruddy, sinewy sailors, the first-class passengers in their fine clothes and jewelry, her fellow refugees, their worn tired faces. She sketched Bora and his friends in Berlin, as she remembered them. A wedding scene in the D.P. camp...

One family on board with them in particular caught her eye. An older woman, her hair just graying, who seemed to be crippled, had trouble walking. The woman had a beautiful face. Her features were aesthetically pleasing, as if sculpted by a master artist. Her complexion was so smooth that it was hard to believe she could be old enough to be graying already, but her bent back and shaking hands countered the angelic face.

She was accompanied by two adolescents: a girl who looked so like her that there could be no doubt about her maternity, and a blonde boy. The girl, 14 or 15 years old, was always by her side helping her and talking with her in Yiddish. The boy, perhaps 12 or 13, was busy exploring the ship, only occasionally rejoining his mother and sister. She noticed that they spoke Polish with him when he was with them. There was no doubt in her mind that the mother and daughter, both swarthy beauties with dark eyes, were Jewish, but the boy could have passed for an "Aryan." He must look more like his father, she thought.

Where was the father? She wondered what had become of him. Had he abandoned his Jewish wife during the war years, been killed in the fighting? Murdered? There were so many widows and orphans on board, so many sad, lonely men. This little family aroused many questions, but she never spoke to them and never learned their story. Something about them attracted her attention. Something about them led her to respect their privacy.

Perhaps it was the delicate, tender love she perceived in their family interactions that attracted her. There must have been a very special relationship in the past, which had created this family. She began to add an imaginary, missing husband-father to her many sketches of them, making him look like the boy. She enjoyed doing so; it repaired what the war had probably destroyed. If only it was so easy! She could, of course, have spoken to them, found out their story, but she avoided doing that, was too shy and did not want to disturb them. It was a wonder that they never noticed her sketching them. Others had, and had commented on her artistic skills.

June 18, 1946, Port Said

I have never seen anything like this place before. The heat, the flies, the squalor, the noise, the filth in the streets. The sheer blue sky. Not a cloud!

We wandered through the "shuk" waving flies away and examining the wares in the stalls. I bought us a lump of very sweet, sticky stuff they call "baclowa," which we ate in the shade of a very tall palm tree. The sun was fiercely bright.

The haggling Arab shoppers in the market here remind me of the Jewish quarter of Warsaw. Many of the poor Jews there were as dark as these local Semites. Their faces lined with worry wrinkles, black eyes, prominent hooked noses, sensuous mouths, expressive hand movements, even their body movements appear Jewish to me. They are less proud. Less other-worldly, too.

And their clothes are different. Not only black, but also white or light hues of blue and green. Not heavy hats, but cloth turbans, bright scarves. More like gypsies than Jews! Many of the women wear veils, only their raven eyes visible, and they walk with slow but heavy grace carrying their large baskets on their heads as they move through the marketplace.

Everyone came running up on deck. The ship's sirens were sounding out their hoarse warnings over and over again. Sailors were running everywhere, carrying things: emergency equipment, rubber boats and rafts. Some were directing the traffic, calling people out of their cabins, escorting families with children.

"Move out of the way!"

"Over there! ... Over here!"

"Out of the way, sir. Excuse me, madam..."

"Right! Right, turn right!"

The big lifeboats were already being lowered into the water, chains removed, ropes loosened as the pulley system creaked into movement. Crowds surged to and fro, frightened, frothing waves of noisy mayhem. The sea, however, was calm.

"We have hit a coral reef," someone explained to his neighbor.

"How do you know that?" Yanosh asked.

"I overheard one of the sailors talking about it," came the answer.

Yanosh took Eva's arm, trying to protect her from the flailing limbs all around them. He was worried that in her present state she might not protect herself adequately, that they might lose the baby. He saw the horror on her face as they moved forward in the crowd towards the nearest boat. The ship rocked heavily a couple of times and then seemed to ground to a sudden halt. Some people tripped, fell, rolled past them along the deck. He grabbed the deck-rail and held on to it as best he could. Eva screamed.

16

Revelations

Yanosh woke with a start. He looked over at Eva. She was lying there peacefully beside him. It was dark. He felt the ship rolling on the waves. Perhaps a storm was starting. He heard others moaning, restless from the disturbance. It had been a dream, a nightmare. He felt relieved.

Quietly, he got up and felt his way down the dark corridor to the toilet cubicle. There was a light on in there. Someone inside. He'd have to wait. If whoever it was didn't come out soon, he would have to go in the corridor. The door finally opened and out came Pawla. She smiled at him apologetically as she passed. Then she turned back and called out after him:

"Wait a minute, Yanosh. I want to talk to you about something."

"What do you want?" he asked, irritated.

The ship's constant swaying movement was making him feel queasy. He rested his hand on the wall to steady himself.

"To talk to you, Yanosh. There is something I must tell you before we reach Australia, before we get off this boat."

"Now? Here? Is it as urgent as that? I'd like to get back to sleep. Can't it wait till the morning?"

"Yanosh now is a good opportunity. Eva's asleep. Marek is too. Please listen to me now. It is important. It is about Bora."

"Okay, so wait here. I'll be out soon."

Yanosh went in and finally relieved himself. There was a gentle knock on the door. Someone else waiting out there? I didn't see anyone else, he thought. He opened the door and saw that it was Pawla. In the short time, she was impatient waiting outside the toilet door.

"I thought you might be drowning in there," she joked.

He didn't feel very humorous.

"Let's find somewhere more comfortable than this dark corridor to talk. It smells here ... people will be looking for the toilet sooner or later."

"We could go up on deck. I will get my coat. You should get something warmer to wear than that, okay?"

She went off and was soon back wearing her grey overcoat. Yanosh had grabbed his own jacket meanwhile and had draped it over his shoulders. They silently climbed the circular stairs together. Yanosh was now curious about what news Pawla had to share with him about Bora. Why was it so urgent? Why didn't she want their spouses to know as well? Was there more about Bora that he didn't already know?

It was cold and windy outside. The waves were crashing roughly onto the sides of the ship, which was being tossed up and down by them. Yanosh felt vulnerable faced with the angry sea's power.

It started raining.

He pulled Pawla back down into the stairwell, closed the iron door with difficulty against the wind. They stood on the top landing of the stairs recovering from the sudden sting of the cold. Pawla lit herself a cigarette, offered him one. He refused, preferring to keep his hands inside his jacket pockets to stay warm.

"Yanosh, you look cold."

Pawla's voice disturbed his thoughts. He remembered why they had come up here.

"Yes, Pawla, I am. You wanted to talk."

"It wasn't such a great idea to come up on deck, I think."

"No, it wasn't, but we are here now. It is sheltered and private here. Go ahead..."

"There is something I must tell you now. While I still can, now that I have the opportunity to speak to you."

"I am listening."

"You remember you once asked me about the scar on my neck, that I told you how I had been beaten by a German soldier, that he had tried to kill me, had begun to cut my throat with his knife, that I managed to shoot him just in time..."

"Of course I remember that. How could I forget a story like that? I'd always wondered how your neck had been scarred so badly."

"Did you believe me?" she asked, blowing smoke rings, as she waited for his response.

"I wasn't sure, it sounded possible."

"I'd like to tell you the truth, but you must swear that you will not tell anyone. Do you? Will you keep my secret?"

"Why are you telling me this?"

"Because of your dealings with Borowski, because you once planned to go into business with him... We know he is here on this ship. I want to warn you to be careful."

"Bora? Borowski? He is connected with your scar?"

"Yes, he is."

She flicked the long ash off her cigarette.

"What's the story?" he asked, clenching his fist and releasing it again and again.

"Well, you know that I was often sent on missions to various parts of Poland for the A.K. I would carry money, sometimes weapons, messages from one underground group to another. The Gestapo knew about me after a while so I had to stop. They posted my picture everywhere, offered a reward."

"Yes, I've heard something about that. Marek told me that you were caught once but managed to escape. I thought that might have been when you got the scar, when those bastards tortured you."

"A lot of people think so, and I encourage them to think that to protect the good name of the Polish resistance. The truth is this scar is from my fellow Poles, not from German Nazis."

"So what happened? What does all this have to do with Bora? What do you have to warn me about?"

"I had reached Vilna in 1943. August. They were liquidating the ghettoes, killing the last Jews in the area. Many had fled to the forests. In the Naroch forest there had been clashes between the A.K. and the Russian partisans. My mission was to reach the A.K. in Naroch and appeal to them to work for cooperation with the Russians, to reach a cease-fire agreement so they could concentrate on our common enemy."

"Yes, Pawla ... go on."

"I moved towards the Naroch forest from Vilna, going from village to village ... disguised myself as a peasant woman returning from market. I was actually carrying a letter from General Mashinski, which got me cooperation from the A.K. people on the way. In Vileika I heard stories of the brutality of the Russian partisans, that they were active in the area. It was there that I met an agent of the A.K. who told me we also had people in the area, that there had been battles between our partisans and the Russians in Naroch. I told him I wanted to reach our men in the forest. He led me to the edge of the forest, pointed east, said that their encampment was near the marshes, two days walk away. He wished me good luck, crossed himself and left me there."

Yanosh put out his cigarette on the metal top of the stair-railing, and then threw it out the door, which he closed again against the wind and rain.

"I began walking," she continued, "it was almost dark and growing cold. I was terrified of wolves, perhaps more than my fear of the Russian partisans. I wrapped myself in my fur coat and trudged on into the forest. After two days I finally reached the A.K. camp, hungry and exhausted, but still convinced of the importance of my mission."

"I was lucky they didn't shoot me as I approached. I called out the password as I'd been told in Vileika by the A.K. contacts there. Luckily the guard had his wits about him. It was the previous password, but he still remembered it and let me through."

"I spoke to the commander soon after I'd rested a little, eaten and warmed myself by the fire. It was evening when I reached them. He was quite gracious, he'd known my father. They had served together in the Polish Army in the battle for Warsaw in

1939. He read the letter, conferred with his fellows and decided to send a group out to meet with the Russians. Colonel Markov, the Russian commander, was contacted and agreed to meet, but insisted we come to his camp, unarmed."

"What you are telling me is incredible," remarked Yanosh. "The Russian and Polish partisans who had been fighting and killing each other agreed to meet and negotiate an armistice between them? And all of this because of a letter you brought them?"

"Yes, it is pretty incredible, but they were getting desperate, the Germans were planning a major offensive against the partisans about which they'd been informed. It was a matter of survival."

"And what about Bora? Where does he figure in all this? What does this have to do with your scar?" Yanosh asked.

"Well, when we reached the Russian camp we were escorted into Markov's hut. There I met Borowski for the first time. He was some kind of deputy of Markov's, barking orders at people, posting guards outside our meeting place. He brought in the maps we needed for our meeting, ordered tea be made and so on. Something about him disturbed me more than the others there. His piercing stare. I felt as if he were reading my insides during the meeting, studying me carefully."

"What happened during the meeting?"

"Colonel Markov was a fairly cultured man, a former school teacher, who had been the regional secretary of the local Communist Party. He spoke an excellent Polish. The chemistry between him and Zabronski, the local A.K. commander was very good. They divided up areas of control between them, marked them on the map and agreed to set aside differences until the Germans were defeated. Everyone agreed that too many lives had been lost and energy wasted in the intra-partisan struggles."

"Bora was silent throughout, carefully listening, making notes and studying the A.K. people. It was unnerving. When the meeting ended, Markov asked Bora to escort us out of the camp. He called a couple of other men, and they marched out of the camp with us. The tension was terrible. They supposedly were there to protect us but I felt they were escorting us away to get rid of us as quickly as possible. I had trouble keeping up with them. They walked so fast. Their rifles seemed to be trained on us a lot of the time. They watched our every movement suspiciously. I feared they might be planning to shoot us right there in the forest."

The wind had died down outside. It had stopped raining. They heard the sound of footsteps – a young couple soon came up the stairs and passed them, out into the cold night. Pawla waited for them to disappear. She looked at Yanosh nervously before speaking again:

"He raped me," she said.

"What? He what?"

"What you heard. He took me aside while everyone waited, resting. He told me he wanted to talk to me privately. We walked about 100 meters into the forest. Suddenly I felt his arms around me, pinning me to a tree. I tried to push him away, but he was too strong. I slapped him. He kissed me, began stroking my neck, talking to me about how attractive he found me. I stopped resisting. I was frightened, terrified. He forced me down and before I could think he was on top of me, had taken off my pants, was inside me. He hurt me. I was bleeding, sat there on the ground crying. It was so shocking, happened so fast that I was overwhelmed, didn't scream."

Pawla was crying as she spoke, she seemed to almost choke on the words, stopped abruptly, then stepped outside. Yanosh stood there watching her, dumbfounded for a moment, saw her toss her cigarette overboard, watched the arc of red light descend into the darkness, heard her sobbing. He followed her out onto the deck.

"What could you have done? Don't blame yourself for what happened."

"I should have screamed, should have resisted more. I have never told anyone before, not even Marek."

"So why did you tell me?"

"To warn you, Yanosh. Don't trust him. He is an animal. He is capable of almost anything."

"Bora, an animal? It's so hard to believe. He is such a cultured, civilized man... Perhaps that was a crime of passion, a momentary failure... It was wartime."

"Don't defend him, Yanosh. How can you explain what he did to me! I wasn't the only one. That wasn't his only crime... Don't you know what he was doing there in Berlin?"

"Yes, I do. But, Pawla that was different. It was a matter of national honor, revenge. I didn't agree with him, but I understood his motives, and he was very helpful to his fellow Jews when they were in need. He saved many lives..."

"He saved mine too, Yanosh, but he is no angel. I have met the bastard many times since then. He is always polite to me, never refers to what happened. It's as if nothing happened between us, as if he never raped me, never saved my life from my fellow Poles. Never used me again and again there in the forest. I hate the man, wish I could kill him, but he has some sort of power over me every time I am near him. He has never said anything about what happened that day, but I can never forget what happened, that the same day that he raped me he also saved my skin, that I owe him, my life."

"How did he save your life?"

She fingered the scar on her throat, caressed it. Lit yet another cigarette and started talking again:

"You asked about my scar. It is a memento of the reception I received from one of my fellow Poles there in the forest. When we returned to the waiting group to renew our trek, I was met with angry, sullen stares from the Polish partisans. As we walked on, some of them began to poke me, whispering insults, hissing words at me like 'whore', 'slut' and such. They asked me if I wasn't ashamed having had sex with a Russian partisan, worse – a Jew. My denials didn't help matters, nor my tears. They didn't believe me at all. One of them came at me with a knife. While we were resting, after having walked about an hour ... he crawled over to sit next to me ... before I knew what was happening I had his knife at my throat. He started yelling 'Bitch, traitor, Jew-lover!' at me. The others just sat there, frozen, staring. I screamed. I was bleeding, felt the knife tearing at my throat. I struggled, managed to push him off me, grabbed his knife. Before I could use it on him, a shot was fired."

"It was Borowski. The man fell, screaming. He'd been hit in the face. His right side turned into a torn bleeding mass of flesh. The man writhed on the ground until another bullet hit him in the chest. He stopped moving, let out a death rattle and was gone. I had rolled out of the way. Borowski came over to me carrying bandages. He dressed my neck wound, telling me I was lucky not to be dead, too. He forced me to drink some water, and a little vodka. I couldn't bare his touch, even though he was making a great effort to be gentle. When he had finished, he ordered everyone to get up, pointed the A.K. people in the direction of their camp and told them to go. 'Take your dead friend with you,' he told them. 'You are coming back with us,' he told me. I must have passed out on the way back. I had lost a lot of blood, had not drunk enough. The next I knew I was in Markov's camp again – the next morning.

"I spent almost a month with the Russian partisans. They would not let me go. Bora had saved my life, now he made sure I recovered from the wound in my neck and that enough time passed for me to be safe from my fellow Polish resistance people. The longer I stayed with them the more I feared for my future in the A.K., but I really had no choice until I recovered.

"During that time I learned about Borowski's family, all of whom had been murdered by the Nazis. He had initiated a Jewish resistance group in the forests, made up of young people who had fled the ghettoes. They'd called it Nekomma, which means Revenge, had been in action for six months until the Soviets decided to disband it since Stalin said the Jews were not a nation and had no right to a separate fighting unit of their own. Bora described one action in which they had burned a

Byelorussian village to the ground, killing all the inhabitants. I was shocked to hear this. How could Jews initiate a pogrom?

"Bora seemed to enjoy my shocked response to his story. 'Why not?' he asked me. 'Jews are no different than anyone else. We had weapons, we knew this village had participated in the local massacre of the Jews,' he said to me."

"Yanosh, I thought the Jews were supposed to be a holy people, God's chosen."

"Bora justified burning down a village? I admit I am also shocked. The man is a rabbi's son. How could he participate in something like that, justify it?"

"Well, he did. Why are you so surprised? You know as well as I do what he has been doing in Germany this last year and a half, the real reason the Americans arrested and then exiled him."

Yanosh took a deep breath.

He was disturbed that she might know something, but tried to keep a straight face, to hide his concern.

"You have heard about the poisonings, haven't you? The former S.S., who have disappeared and then been found dead."

"I know, Pawla, I know."

He did not want to say more than necessary.

The wind had died down, it had stopped raining, but there was a chill in the air. They stood looking out over the water, which lapped the side of the ship incessantly. Yanosh looked up at the myriad stars, then over at Pawla, who stood pensively looking out at the dark waters. He was tempted to take her in his arms, felt an attraction to the woman, which he resisted with difficulty.

"Pawla, I am going back to bed. Eva will begin to worry if she wakes up and doesn't find me nearby. I've been gone a while and I need to get some more sleep. You look tired too... You have given me a lot to think about and I appreciate your sharing all this with me. It must be hard for you. Are you coming down?"

"No, Yanosh, I'd like to stay up here and watch the dawn break. I don't think I can sleep anymore tonight. Sleep well."

"Good night."

Yanosh turned, went back through the doors, intending to go down the stairs and return to his wife. He looked back over his shoulder to see Pawla still standing there, smoke curling up above her long blonde hair as she looked out into the ocean's blackness. Then he turned around, went back to her, put his arms around her waist and kissed her. She pushed him away.

"I must go," he said.

She smiled sadly.

"Go, Yanosh, go back to your Eva ... and ... and ... sleep well."

Yanosh climbed the metal stairs. Everyone was sleeping below him. He had been restless again. Couldn't sleep. A walk on deck would help him, he thought. The sound of the waves, the night sky ... they would help him relax, calm his nerves, his turbulent mind.

He continued climbing, listening to the clanking sound his shoes made, the echo produced in the hollow space below, as he ascended. He could hear the ship's engine churning nearby. The odor of the oil and sweat hit him when he passed the engine room. He thought about Pawla's confession the night before. It was an incredible story. Hard to believe, despite all he knew about Bora. He felt shocked.

When would he meet Bora again? He would like to confront him with what Eva had told him to get some answers to the many questions which now tortured him about the man.

The steam hissing past in the pipe beside him was speaking to him, he thought.

"He is dead! He is dead," it said.

"Why? What do you mean?" he asked into the night.

No answer. Just the rumbling of the machines below and the steam hissing into the sea-framed night.

"He is alive. I saw him," he said to himself, arguing with

the seething silence around him. He continued climbing. The pipe hissed.

On the platform atop the stairs he stopped to catch his breath, lit a cigarette, pushed open the heavy, blue metal door and stepped outside into the cold.

The wind hit him hard in the face, his cigarette went out. The raw cold numbed him momentarily.

Yanosh walked the length of the deck and back, feeling the biting wind striking his neck one way, against his forehead the other. It was dark. No moon to be seen, few stars. A cloudy night, but no rain... His mind rolled with the waves.

What had become of Bora? He had seen him only twice since they'd set out. He had left him a note in his cabin, but there had been no response. More than a week had passed. Eva's belly now was very big. They had chosen names for a boy and for a girl. They had traveled halfway round the world.

He thought about what Pawla had told him... Bora a rapist? It wasn't possible. Yes, he could be rough. He had seen that. But he was a rabbi's son! He was an honorable man. He had spilt some blood, but that was the thing to do at the time. Killing Germans after all that had happened made sense. He had assassinated S.S. men, mass murderers ... So what! But rape?

No, it couldn't be. Must be a misunderstanding. But where was he now? And why was he on this ship and not on a ship to Palestine, or already there on one of those Zionist communes? He had so many questions without any answers! If he could contact him he would ask, he would hear Bora's version of what had happened in the Naroch forest during the war. He must speak to him about it. But how? The man had vanished, was nowhere to be found.

Bora was sitting on deck, basking in the sun. His hat was pushed forward, shading his eyes, but there was no mistake. It was him. Yanosh knew that body, its stocky, muscular look. He approached cautiously.

"Bora, hello. I am happy to find you here. You are enjoying the sun, I see."

"Ah, Yanosh. Nice to see you. Yes, sitting in the sun is relaxing. I enjoy the warmth. How are you, young man?"

Yanosh stood looking down at his old friend, staring despite himself, at the scarred side of his face.

"How are you, Yanosh?" he asked again, smiling up at him.

"All right I suppose, but what happened to your face?"

"You can pull up a deckchair – there are some over there – and I will tell you the story. Come, Yanosh. I am happy to tell you what happened; I would like to catch up with your news as well."

Yanosh brought over a chair and sat beside him.

"Right. I suppose you are wondering why I am here on this ship and why I have been avoiding you and your friends."

"Yes, that, but even more than that I was surprised to see you at all, to see that you are still alive."

"What do you mean?"

"I was there in Berlin that day, the day of the explosion at the Blichner Hotel. I saw you go into the building; you must have been in the lobby when the bomb went off. I was sure you were dead. That's what Moniek told me, the others thought so as well. And then you were not heard of again, not until I saw you on this ship."

"There was no funeral, was there?"

"No."

"No death notices or eulogies?"

"No."

"Well I am very much alive as you can see. It is true that someone was trying to assassinate me and twice came close to succeeding, but I have an angel watching over me, a very cunning and resourceful angel, at that."

"But what's the story? What are you doing here now? Weren't you planning to leave for Palestine, to serve the Zionist cause there?"

"So, Yanosh, I must start my story earlier, start telling what happened after we parted at the *Pesach Seder* a few months ago."

"Yes. That too was pretty dramatic."

"That it was."

"So what happened after they arrested you?"

"After keeping me incarcerated for a while they expelled me from the country, told me to stay away for my own safety, that I was causing them too many headaches."

"Where did you go?"

"To Paris. I have a cousin there, some other friends, Yiddish writers I knew before and during the war."

"So how is it I saw you again in Berlin after that?"

"Let me tell you a story. You know I love the Chelm stories. There was once a Jew from Chelm who went to great efforts to attain a fish for his family for Shabbes. As he was coming home, happily carrying his catch, the fish still very much alive and struggling, swished its tail. It hit our Chelmer friend in the face, cutting his nose and causing the poor man to bleed. The gentleman was very upset about this. He came before the Chelm Beit Din demanding justice, showing the judges the culprit, still wriggling in his hands and the damage caused him. The dayanim deliberated on this and in their Chelm wisdom decided that the appropriate sentence to punish said fish was death by drowning!"

"Very droll. I see. So you were the fish in this case?"

"Yes, you might say that. I wasn't going to stop swimming, I was not going to let their Chelm wisdom stop me from doing what needed to be done. Letting me out of prison was their mistake."

"Perhaps coming back to Germany was yours?"

"No. I have no regrets. I will go to my grave happy in the knowledge of having settled accounts with some of those Nazi mass murderers."

"But Bora, you still haven't explained what you are doing here on the Aurora."

218

"I can't tell you everything, but let me just say that I am on a special mission for the cause, and after it is completed I will be going to Palestine ... if I'm not killed before that."

"You sound fatalistic."

"I have survived much already but I must be realistic. As you know I am a fighter, and I do have a certain love of life as well. Now Yanosh, I would like to hear something about you and Eva, and your friends, Marek and Pawla. What have you been up to? What are your plans?"

"There isn't much to tell. You know that we were married, that Eva is expecting, that we are migrating to Australia. If I remember well, we got the idea from you originally. Marek and Pawla have similar goals. To start over, to forget the past."

"The past won't go away, Yanosh. Don't fool yourselves. You have to confront it, struggle with it and only then can you transcend it."

"I think you are wrong, Bora. Too much obsession with the past can be soul-destroying. Talking of the past, there is something else I wanted to ask you about."

"Yes?"

"Your relationship with Pawla. She told me about your time together in the Naroch forest, that you forced yourself on her, exploited her."

"And you believed her?"

"I am not sure what to believe. That is why I am asking."

Bora laughed. Tears came to his eyes, which he wiped away with a large white handkerchief he'd pulled out.

"She is lying, Yanosh. The sex was as much her idea as mine. Let me tell you she was passionate. I find her choice of your friend, Marek, as a lovemate surprising. He is so pious, such a 'saint.' And she? Well I wasn't the only one, I can tell you that."

"People change."

"Some do, but not her. I don't think so. I have observed you two on the deck below talking in the evening. Be careful, Yanosh. Eva is a fine woman, will be a devoted mother. I know pregnancy can be a strain, but ... Keep clear of Pawla. She is a cunning, scheming woman. Not to be trusted."

Walking along the deck one evening some days later, he heard someone behind him. The door swung open and out stepped a woman wrapped in a coat several sizes too big. It was Pawla. She came up to him and took his right arm.

Pawla and Yanosh walked the deck together. They watched the sunrise and spoke.

"He didn't exactly rape me," she said.

"What? What did you say?"

"It wasn't rape. I let him; I wanted him in my passion at the time. I was attracted to him, but I was angry with myself and him afterwards. I felt used, saw that he didn't really care about me and I began to hate him. So it felt like rape to me. I convinced myself that that's what had happened."

"Why are you telling me this now? You are confusing me, Pawla. I no longer know what to think."

"I understand. I suppose it is me who is confused."

"I think so."

"Talking to you yesterday was cathartic for me. I felt a powerful sense of release, but I know how important the man is to you, how much you admire him."

"Yes, I did, Pawla, but I have become disillusioned, less enamored of him, and I am baffled by his behavior since last spring. There is a mystery about him I can't fathom."

Pawla was smoking again. She was listening, so he continued.

"Yesterday I pinned him down at last. We spoke at length, but I remain mystified. He answered my questions, but spoke in riddles. But about your relationship with him he was unequivocal. He laughed. He denied your charge of rape, said you were as passionate as he."

"Yes. That sounds like the old Bora. He is strange. I don't understand him. Nothing he does surprises me, Yanosh."

They walked silently together for a while, then he turned to go, to return to Eva, to his life.

"Yanosh…"

"Yes, Pawla?"

"Where are you going?"

"I'm going to rejoin my wife."

"But I have more to tell you…"

"Not now, Pawla. I've been gone awhile now. Some other time, okay?"

"All right. We'll talk later."

"Bye."

"Bye."

He opened the metal door and went inside, feeling the sudden warmth of the sheltered space. Looking out behind him he saw Pawla light another cigarette and lean out over the water.

As he climbed down the stairs, he heard the sound of gunfire. Three shots. A woman screaming. The sounds had come from above him, from outside.

He ran back up the stairs, pushed the door open and emerged into the cold wind.

A siren was sounding. There was shouting on the upper deck. He looked up to see people running. A man lay bleeding up there. Blood was dripping down the side of that deck, landing onto the lower deck, forming a growing red puddle a few meters away from him.

Pawla stood there, leaning on the railing and smoking, watching the events on the upper deck. She seemed to be calm, collected, standing there. He was relieved to see her, but surprised at her response to what was happening above them.

"Pawla, you're all right! Something terrible has happened up there."

"Not so terrible, Yanosh. It was expected. I expected something like this to happen to him."

"What are you talking about?"

Movement above distracted them. The wounded person was being carried away on a stretcher, writhing in pain, groaning, still alive. Sailors were swarming along the near side of the deck shouting and competing for a better view of what was happening. A man, a young sailor, appeared, carrying a bucket and some rags. He began mopping up the blood, causing waves of movement in the milling crowd.

"Get out of the way!"

The stretcher-bearers yelled at those congregating by the upper deck's stairs. The doctor came running through the crowd, and examined the man. He led them into the infirmary.

Yanosh turned back to Pawla: "What were you talking about before?" he asked.

"I saw the man who was shot. It was hard to see, the sun was in my eyes, but I think I recognized him."

"Bora?"

"I think so. He was wearing a brown peaked cap. There was something strange about his face."

"What do you mean?"

"It was scarred on one side, looked as if part of his face had been blown off. He only had one ear. I remember you mentioned something like that, when you told us you had seen him. A short stocky man … he was shot in the back of the head from inside, from one of the cabin windows."

"So you think it was him?"

"Yes, but I'm not sure."

"I am going up there to find out if it was him."

"They won't let you near, Yanosh. I'm sure they won't."

"I'm going to try. Do you want to come with me?"

"No, I am staying here. I'm not interested in what happens to Bora anymore," she said bitterly.

Yanosh went inside again, ran back down into the ship. He soon rejoined Eva.

"What happened," she asked, rubbing her eyes, "You look agitated."

"Someone was just shot. I think it might be Bora."

Eva was awake now. In the dim light he could see that her brow was knitted. He decided to ignore her alarmed look.

"I'm going back up ... to find out more about what happened, to see if it was him."

"Why?"

"Pawla said she saw him on the upper deck; saw that he was the one shot."

"You were up there with Pawla?"

"Yes, we were talking when it happened."

"What happened?"

The man who was shot was carried away on a stretcher. He was still alive, but bleeding a lot."

"I knew that if Bora was here there would be trouble."

"I know where the infirmary is. We were there, remember?"

"Of course I do."

"Well, I am going up there."

"Be careful, Yanosh."

"Of course I will."

He left her for the stairs, then turned back to wave. Seeing her concerned look, he blew her a kiss, which she returned. He started climbing the stairs again, passed the churning engine room quickly on his ascent. He was soon at the blue door, breathing heavily.

He came out into the mist of cold sea spray. Some sense of sanity had returned to the lower deck. No one was shouting, the blood had been cleaned away, but he heard people talking above. There was a small group of people standing right over his head... He could hear their conversation.

"I heard the shooting!" one said.

"Really?" responded another.

"Ah ha. They carried a man away about half an hour ago, maybe more," he said.

"Was he dead?"

"Don't know. Might be. He lost a lot of blood."

"Who was he?"

"Who cares," a mousy-looking woman interrupted the two Englishman. She spoke with a strong Slavic accent.

"There are so many dead already. The war, the war... What does it matter anymore if another gets killed!"

They ignored her and continued talking.

"Perhaps he's still alive. Maybe they can save the guy?"

"Wonder who shot him and why?"

"Yes, so do I, but I am sure there will be an investigation."

"And a funeral," added the woman.

"A funeral? Yes, a funeral, if he dies."

Yanosh had heard enough. They didn't know anything, it was just empty talk. He continued across the deck, went through the door under the other side of the upper area, found the stairs winding up inside and started up towards the infirmary. He reached the metal grate at the top. It was closed and locked. He climbed over it, squeezing through the gap between the ceiling and the top. The door on the other side was not locked. He opened it and went through quietly.

There were some people standing outside the infirmary talking about what had happened. Maybe they knew something. He listened to them.

"There are two men in there. One is dead, shot himself in the head. I heard them say that just one bullet hit him. He had a strange tattoo on his shoulder according to one of the sailors who had carried the stretcher."

"What do you mean?"

"Some kind of Nazi symbol or something."

"You don't say!"

"Yep."

"What about the other one?"

"They are trying to save him. Lost a lot of blood, but his heart is still ticking they said. Still has a pulse."

"Is it that strange guy from Poland? The one who always wears a hat."

"That's the one."

"He was strange. Didn't talk to anyone, except the blond he was with."

"Where's she?"

"She is in there too. I saw her come running and force her way in not long ago."

"Guess that was his wife."

"Don't think so. She wasn't wearing any wedding ring that I could see. She looked pretty crazy to me, was screaming in a foreign lingo, maybe German. Yeah, sounded like German."

Yanosh listened to the conversation. He was fascinated with what he was hearing, but frustrated that he couldn't get any closer to see what was happening inside. He wanted to know if it was really Bora in there, as he feared.

"Who was the other guy? The one they said shot himself? Did you see him?"

"No, I didn't see him. No one knows anything about him. I heard he wasn't on the passenger list, a stowaway."

"A stowaway?"

"That's what I said! Are you deaf or something?"

"Don't shout!"

"One of the sailors said they've got the gun – a German handgun, a Luger."

"You don't say!"

"Yeah, the kind of weapon the German secret police used. What did they call 'em, the secret police of theirs?"

"The Jeestaypo."

"Yeah, that's it. The Gistaypo."

"You're sure about all that?"

"Yeah, that's what I heard from me mate Joe. Ee'd know. Ee's a friend of the capp'n, Eey is?"

"You don't say!"

"Yeah, that's what he told me."

"Those Germans are a nasty bunch."

"I wouldn't say that. I met some nice German ladies when we were in Berlin. They were very accommodating, if you know what I mean."

225

The two men walked off, talking. Yanosh couldn't hear what they were saying any longer, but he had heard enough.

August 13, 1946

They "buried" Bora and another man, a stowaway, yesterday at sea. Two bodies were thrown overboard, draped in white sheets, weights attached. I watched as the bodies sunk into the water leaving two circles of white froth and then rising bubbles. A woman shrieked when they plopped them over the side of the ship, otherwise it was a silent funeral. No speeches and no eulogies, no priest or rabbi to perform any ritual either. Would it have mattered to him? I don't know.

The woman who was with Bora on board isn't saying anything about what happened or about her relationship with him. The ship's captain made it clear that the investigation into the crime is over for the time being, until we reach Australia. I think it was probably the Nazis, someone from the S.S. Organization, Odessa, but we will never know. How will they prove anything now, anyway?

Bora was a violent man. He killed many people, I know, but he was also a good man, loyal to his people. He saved many lives, the lives of fellow Jews when that was difficult, almost impossible to do, and dangerous. He told me once in Berlin that he had fed and protected about 250 Jews in the Naroch forest during the war under his commander Markov's nose.

He risked his life nightly organizing help for them, posted guards there, brought them special gifts to celebrate Jewish holidays when he could. I remember the story he once told me of how he arranged a hot bath in honor of Purim for a family who were hiding in a hole in the ground.

After the war he helped people escape the Russians and the new communist regime in Poland. And, of course, he helped Eva and me, and our friends when we were desperate. We owed him our lives too!

Now he is dead. Why? Did he deserve to end like this? Dumped in the sea! There is no justice. The pigs who couldn't stop him all those years during the war, and after it, got him after all!

And Pawla? She frightens me. She was so cold and unfeeling about this tragedy. Almost seemed pleased. He warned me that she was not a person to be trusted, had an evil streak, to keep away from her, just as Eva warned me to stay away from Bora. Did she have something to do with Bora's death? How can Marek be so unsuspecting and oblivious to it all?

Will I never find peace of mind, sanity? When we reach Australia I would like to distance myself from her and all that she reminds me of, to forget the past and move on. But I know I can't. She and Marek are all the "family" we have, apart from our soon-to-be born child.

If I believed in a God, as Marek does, I would pray for one thing, that our little one will live in a better world than we did. But is that possible?

The ship approached the shore after weeks of the rough southeastward journey across the Indian Ocean. Everyone went rushing up to the top deck when the announcement came that the Australian shore was first sighted. It was night and in the distance they could see the twinkling shore lights. They came and went from view as the ship bounced on the waves.

Yanosh looked up at the sky for a moment and was astounded. It was different from what he had known in Europe. There were many more stars. Someone had told him that the southern sky would be different. He had mentally registered that information. Now he remembered. He had heard that one could see the Milky Way. This must be it. Beside him Marek pulled on his arm and pointed to a cluster of stars just above the shore lights.

"Look," he said, "that must be the famous Southern Cross, the stars they have on their flag."

Marek crossed himself and mumbled a prayer. Yanosh felt annoyed at this. Yanosh loved the man. He and Eva owed their lives to him. He knew that Marek's Catholic faith was important to him, kept him going, but he hated his piety. How could he go on believing in God, in the face of the horrors of Poland?

He looked around at the crowd along the edge of the ship, all those hands, some old, bony and thin, others smooth and young, holding the railing on either side of him. So many people were hoping to rebuild broken, shattered lives in this new country, those distant lights in the fading dark. Here and there some people were praying. Some men, obviously Jews, were wearing hats, or yarmulkes, women wrapped in scarves. They were, he knew, mumbling their morning prayers or reciting psalms as the first dawn began to break and the lights disappeared. How could they still be praying? He could not understand it.

They couldn't see the shore anymore. With daybreak, all they saw was the endless water again. They would have to wait. People began to leave the railing along the edge of the ship, and return to their usual places, to their huddled corners. He found Eva. She looked peaceful, curled up under her blanket, her form round with child, so vulnerable. She was due any day now. He hoped the baby would wait to be born in Australia, not here on the ship.

He let her sleep on, searching meanwhile for his notepad and pen. He wanted to take advantage of the opportunity to write a little, as they approached the Australian shore. It was time to do an accounting of their journey, now that it was coming to an end. It was time to let go of Europe and all it represented, to meet the future cleansed of that past. He would not let it weigh him down. He began to write, stopped. Crossed out what he had written... Started again. He gave up. Went back up on deck again and stood looking out to see if the Australian shore could be seen. It could not. Not yet.

Yanosh left the rail again, disappointed. He wandered about the deck, impatient. He noticed a young couple kissing, an old woman mumbling her morning prayers. He saw Marek across the way. He avoided him, not wanting to get into a conversation now. He wanted to be alone with his thoughts. He had to make some sense of it all, to clear his mind before the shore would be sighted again, with all the excitement that aroused.

Then he felt her touch, her gentle caress of his shoulder. Eva was up. She looked at him, concerned, frowning. He took her arm and they walked on together, silently. She understood him, he felt.

"You are moody again, Yanosh."

"Yes, I am."

"What is on your mind?"

"I cannot get Bora out of my mind; his murder, his story, what Pawla told me about him. I just do not understand what happened. Cannot believe it."

"I wasn't surprised by what happened, Yanosh. Something was going to happen. I could feel it."

"I know. You told me weeks ago. You were right, but that doesn't help me understand it, doesn't make it right."

"It doesn't matter anymore. You just have to accept what comes and move on."

He nodded. She was right about that, too.

They went back below deck.

They passed a young lad in the passageway carrying a bag. It was an army bag, green or grayish-brown, with many patches and a long rope tied to the top, with which he carried it. He moved aside to let them pass. The bag tore, caught on a jutting nail in the wall. It flew open and out tumbled his things. The boy quickly bent down to pick up the contents. They bent down with him as well, to help him, apologizing to him for the accident.

Then he saw the little bag with the Hebrew letters and the embroidered symbol, the Star of David. It shocked him. He watched the boy pick it up, kiss it piously. He was angered by it. He wished they hadn't bumped into him. He knew that the bag must contain tefillin, that the boy certainly must be wrapping them around his arm and on his forehead every morning when he prayed. He had seen them do that before the war, during the ghetto years and in the D.P. camps after the war.

It reminded him of so much he wanted to forget. Of his grandfather, Max, of his Uncle Simcha, and Aunt Sheina and their many children. All gone. All murdered. He remembered his bar mitzvah. How much he had hated being made to put them on. He watched the lad back away from them and disappear.

"Notice the terror in his eyes?" he asked Eva.

"Yes, I did," she said, "of course I did."

They walked on down the narrow corridor, the sound of the engines had become deafening as they moved deeper into the bowels of the boat. They went around the corner and down the mighty metal spiral stairwell. The air was now stifling. There was little ventilation. All kinds of human smells, particularly sweat, but also less pleasant ones invaded their nostrils. It took a while to get used to it again, but they always did. The worst was when people vomited. People often did, especially the children. So many suffered from the motions of the sea. There was little that could be done. The deck was always crowded with people escaping the intestines of the ship, but they had no choice but to descend again to escape the cold or get some sleep.

They had barely settled down in their usual spot, which they had marked off with their blankets and bags, when a siren sounded. Everyone started moving, tumbling out of their cocoons, getting up out of their huddled groups, pushing, shoving, helping each other, up and forward. A human mass, accompanied by a cacophony of shrieks, screams, calls, babble, heavy breathing, coughs, and sneezes, arms, legs, moving bundles of rags, carrying bags, clutching loved ones, surged up out of the ship's innards, and then were spewed up on deck.

There they were met with the rush of sailors making all kinds of preparations. Yanosh was attacked by a powerful sense of dejavu, it vaguely reminded him of a nightmare he had had not long ago.

"Land!" someone shouted, "It's Australia, the coast of Australia."

Yanosh and Eva joined the crowd which had gathered on the stern brow and looked in the direction some were pointing to. They saw seagulls, many birds, circling in the air. And then ships and boats, sails, and just beyond them some distant green hills, marked by a mass of clouds just above them.

"It must be raining over there. Look at those dark clouds."

"It must be Fremantle, the port we are headed for. So many seagulls, all those sailboats... We are close to our final destination."

Yanosh gathered Eva into his arms, and gave her a hug.

"Yanosh, stop that! The baby. Remember I am expecting the baby any day now."

"Oh, I haven't forgotten, Eva. How could I, with you having a belly like that?"

"That was not funny!"

"Do you realize what this means?"

"What do you mean? What are you talking about? You are so excited, my love!"

"Our child will be born in Australia, will be an Australian."

Eva squeezed his hand.

He remembered that Bora always carried a crust of bread in his pockets. He would have had something to feed the birds with, he thought. He remembered how gentle Bora could be with animals, his love of nature, of all creatures.

Yanosh sighed at that thought, let it float away, and holding his wife's hand, he looked out to sea.

Above the excited, babbling crowd, the seagulls circled, squawking, hoping to be fed. But Yanosh and Eva didn't have any bread. Just bloody memories, and hopes for a new life, and a better future.

The Author

Yehiel Grenimann is the eldest child of two Polish Holocaust survivors.

After completing his MA in Holocaust Studies at the Hebrew University's Institute for Contemporary Jewry, he spent ten years in Holocaust education and was Director of the Ot Ve'Ed Institute in Jerusalem, where he focused on teaching teenagers, young adults, and educators about Jewish resistance during World War II.

Since receiving his rabbinical ordination from the Schechter Institute of Jewish Studies in 1991, he has worked as a rabbi and educator in the Masorti movement. For many years, he has been active in peace-oriented groups and currently works for Rabbis for Human Rights.

A published writer, Yehiel's following work has appeared in many publications:

"A Theological Confrontation with the Holocaust," *Et La'asot* (Journal of the Seminary of Judaic Studies and the Masorti Movement in Israel), Winter 1996 (in Hebrew).

Commentaries on weekly and festival Torah portions, in Hebrew and English. 1991-2003.

"Bitter Conflict - Can Judaism Bring Hope?" published in an anthology edited by Prof. Gerrie ter Haar, "Religion, Violence and Visions for Peace" (Brill Publishers, 2005).

"Letter From Jerusalem: Masorti Giyur", Conservative Judaism, Vol. 57, No. 4, Summer 2005 (Publication of the Rabbinical Assembly and J.T.S., New York).

"Purim In The Forest" (short story), in *The Beauty Of The Story*, ed. Rosally Saltsman (Judaica Press, New York, 2009).

The chapter "The Seder" of this novel was previously published in *JewishFiction.net* Volume 1,No. 3, February 24th 2011.

A long-time Jerusalem resident, he is married to Deborah and the father of four adult children.